As the first part of his session neared the end, Joshua heard the door at the rear of the classroom open. He looked up to see Desiree, in dress blues, step into the class. She stood, her hat in her hand, at the rear. Joshua became fixated, his train of thought lost as he looked at the woman who made him wonder, made his emotions ramble out of control. He looked at his notes in an attempt to gain control over the feelings. He had thought a lot about her the last two days: their date to the movies, his overwhelming desire to kiss her, once after their date, then the abrupt kiss at the stationhouse, and Heaney's words. He purposely hadn't called her. He needed time. Besides, she hadn't called him either, and he still smarted over her insinuation that he had a problem working with, or for women.

BLAZE

BARBARA KEATON

Genesis Press Inc.

Indigo Love Stories

An imprint of Genesis Press Inc.
Publishing Company

Genesis Press, Inc.
P.O. Box 101
Columbus, MS 39703

ISBN: 1-58571-172-1
Manufactured in the United States of America

First Edition

Visit us at www.genesis-press.com
or call at 1-888-Indigo-1

DEDICATION

This book is dedicated to Robin D. Johnson—Only the Lord knows
how much I miss your laughter and your spirit.
God willing, we will meet again.

ACKNOWLEDGMENTS

First, foremost, and always, thank you to my heavenly Father and his Son, Jesus Christ, from whom all of my blessings most certainly flow. A million-and-one thanks to Annette Nance-Holt, one of the Chicago Fire Department's first African American, female Lieutenants! You Go Girl! To the African American Firefighters and Paramedics League. Much love to the men and women of Engine Company #75 (thanks for the meal—a sistah was hungry!). And last, but not least, to the countless Chicago Firefighters, who put their lives on the line everyday protecting the citizens of Chicago! Thank you for answering the call, and may God bless and keep each, and every one of you.

PROLOGUE

The image crept around the side of the house. Its head turned from left to right. The moon shone on black gym shoes with red laces. Looking up, the image poured a clear liquid from a container, pausing only long enough to inhale deeply. Removing a book of matches, the image struck the match then smiled wickedly as the fire danced, first yellow, then blue-green. When the match hit the soaked ground, a blaze formed and began to burn, slowly at first as it made its way along the created path, then more intensely as it snaked up the side of the house. The image stood stark still and watched the blaze take form, the colors bright and inviting as it licked at its feet.

"They'll see. They all will see who's the best." The image snickered sourly then ran into the darkness of night.

CHAPTER 1

"The only thing you take with you when you're gone is what you leave behind." John Allston

Desiree Charles turned over onto her right side and placed a pillow over her head. The shrill siren drilled through her, a piercing sound so evasive, she unconsciously added the covers to the pillow and pulled them both tightly around her head. At first she thought she was dreaming, free falling into a dark abyss of fire and smoke; the recurrent nightmare she'd been having for more than ten years. The loud siren continued, raised an octave; followed by the lieutenant's voice over the loud speaker. It was no dream—the siren spoke of a fire in progress.

Desiree jumped out of the twin-sized bed; her sock clad feet hit the floor. She snatched her white shirt and navy blue pants from the foot of her bed. She shook her head. No matter how wild she slept, her uniform always remained untouched at the foot of her bed, at her disposal. She slipped her uniform over her white boxer shorts and navy T-shirt. Desiree pulled the St. Jude medallion from the pocket of her pants, kissed it, placed it back in her pocket, then ran to the pole. As she slid down the pole, she could see her fellow firefighters running toward the parked red and black fire engine, their boots lined neatly beside the truck. She took a quick count of her men, a mental roll call, as her eyes met each one: Heaney, Moose, Tulley, and Carroll. All present and accounted for.

Once her feet hit solid ground, Desiree pulled her overalls over her body. She snatched her heavy, heat resistant coat from the front seat as she simultaneously slid her feet into her boots. She grabbed her helmet from the front seat and flipped the eye shield upward after she placed the protective gear about her head. She secured the chin guard around the back of her head as she stepped up on the engine's sideboard and effortlessly pulled her 130 lb., supple frame onto the passenger seat of the large engine. The heavy vehicle came to life. The red mars lights and loud siren blaring out into the darkening sky.

Speaking into the handheld microphone, Desiree communicated with dispatch as she repeated the address. She informed the dispatch operator of Engine Company #19's estimated time of arrival. She glanced over at the driver, the Lieutenant of Engine #19. Seamus Heaney had been a firefighter for thirty years. The son, and then father of Chicago firefighters, Pappa Shay, as she affectionately called him, was not only her godfather, but had become her protector and friend. She smiled at him, tapped his hand and nodded—a motion that had become their secret agreement that they were on their way, once again, to fight the beast.

Heaney expertly maneuvered the engine east down Seventy-ninth Street, always amazed at the amount of cars and people lining the street at this time of night. As if reading his mind, Desiree sounded the horn, a warning shot to vehicles ahead to move out of the engine's path. She was incredulous at the lack of respect people showed for an emergency vehicle. This vehicle could be on its way to save their own home from burning to the ground, or worse to save a loved one. Desiree sounded the horn again.

As the engine barreled down the street, Desiree added the last of her turn out gear, or PPE—Personal Protection Equipment. She placed her slightly muscular arms through the loops of the oxygen tank, checked the gauge and the alarm attached to it. She ended by placing her hands in her fire protective gloves. In all, Desiree's frame carried some seventy pounds of PPE.

With her left hand, Desiree reached behind her to retrieve the heat-seeking camera and secured it to her utility belt moments before her right hand reached out and automatically gripped the grab bar. She steeled herself for one of Heaney's infamous turns, which always made her wince. After years of experiencing his driving, first as a candidate, she had never quite become accustomed to his handling of the forty-foot fire truck. Heaney grinned at her.

"Lass, we're on our way," he said, his Irish brogue clear, as he made a left turn onto Rev. Martin Luther King, Jr. Drive, known simply as King Drive, and headed north to the address.

Arriving seven minutes later, Desiree and Heaney jumped out of the cab, followed by their fellow firefighters, and went into action. Desiree stepped to the curb. Her eyes darted up and down the street as she made a mental note of the number of fire hydrants in her vision. Two cars blocked the hydrant closest to them. She glanced at the cars, then to the house on fire. The flames from it dangerously licked the one next to it.

"Carroll and Moose! Get those cars out of here!" she ordered as she began to assist the other firefighters pull the hose from the bed of the engine. She smiled to herself as she watched her men pick up one of the vehicles and move it to the middle of the street. They would have the vehicle promptly ticketed and towed once officers from the Chicago Police Department arrived.

Once the hose was secured to the nearby hydrant, Tulley turned the heavy valve with a large wrench and the hose came to life. As she stood behind Moose's six-foot-five large frame, Desiree braced herself for the rush of water, some 150 gallons being forced through the four-inch hose. She signaled to Carroll to take her spot, and then signaled to Heaney, who joined her side as she walked down the side of the house.

Flames jutted out of a window, mere feet from the top of her helmet, but she was accustomed to it—had become used to the searing heat. She loved her job, had wanted to be a firefighter since she could remember. Her father had been a firefighter just like his father and grandfather, who once belonged to the first colored stationhouse, Engine 21, which was destroyed in the second Great Chicago Fire, which occurred on July 14, 1874 and destroyed a large section of what was then known as Black Chicago. After the second Chicago Fire, Desiree's great-grandfather moved back to Alabama to join the first black volunteer firefighters in the community.

All the men of her family had a fear and great respect for fire—and the ensuing damage it could cause. But even more so, was the personal battle each had waged to gain respect in a company that hadn't always accepted or been kind to black firefighters. The charge was even more important to Desiree, for she was the only female in the Charles clan to become a firefighter.

Head tilted to the left, she asked, "Hear that, Pappa Shay?"

"Yeah."

Both rushed to the rear of the residence. Desiree spoke into her two-way radio. "10-51 a ladder to 900 E. Seventy-eighth Place." Coming to a halt, they simultaneously looked upward then trained their ear to hear the cries of what sounded like children.

"Lass, someone's up there," Heaney said as they rounded the rear steps. He pulled off one of his gloves then lightly touched the doorknob. It was cool. And locked.

"Damn," Desiree spat out.

"Gonna hafta break it down," Heaney replied as he spoke into his two-way. He ordered two men to come to the rear. In less a minute, the door had been hacked away. Each bowed their heads, Heaney and Desiree crossed themselves. She handed Heaney the safety line and watched her men loop the solid rope through the loops of their heavy jacket, giving no less than a two-foot lap between them. They placed their oxygen masks over their faces, took a deep breath of the pure gas, then entered the dark house that was filled with blinding smoke.

Desiree stopped near the wall she assumed had stairs leading upward. Head cocked to the right, she tried to listen for the voices she had heard. She pulled a flashlight from her heavy protective coat then pointed the bright light upward. The illumination from the flashlight did little to penetrate the thick, black smoke. She grabbed the heat-seeking camera and trained it along the area in front of her. The glowing screen indicated two hot spots inside the wall to their right, which led up toward the stairs. She spoke into the earpiece attached to her helmet.

"We've got two live ones, gentlemen. Both to the right and snaking up the stairs. We're going up. Be careful." She tapped the side of Heaney's helmet, followed by a tap on Carroll's shoulder.

She tugged on the line then led her men forward as she felt along the wall of the two-story frame house. Desiree knew, from studying the various layouts of houses, that the stairs were approximately ten feet forward and to her right. As she got closer, she could see the illumination from the mars lights of the fire truck through what appeared to be partially opened vertical blinds at a front window. She knew the front door wasn't far away. As she reached the stairway, her gloved hand grabbed the wood molding. She took the first step upward, then halted. The beast had met them and was coming on strong. Flames whipped angrily along the walls then snaked quickly above their covered heads.

She felt the line go slack and knew Heaney was gone.

Heaney rushed to the window, tore the blinds away with one swipe of his large hand. "Down," he barked into the headset. They didn't hesitate and quickly laid down on their stomachs, their chins tucked tightly in the top of their chests. The sound of breaking glass assaulted their ears as Heaney took out the large picture window with an ax. They couldn't afford to wait for the ladder company to arrive, even though Desiree could hear the sirens in the distance.

Mere seconds passed. The prone team felt the sudden gush of air followed by searing heat as the flame shot across them. She felt it as it skimmed across her jacket and helmet. Desiree continued to lay prone on the bottom of the stairs and let the beast run its course before it calmed. She sighed deeply. A cold rush of water covered her.

Desiree peered from under her helmet into the facemasks of her fellow firefighters. Cold water at her back, Desiree took a deep breath then gave the order for them to stand.

Together, one behind the other, they began to climb the stairs. She stopped on the top landing, the smoke less dense, and pointed the flashlight upon four doors surrounding her. Removing the safety line from their jackets, each firefighter took a room. Crouching low, Desiree removed her protective glove from her right hand and felt under the door, then the doorknob. Cool. Slowly, she opened the door, her flashlight swept across the room. Upon noticing a closet, she stepped to it, opened it and pushed back the clothes. Her light came upon two children, a boy and a girl, who began to scream loudly.

"It's okay. Come with me," she pushed her mask from her face. She had to get them out of the smoky house and fast. Scooping one child into her arms, a girl who looked no more than five, Desiree turned and handed the child to Heaney, who was right behind her. She then opened her jacket, picked up the little boy, who she guessed was about three years old, took him into her arms, cradled him close to her chest, then secured her coat around him. She smiled as the little boy's wide eyes, full of fear, peered up at her from the top of her coat.

"I've got you, baby. We're going to be okay," Desiree spoke as the child nodded then ducked his head further into her coat. As they turned to leave, she heard another yell. The voice in the earpiece told them that the front of the house had collapsed. They were trapped.

"Shit! Where's the ladder company?" Desiree moved to the bed-room window, pulled back the blinds and peered below. Praying the flames wouldn't engulf them, she tried to steel her mounting emotions. *I heard the siren. They'll be here.*

Desiree tightened her hold on the child she held. *Never again. I will not ever lose another one.* Heavy footsteps coming toward the rear of the burning house sent relief through her. She ticked off the seconds to when she would see a ladder at the window.

Heaney placed his mask on the child's face. "They're here. No need to worry." The little girl was wrapped up in his coat, close to his heart.

In spite of the situation, Desiree found herself smiling. *Just like Heaney, always putting others before himself.*

From the window, Desire could see the steel ladder. She sighed a breath of relief as the top of a helmet appeared at the base of the win-dow, an ax in hand. Desiree and Heaney turned their backs as a rain of glass showered them. They stepped through the broken window and carefully climbed, backwards, down the ladder; each clutched precious cargo tightly against their chests.

Safely on the ground, Desiree walked with the child still clutched to her chest to the front of the house. A panicky female voice grabbed her attention. The child Desiree held squirmed in her arms.

"Momma," the child cried out as his head poked through the coat.

The woman, wearing a blanket draped over a gown, ran to take her child. Desiree's heart smiled as she freely reunited the pair.

The woman hugged the child close then her eyes darted around. Heaney appeared and handed over the other child. The woman had both children in her arms. Tears ran down her cheeks unchecked as she thanked God. The woman then set her eyes on Desiree. Somehow, the woman pulled Desiree to her and hugged her tightly, the now crying children between them.

"Thank you," the woman breathed as paramedics walked over and escorted her and the children to a waiting ambulance. Heaney followed and waved at the children. He then joined Desiree as she stood on the sidewalk. Together they watched as the beast's power diminished, until finally the fire had been put out. They had been at the scene for nearly four hours. Desiree thanked God, then turned and headed back to the fire engine.

At the stationhouse, as Desiree showered in the only shower for women, she thought of the face of the child, its eyes wide as she coaxed the child from the hiding place in the closet. She smiled sadly. This time, she mused, she had been lucky. She had been blessed to get to the child on time.

Too wired to relax, as she always was after a two-alarm blaze, Desiree went downstairs to the desk, which was near the front of the stationhouse. She turned on the television and absently watched the beginning of the local early morning news. Her attention was averted when Heaney sat across from her.

"Can't rest, ugh, Lass?" his steel blue eyes stared at her.

Desiree shook her head.

"Neither can I. Anything good on this thing?" He tapped the top of the small television on her desk.

"Nope, same old stuff. What you think about that fire?"

"I smelled something funny when we came around the side of the house. It wasn't gasoline, but it was definitely something."

"I did, too. Smelled like ammonia. Think it was arson?"

"Not sure, but I did smell something strange…"

"Did you tell the investigators?"

"Naw—they think I'm nuts anyway." Heaney chuckled.

For the past five years, Heaney had begun to slow down, his responses were not as sharp, and he had become reckless. Like at the fire. It was the job of an engine company to bring the multitude of varying size hoses to the fire, then extinguish the flames. The ladder company's job was to force the fire out of any hiding places so that the engine company could successfully extinguish it. Heaney breaking that window was not a part of the engine company's responsibility and the sudden rush of air could have caused the fire to rage out of control. Though she knew that he had done what he felt compelled to do, seconds always seems like hours, the ladder company was only a step behind them.

Sixty-one, Heaney had been a firefighter for nearly forty years and could walk at any time. In another four years, the department would force him to retire.

Desiree had once talked to him about retiring, but Heaney had waved her away and stated that he wanted to die with his boots on. She had chided him for such talk, but the reality was at the rate he was going, he might just get his wish.

"Well, two more hours then we're free for three days. What are you going to do?"

"You know me. Letty has some house work for me, so I'll be a bona fide member of the 'Honey-Do' club," Heaney said as he chuckled.

They laughed, then settled back to watch the beginning of the early morning local news as they waited for the hour to signal their shift change.

While they waited, Desiree thought of her firefighters. Four in total, all men, two of whom were black, Tulley and Moose, hadn't always been crazy about her arrival at Engine Company #19. One of the oldest in the city, the stationhouse had been built at the turn of the 19th Century; its dark, red bricks spoke its age. Once there had been talk of demolishing the old stationhouse, but it was saved from the wrecking ball when the city of Chicago granted it landmark status at the behest of the community in which the stationhouse was nestled. And though the accommodations were rustic at best, it was the stationhouse her father served in for over twenty years.

Desiree pulled open the desk drawer and glanced at the photo at the bottom, the only photo she had with her mother and father on the day she graduated from the Fire Academy. It was exactly one year later that her father had been trapped in a fire. While he hadn't been seriously injured, he felt that he had been abandoned by his fellow firefighters, left to perish at the hands of the beast. He saw the experience as an epiphany—as a sign to walk away before they had to carry him away. Still, the incident left her father sullen and depressed for many years.

Heaney had been at the same fire, yet he refused to allow Trenton Charles to believe that black or white, a firefighter would allow a fellow fighter to parish.

Heaney and Trenton had been cadets together, her father one of few to be granted the opportunity to join the department in 1973, which at the time was considered a bastion of pure racism.

Back then, the instructors had thought it would be comical to pair Heaney, a hard-line Irish man from Liscannor, County of Clare, Irish Republic, and her father, a radical Negro from Mobile, Alabama.

For Heaney, he had witnessed countless bloody street brawls in Liscannor between English Protestants of the British rule and Irish Catholics, who wanted to worship freely. He felt he was in no position to judge a man based on his color, when in fact he himself had been judged because of his religious beliefs. But their instructors were hard pressed when the two, both staunch Catholic's, had become fast friends. That was thirty-one years ago.

Most of her life, Desiree had been a part of the Heaney family. Being an only child, she had played with Heaney's four children, and often-celebrated birthdays and Thanksgiving at their home. She considered Heaney more like her second father, versus just a godfather.

Desiree looked up into Heaney's face. His warm blue eyes, surrounded by long blonde eyelashes, were set in a round, pie face, tanned burnished beige by the sun. She smiled and shook her head. *My Pappa Heaney.*

For two hours, the two sat at the desk and absently watched the local news. They stood as the next shift of firefighters began to stream into the stationhouse. Desiree nodded at each as they began the shift change ritual. The candidate, who had undergone six months of training, three for emergency medical technician and three for fire protection, had to have a full year on the force before being qualified as a full-fledged firefighter. The candidate walked over to her and smiled.

"Hey Timmons, how's it going?" Desiree inquired.

"It's going. But I'm glad I'm here and not where Janice is. She'd ride me harder than these guys on B shift ever would."

Desiree shook her head. Lena Timmons was in her sixth month of candidacy. She had followed her older sister, Janice Timmons, who was a ten-year veteran with the department and a Lieutenant with Ladder #12. Word had it that Janice Timmons was hard on her charges and a take-no-prisoners leader who was hard pressed to give praise and even harder to give her support.

Desiree had taken the younger Timmons under her wing, being an ear for her when the young, twenty-three year-old candidate needed one. As for her sister Janice, they had never been friends, even when she had been one of three black women, along with Desiree and her best friend, Annette Bishop, at the Fire Academy. Back then, Janice had told Desiree that she didn't need or want her friendship.

"Well, you know where I'm at. Call me if you need me, okay?"

Timmons nodded, a strand of her sable lock lay flushed against pear shaped mocha complexion, her dark eyes filled with gratitude. Desiree took her hand in hers and smiled. They both understood the need, the importance of the camaraderie between two black women in a man's world—a mostly white man's profession.

"Be careful, hear me?" Desiree said as she lightly squeezed Timmons's hand.

Timmons then went about checking the equipment. Desiree stood by and observed her. She watched as Timmons's arched eyebrows raised high, confusion darted in and out of her eyes. Desiree decided to stay behind a few moments to assist when she noticed that Timmons was not adequately checking the oxygen tanks. Desiree knew that the three guys and the captain of Timmons' shift wouldn't give her a hand, which could be dangerous for them all. One of the candidate's primary responsibilities was to check the oxygen levels of the tanks.

After an hour of going through the ritual with Timmons, she left the stationhouse and headed home. A firefighter's shift consists of twenty-four hours on and two days off. Desiree knew that those two days would be like manna to her soul, and she was truly looking forward to them all.

CHAPTER 2

Joshua Davis rubbed the growing stubble on his face. He shut his eyes tightly in an attempt to soothe the burning sensation left by not enough sleep and too many hours spent on numerous investigations. Lead detective for the Chicago Fire Department's Arson Unit, Joshua had to take on the tough cases, the ones that resulted in fatalities.

He glanced at the next file in his stack of nearly thirty.

"Engine Company #19," Joshua read the post-it note attached to the front of the file. He opened the file and began to peruse the report of a fire on the South Side of Chicago where two children were rescued. No fatalities, he noted. His eyes quickly scanned the typed words. He made it a habit of reading the files twice, once perfunctory, followed by a more thorough read when there were instances that piqued his immediate interest. He re-read the pages and stopped at the familiar name of the person who rescued the two small children.

Recollections of the attractive captain of Engine Company #19 brought a smile to his face. Proud that she had risen through the ranks to become the first black female station captain, he was impressed with the stories of her leadership and firefighting skills. Word around the various stationhouses had it that Captain Charles was a fierce firefighter and didn't ask her team to do anything she wouldn't.

Joshua hadn't formally met her, but had seen her once at a meeting of the African American Professional Firefighters and Paramedics League. Over the years, he'd also seen pictures of her in the fire department's newsletter. The one picture he remembered vividly had been posted on the inside of her father's locker. It showed Captain Charles posing with her mother and father the day she graduated from the Fire Academy. Now, like then, he couldn't help but remember the warm smile that seemed to touch her eyes as he looked at the picture so many years ago. He hadn't seen her father, Trenton, in years, but his words the day he looked at the picture one minute too long rang loud and clear—"Stay away from my baby girl."

Joshua smiled at the thought. Fresh out of the academy, Joshua had worked with Trenton Charles. He had been hard on Joshua. Every misstep he made, Charles was there in his face. Yet, Joshua had to admit that he had been fair. For it was Trenton Charles who had taken him under his wing and helped shape him into a fearless firefighter. When Trenton had finished, Joshua felt he could fight a fire with his eyes closed and one hand tied behind his back.

Still, he knew little about Trenton's daughter. Oh, he knew that the esteemed Captain Charles had been number one in her class, was a fierce firefighter, and was an expert on causes of fire and the use of accelerant. She taught a class on accelerants at the academy at least once a month. The only personal thing he knew about her was that she had dated a fellow firefighter, Donald Anderson, who, in his opinion, was a real asshole. He couldn't fathom what she saw in Anderson.

Joshua dismissed the thought and continued to read the file, scribbling notes on a pad of paper. He suspected arson, and his suspicion was confirmed when he came across a handwritten note that stated a strange odor was detected along the east side of the two-story house. Since there were no deaths, he'd assign the case to one of the five members of the unit.

For several additional hours, Joshua poured over cases, assigning investigators to them. A heavy sigh of relief escaped him when he came upon a file marked "solved." In that case, Joshua had worked relentlessly, nearly around the clock, as he investigated a rash of fires in the stately Pill Hill community of Chicago, one of which resulted in the death of two small children. After nearly two months of dead end leads, he received an anonymous tip that led him to a serial arsonist, who had just been released from prison six months prior.

Joshua looked up as the day shift began to filter into the large room, located in the bowels of the Chicago Police Department headquarters. He nodded at several as they passed his desk. Their arrival was a signal that his shift—the night shift—had ended.

"Davis," a voice bellowed from the doorway. "Time to go home, my brother."

Joshua laughed at the sight of his best friend, John Paglinini, as he stood in the door with his arms folded across his chest. He watched the faces of the men in the room as their eyes traveled from Joshua's to John's. One could clearly see that the two were far from brothers. Joshua stood six-feet even and John stood at five-eleven. Joshua was a warm chestnut color, while John's face was a tanned bronze and put you in the mind of the actor George Hamilton. But no one dared to utter a word. John Paglinini was second in command of the Chicago Fire Department.

"What brings you here this morning?" Joshua asked.

"Nothing in particular. Want to go to breakfast?" John walked over to Joshua.

"Sounds good. The usual joint?" Joshua looked into John's light, toast colored eyes. He knew that whenever John wanted to have break-fast he wanted to discuss his love life, of which Joshua knew was much more interesting than his. Joshua had no love life.

"Yeah, sure." John picked up the file lying on Joshua's desk. "Engine Company #19." He opened the file. "They're a hell of a team. And Captain Charles has whipped that bunch into shape."

Joshua nodded his head as he went about the room and placed files in the in-boxes of several investigators. John waved the file over his head. "What about this one? Where do you want it?"

Joshua paused. He knew anyone on his team could investigate the case, but for some inexplicable reason, he decided to investigate the case himself. To do so would mean having to interview Captain Desiree Charles. "Just leave it on my desk. On top of that pile to the left," he responded then grabbed his coat and black Kangol hat, turning it back-ward on his round head. "Let's bounce, my brother."

As the pair walked out into the bright sun, John paused several times to shake hands with fellow investigators and police officers. Joshua yawned and told John if he didn't hurry, he'd loose his dining partner.

The Original Pancake house on Eighty-seventh Street was a favorite of both men. Joshua loved the large helpings of food the cooks heaped on his plate whenever he entered the restaurant for breakfast. For the past seventeen years that he had been a part of the department, he'd visit the restaurant at least three times a week. As for John, the waitresses loved to see him enter. He called each by her name as he smiled and chatted. He'd give each an abundant view of his white, even teeth. Joshua got a mild thrill out of watching his best friend attempt to work the women. What they didn't know about John was that he preferred women of color, exclusively.

"Okay, talk," Joshua said as the waitress finally left their table. John had engaged her in small talk surrounding her son.

"Man," John rubbed his face. "I broke up with Trina."

Joshua hid a smirk behind his hand. He knew that John would drone on and on about another woman who got away. He glanced at the large, white-faced clock with the black hands then shook his head. He knew he wouldn't get into bed for at least another two hours.

He nodded his head and listened as John talked about the woman he swore he was going to marry. Divorced three years, John constantly talked about remarrying, while Joshua couldn't think of every marrying again. He dated, once and a while, but hadn't met anyone who could stand up to his beloved Serena.

John's words droned on as Joshua glanced out the large window. His attention was averted at the sound of sirens. He watched as the engine roared past the restaurant. He glimpsed the large white numbers on the side of the red truck. Engine Company #19. Joshua thought of the illustrious, but no non-sense, Captain Desiree Charles and made a mental note to stop by the stationhouse over the next couple of days to talk to her about the case sitting on his desk.

"Man, did you hear me?"

Joshua turned his head to look at John. "Sorry. What'd you say?"

"Never mind. You suppose to be helping." John frowned as Joshua laughed at his expression.

"My bad. So, what are you going to do?" Joshua asked, then waited for an answer as the waitress placed steaming heaps of hash browns, pancakes, scrambled eggs and sausage in front of him.

"What can I do?" John shrugged his shoulders, then closed his eyes and inhaled deeply as his plate of sausage gravy and biscuits, with a side of cheese grits, were placed in front of him. He thanked the waitress, bowed his head, then picked up his fork. "Man, she tossed my clothes out on the street!"

"Next time call her like you said you would," Joshua stated between mouthfuls. "But John, I don't understand. Y'all dated for all of what? Three months?"

John poked out his narrow lips. "And?"

"Brother, that's not enough time. Hell, you met her one night at a club, the next thing I know y'all are practically living at each other's houses talking about getting married." Joshua watched the pained expression on his best friend's face. He felt for him, but Joshua couldn't find the right words. He thought of when he first met John.

John had walked into the academy sure and cocky. The instructors had taken an immediate disliking to him and had paired him and Joshua together during the three-month training. After their graduation from the academy, Joshua number one and John number two in their class, were assigned to the same stationhouse as cadets. It wasn't until a bar room brawl, where John had been outnumbered before Joshua stepped in, that they became close. John had called Joshua his brother and the moniker stuck for the past fifteen years of their friendship and careers. And John had been more of a brother to Joshua than Joshua's own brother Abel had. He had been there when Joshua lost Serena.

"Okay, do you really want to marry Trina?" Joshua set his fork down.

John averted his gaze.

"I thought so. Man, move on. Okay?"

A smile slowly crept across John's face then turned into a full laugh as he turned his eyes to look at Joshua. "Yeah, you're right. She wasn't that tidy. And she couldn't cook. Not even greens!" John stated. "Ever hear of a black woman who can't cook greens and corn bread? I still haven't met a woman who could cook like Serena."

Brows furrowed, Joshua didn't want to talk about Serena. "Move on from this, too."

"My bad. But you know I'm here, right?"

"You sound like that shrink."

"I'm just worried about you, Josh, that's all. You okay?"

Joshua rubbed his large hand down his mouth. "Yeah." He looked at his watch. "Look, I'm tired. I gotta go home and get some sleep." He tossed his napkin on the plate, pulled several bills from his pocket and laid them on the table. "And I do think you need to go to work."

John rose from the table at the same moment Joshua did. "I just want to make sure you're alright. It's been nearly four years."

Joshua's jet-black eyebrows rose as his face became steel. "And?"

"Never mind. Call me later. Later, brother." John grabbed Joshua's hand and pulled him into an embrace. "You know you my only brother. I love you, man." He walked out of the restaurant, waving at the waitresses as he exited.

Joshua stood by the table. He knew that John meant well, but Serena wasn't something he wanted to discuss right now. To make matters worse, he had begun having dreams of her again, but this time something about them seemed different.

He shook slightly and strolled out of the restaurant, nodding at the waitresses as he did. Once in his car, he examined his reflection in the rearview mirror. The whites of his deep brown eyes had turned a pale crimson. Sleep. Sleep would help, but wouldn't cure what he had lost. Four years was a long time, but memories and love didn't disappear overnight. And though he had dated, and even selfishly slept with a few women, he hadn't met a woman who made him take pause and dare to dream of a different life, one that he had hoped to share with Serena for the rest of his life.

He started up the department issued, midnight blue sedan, and joined the morning traffic. At a traffic light, he looked over to his right and saw white letters and number on the large red truck as it pulled up next to him. Engine 19. He resisted the urge to lean over and look up to see if Captain Charles was sitting up front. When the light turned green, he sped ahead of the truck and watched through the mirror as it traveled two cars behind. He tried to make out the image but couldn't.

Why am I so interested in Engine 19, much less Captain Charles? Well, he reasoned, *I need to interview her for the case.* A case he knew he should assign to one of the members of his unit. But she was the one who was at the scene, had rescued the children, who had written the report. So, to him, it stood to reason that she would be the best one to talk to concerning the fire.

Satisfied with his reasoning, Joshua headed home with hopes that this day would lend itself to some sound, dreamless sleep. He eyed the rear view mirror one last time and watched as the large red engine turned the corner and disappeared from his sights.

CHAPTER 3

Two days was not enough. Desiree had spent one of her days off with her parents. Her final day off had been spent happily secluded in her house. Yet, during that final day, her thoughts had been intermittently filled with the failure of her last relationship. Being a firefighter was difficult enough, but being a female firefighter, and a captain at that, had proved even tougher on a relationship. Admittedly, Desiree knew many men were hard pressed to date a woman who was employed in a male-dominated profession. She had found it difficult, in the beginning, to shake off the hard "chest of armor" females had to implore just to get a little respect from her fellow firefighters. She hadn't liked it, even though she had been a fierce tomboy from the age of nine until she turned sixteen and found boys much more fun to kiss than to literally chase down a street.

When Desiree had met Donald Anderson, she was in a dating dry spell. Sure the brothers wanted to date her, found her attractive, until the reality of her career dawned on them. When she first met Donald Anderson, a firefighter as well, she was relieved that she didn't have to explain the duplicitous role females had to play in the fire department. He had said his mother and sisters were "strong, black women." In that, Desiree felt that he understood. The night they met at a fund-raiser hosted by the local North Central Region's African American Firefighters and Paramedics League, Desiree hadn't been looking for a date. She just wanted to support the organization. Even though she had a firm stance against dating any of the men on the department, she gave in to his persistent, yet witty, pleads that they go out. Their first date was at the beach after they both had just ended their respective shifts. She had found Donald's deadpan humor and support refreshing. Outside of best friend Annette, Donald had become the one she had laid her head on and cried her heart out when the pressure got too intense. After her promotion to captain, Donald had begun to change. They saw each other less and less. Though she knew why, she wasn't about to give up her life as a firefighter. She had worked hard to get to this point, had studied every facet of firefighting, and she'd be damned if she'd let some man's insecurities stand in her way.

"Water under the bridge," she stated as she climbed from the Blazer and entered the firehouse to begin another twenty-four hour shift.

"Hey, Captain, Tulley's wife had the baby night before last. It's a girl," Moose said as he met her at the door.

Desiree smiled, even though it didn't quite reach her heart. She and Donald had been engaged and had talked often about starting a family. "That's great news. Did he take off?"

"Naw that crazed man is upstairs passing out pink bubble gum cigars."

Desiree joined the men upstairs. Heaney stood in the middle of the large room; ten twin-sized beds lined the walls. Heaney had his signature cigar in his mouth.

"And each of my children came spitting out. Back then, I was a different kind of father—I insisted on watching them being born."

Desiree laughed as he went into story after story of birth and the importance of being a "hands-on" parent. After nearly forty minutes of non-stop stories, Desiree cleared her throat and signaled that it was time for them to get to work. Today, the engine needed to be cleaned— inside and out.

They worked for several hours, glad that the siren hadn't sounded a call to a fire. The reprieve even gave Desiree a moment to catch up several mounds of paperwork, which she hated doing, but knew that it was a necessary part of her duties.

Heaney came and sat before her. "Nice and quiet. Just like I like it. You know, another fire broke out the other day. I talked to the guys. They said it seemed to have started on the right side of the house. One of 'em claimed to have gotten a whiff of something strange."

"Just like the one we fought on our last shift. Any fatalities?"

Heaney shook his head. "Thank God. But I think we may have another bug on our hands."

She winced. The last time there was an arsonists loose on the South Side had been ten years ago. Desiree had been a firefighter for five years, and in that time had fought countless fires, but had yet to experience a fatality. What had started out as a simple one-alarm blaze, quickly turned into a four-alarm blaze that engulfed several houses on one block. In one of those houses hid a five-year-old child, a little girl. After the child's parents informed the firefighters that the child was in the house, Desiree had desperately searched for her. Desiree found her under a bed behind clothes and shoes, but she hadn't been able find her in time to save her.

"Is Arson on it?" she asked absently, her thoughts on the lifeless body of the small child cradled in her arms as she rushed out of the burning house, her mouth secured to the child's as Desiree attempted to revive the child through CPR.

"Yeah, they came to the scene."

Desiree stood and walked over to the door. She stepped outside and closed her eyes. A warm summer breeze skimmed across her face and lifted her ponytail. In the ensuing years, she hadn't been able to talk about that incident. The department had insisted that she speak to a psychologist, hired by the department expressly for firefighters. She had balked at their suggestion, yet her dreams were riddled with the images of the lifeless child on that cold December night. She rode them out, always waking in a cold sweat.

She turned her attention to the three children playing on the sidewalk in front of the firehouse.

"Miss Captain, do you know how to play Hop Scotch?" one of the girls asked.

Desiree beamed and walked over to them. She took the white chalk from the little girl named Christina. Desiree had come to call Christina "bright eyes," because her hazel eyes seemed to twinkle like bright stars. The two other children, Hannah and Miranda, laughed as Desiree drew the boxes on the ground, numbering each. They clapped in glee once Moose came out and gave Desiree blue colored chalk. She drew a wild, billowy cloud, wrote "blue sky" in it, then picked up a nearby small rock.

"Mr. Moose, are you going to play?" Miranda asked as she looked up into the large man's face, her warm brown eyes almost matching the color of her long, shoulder length ponytail. Moose smiled at the little girl. His large, 6'5" frame made many think he would be hard and mean, and the men at the four stationhouses he had worked in his twenty years with the department had aptly named him "Moose." But his wide, easy smile and dreamy brown eyes set in a deep mahogany face disarmed anyone who came his way. A forty-five-year-old divorcee, Moose, whose mother had named him Alfred Johnson, was the second oldest firefighter at the stationhouse and one of the best she had ever worked with. He had been in her corner the moment she had stepped into Engine Company #19's front door. He had told Desiree that he knew discrimination first hand and he had no right to discriminate against her because of her sex. From that point forward, Desiree had a great respect and love for Moose.

Desiree laughed as Moose began to back up, his large hands raised in surrender. She would have loved to see, Moose, who was built like a defensive lineman, jump with one foot inside the chalk drawn boxes. Desiree spoke to the girls. "No, Mr. Moose has work to do. Maybe next time. Okay?"

The trio shrugged their shoulders. Desiree tossed the rock aimlessly toward one of the boxes. She had the girls' line up by height, shortest to tallest, and they each took turns. After an hour of play, the sky began to darken. She instructed the children to go home then watched them as each one headed up the street to their respective homes.

Desiree smiled sadly. She wanted to have children, but at her current pace that dream seemed to become more and more remote. Thirty-seven years old, she knew the clock was ticking. She frowned as she continued to stand on the sidewalk, the children long gone. She allowed herself one final thought of Donald. He was history, and she had accepted that. It was time to move on.

Desiree returned to the stationhouse. The crew sat around for another five hours. She and Tulley talked about his desire to take the upcoming Lieutenant's exam. She was proud to hear that two of her men wanted to take the test, and she pledged her support.

Following a game of pitty-pat, Desiree went back outside. She sat down in a lawn chair and looked up into the now dark sky. She was restless. They'd had one incident the entire day, and it was a small fire in a garbage can three blocks away.

Desiree thought about her upcoming seventeen-day furlough in two months. She had decided to go to South Carolina for two weeks, followed by a three-day shopping and gambling trip in Michigan City with Annette. Her thoughts were interrupted by the loud shrill of the siren, followed by the sound of the dispatcher's voice over the intercom. She ran back into the firehouse and headed to the engine. She paused when she heard the phone ring. She thought not to answer it, but her Battalion Chief, Mike Callahan, had a way of calling at the same time a call to a fire rang out. She picked up the receiver.

"Engine Company #19. Captain Charles."

Words on the receiver came out garbled and hushed. She tried to make out the words on the other end. She caught the words "got to go," and nothing else as the line went dead. She hung up the phone and rushed to join her men at the engine. She put on her turn out gear, jumped in the cab and held on for another of Heaney's wild rides. She glanced over at him. He had on glasses. She tilted her head to the side. She hadn't seen Heaney in glasses before.

"I almost ran over that car the other night," he said simply and focused his attention on the street ahead of them.

Seven and a half minutes later, they arrived at another house. As Desiree and her team rushed from the truck, they could see that the right side of the house was engulfed in flames. Quickly, four hoses were attached to a nearby fire hydrant just as Desiree and Heaney rushed toward the front of the house.

They bounded up the concrete steps then frowned. The entrance was guarded by a wrought iron door with a screen attached near the top behind the iron. Heaney removed his glove, felt around the seams. He pulled his ax from his belt loop, sliced through the mesh, then placed the blunt end though the bars and pried the door from its jam. He felt the door again. Satisfied at its coolness, he stepped back then raised his right leg and kicked in the door.

Desiree raised the heat seeker upward. The device picked up countless hot spots, hidden areas of fire, along the walls and ceiling.

For hours, the crew battled the stubborn blaze as adrenaline pumped furiously through their veins. The natural drug worked to take each of them over the top as Desiree led her men further into the house armed with axes and hoses. Another engine company joined them and battled the blaze from the outside, while Desiree and her men battled the hidden blaze from inside.

"Right here," Desiree spoke into the mouthpiece attached to her helmet as she lowered the heat seeker and pointed to the wall. Without prompt, Carroll removed his ax, stepped up to the wall and raised the ax over his head. He swung upon the wall twice. The plaster crumbled as flames from the fire reared upward. Carroll stepped back as Moose and Tulley raised the hose to the left support wall, the cold water rained down on the wall and splashed back on them. Several times, Carroll, followed by Heaney, tore pieces of plaster from the walls that surrounded them, with Moose and Tulley saturating the spots with the force of one-hundred pounds of water.

Once extinguished, Desiree stepped over burned debris as she made her way from the front of the house to the rear. She raised and lowered the heat seeker. She was relieved to find no additional hot spots.

"It's a wrap, guys. Let's finish up and head home." Desiree stood in the charred living room. She and her crew laughed easily as they began to inspect the rubble. Desiree thought how people wouldn't understand their lively banter. To them it was a way to ease the tension, release some of the pent up frustration and adrenalin that consumed each of them every time they responded to a fire.

Desiree smiled at each of her men as they began to go through the house to ensure that no sparks remained to rear their ugly heads later. She thought back to when their now easy camaraderie hadn't always been so. When Desiree first arrived at the stationhouse one year ago, Carroll and Tulley felt that she was too young to be a captain of a stationhouse. With the exception of Heaney and Moose, her arrival had been met by silent stares and tight lips.

For nearly one month, Carroll and Tulley only responded to her when she posed a question or gave an order, but outside of that, they didn't interact with her at all. Heaney had advised her to bid her time and act accordingly, "The opportunity will present itself." As for Moose, he thought it best that he not intervene, for though he was all for her as Captain, he needed to know that the captain of his shift could handle herself.

To Desiree, Carroll and Tulley's treatment was nothing compared to the dog food in her boots incident. At her first stationhouse as a cadet, the all white, male team had placed wet dog food in her boots. The squishy feeling she received as she had placed her foot, covered only by a sock, into her boot caused her to nearly wretch. But she sucked it up, forced her feet into the moist boots and fought that fire like she was trained to. She had wanted to cry back then, but to shed tears would prove their senseless point: that she wasn't tough enough to be a firefighter. *Umph,* she huffed. The silent treatment they gave her was nothing in comparison to what she had already experienced.

Desiree had laughed the day a picture of a naked, white woman had been plastered on the door to her quarters. Below the picture was a note, horribly scribbled, which instructed her to *"go home and have some babies. That's where a woman belongs—in the kitchen, cooking and pregnant."*

Though the picture hadn't bothered her in the least, she knew that it was time to put those two in their places and show them that she wasn't going anywhere anytime soon.

A week after the picture incident, the company responded to a house fire, tame in comparison to some they had fought. Carroll and

Tulley had gone around to the rear, without informing Desiree. As captain, it was her responsibility to know where her team, which consisted of the four men, was at all times. Now was not the time to make a point or engage in heroics.

Once the fire was out, the crew returned to the stationhouse. Instead of heading to her quarters, Desiree had gone to the kitchen. She had ordered Tulley, who was the stationhouse cook when on duty, out of the kitchen. She closed the door behind him. For over two hours, the men of Engine Company #19 heard pots and pans clatter and clang, but none dared to open the kitchen door to peek inside.

A half-hour later Desiree stepped out of the kitchen, an apron secured around her small waist, and called the firefighters to the dining area. Desiree placed heaping servings of mashed potatoes, with home-made gravy, short ribs of beef, cabbage and corn, hot water corn bread and dinner roles on the table. She topped it off with two pitchers of sweet tea. As she served the sumptuous meal, she asked each one seated in a voice dripping with honey if they had enough on their plates.

The men only nodded and stole curious glances at each other. Desiree watched them; her eyes went from focusing on Tulley, then back to Carroll. She stood at the head of the table and waited until each member of her team had a small portion of food left on their plates. Desiree snatched the apron from her waist, tossing it carelessly onto the table, then gripped the edge of the table and flipped it over. Broken dishes strewn the floor as startled men fled in several directions.

"Halt!" she yelled. "And that's a direct order. Any man who moves will get twenty-nine days for failure to follow a direct order." No one moved. "Now, come back here and sit down!"

The four men, which included Heaney, returned to the dining area and sat in chairs. They looked at the broken plates and glasses on the floor, the overturned table. Desiree dared not look at Heaney for she knew he would have a bemused expression plastered across his face.

"Since my arrival, Carroll and Tulley, you two have tried to make me run. But I've got news for you. I'M HERE TO STAY," she announced every word through clinched teeth. "And you two are hereby suspended for three days. You will never," she walked over to Tulley and Carroll, and leaned into their faces, "and I mean *never*, go out on your own. Something could have happened to you at that fire today. What would make you," she pointed to Tulley, "think I want to call your wife and tell her you were killed fighting the beast? Or you Carroll," she pointed her finger at him, "call your parents and fiancée and tell them the same?!" She straightened, then began to circle her men. The soles of her feet stepped quietly over broken dishes. "We are either in this together or not at all. I'm here to stay, gentlemen. And if you can't get with it, then get out!" She pointed to the door.

Ready to walk away, she stopped herself. "Oh, and wasn't that a mighty fine meal? Oh, and by the way, I like my meat tall, dark and handsome with three legs. Not skinny and colorless with two."

From that day forward, Carroll and Tulley had a newfound respect for their captain, with Tulley becoming one of her staunchest supporters. And Desiree had been glad Heaney hadn't intervened.

Desiree nodded at the thought and looked at her men proudly as they continued to sweep the house for smoldering embers.

"Wait," Moose called out. "Looks like bodies."

They paused. No one spoke as Moose, followed by Tulley, moved closer. Tulley sighed loudly. "Somebody call the coroner."

No matter how many fires Desiree had battled over fifteen years, she still hadn't gotten accustomed to the fatalities. The first one, ten years ago, had been that of the five-year old child. The incident had scarred her, as if she had been burned herself, and much to her chagrin just like the scars her father wore daily as a reminder of the fury fire could unleash.

Outside, she sat on the large, chrome bumper of the engine, hung her head and said a silent prayer. She raised her head slightly and watched absently as the coroner, followed by the paramedics, entered the shell of the burned brick house. She was still on the bumper when she noticed a midnight blue sedan pull up and park in the middle of the street. A tall man exited, his wide back clothed in a black polo, a black Kangol turned backwards on his head, his lower body encased in black slacks and shoes. She glanced at him then averted her eyes. She looked up again. *Joshua Davis.*

She had seen him from a distance many times over the years—the fine brother who didn't play games, didn't smile and had risen through the ranks to be one of the department's best arson detectives, but he never seemed to notice her. Her father had bragged on him saying, "Joshua Davis is one hell of a firefighter." Her father's glowing accolades of the then young firefighter had made her wonder about him. The first time she saw him, she had been attracted to him.

The one opportunity she had to speak to him, he had been whisked away by fellow firefighters following his election as president of the African American Firefighters and Paramedics League. She hadn't even congratulated him. Instead, she stood and watched as he exited the union hall surrounded by a crowd.

Shortly after the election, she had begun dating Donald and hadn't really given Joshua much thought, especially since she had sworn off dating firefighters.

Desiree watched as he paused and looked into her eyes.

CHAPTER 4

"Davis. In here," the coroner called out from the porch.

"What you got, Bill?" Joshua asked as he looked toward the voice. He scanned the various faces of the onlookers standing along the sidewalk at the scene as he approached. He searched for that knowing glance, the wildness in ones eyes—a wildness that typically belonged to an arsonist. He saw none then stole a glance at the firefighter sitting on the bumper of the fire engine, his head hung. He noted the somberness surrounding the scene. Felt it. Knew it. A part of him wanted to go over and put his arm around the firefighters shoulder, assure him that it wasn't his lack of knowledge and skill, but it was a part of the job that no one ever got use to, no matter how much they pretended they had. The other part of him, the no-nonsense part of him, shrugged off the emotional pull.

He paused near the truck. The firefighter raised her head and met his eyes. It was Desiree Charles.

He nodded absently at her then continued toward the house.

"It's two bodies. This one," the coroner pulled back the sheet as Joshua stepped into the charred living room of the house, "isn't as badly burned as that one." He pointed to his right. "That one is burned beyond recognition. Looks like they were trying to escape. The guys found them as they began to go through the rubble from the roof."

In Joshua's ten years as a detective for the Chicago Fire Department, he still hadn't gotten used to seeing burned bodies. He squatted over the body. The odor could be so overwhelming that it seeped from his pores for days following. When he was a firefighter, he had named it "the smell of the beast." Joshua thought of the countless individuals who had been badly burned in fires and survived, yet the scars had distorted them completely.

"God bless their souls," Joshua said as the coroner covered the victims. "This is going to be ruled an accident until I finish my investigation. Anyone got anything else?" Joshua rose and looked at the firefighters and police officers assembled. No one spoke. "Well, guys, let me get started."

The men left Joshua alone among the rubble, the bodies now removed. Joshua placed latex gloves over his hands, pulled a flashlight from his pocket followed by a small notebook and pencil. He began to make notes, sniffing the surrounding air for any traces of gasoline or other unnatural odors. Hours passed as Joshua turned over burnt items and examined them. He had placed several items in a pile near the front door, then stepped outside and headed to his car. He looked up and down the block and watched as a couple sauntered past the burned out shell, oblivious to the life lost there.

A familiar scent stopped Joshua suddenly. Unable to recall the odor, he was certain the strong, acidic odor had been used to start the fire. He rushed to his car and grabbed another kit then rounded the side of the house. He squatted over an area of charred grass, pulled several blades from its base, placed them in a plastic bag, then sealed the contents and marked them. He repeated this several times then retrieved the items he left in the house.

He looked back over his shoulder one last time at the house, shook his head, then headed to the stationhouse of Engine Company #19.

Desiree pulled her gym shoes onto her feet then stood and raked her fingers through her shoulder length hair. She smelled like smoke from head to toe and was glad her shift had finally ended. The last hours of her shift had been pure hell. She thought of the two bodies at the last fire. She shook her head then thought of the next three days, her scheduled days off.

Another three whole days of total rest and relaxation! This time she would do something she hadn't done since she and Donald broke up. She would soak in her whirlpool tub, then she would sleep in her queen-sized bed until she couldn't sleep anymore, followed by lazily lounging on the chaise situated on the wooden deck she'd had built behind her two-story Victorian, which was located less than fifteen miles from the stationhouse.

"Guys," she said as she joined the men from her shift. "I'll see you all in a few days. Be careful. And, Tulley, take some time off to be with your wife and baby. Hear me? That's what FMLA is for. Use it. I don't want to see you here in three days."

Tulley nodded as Moose and Carroll smiled and saluted her. She smiled back as she returned the salute. The three men, much like Heaney, had become her protectors of sorts. And now, just as Heaney had from the very beginning of her career, each had made it their personal credo to ensure they supported her as stationhouse captain. And she loved them for it. She knew her men were some of the best firefighters in all of Chicago.

"See ya, Pappa," Desiree whispered as Heaney joined her, and they headed toward the door of the stationhouse.

"Hey, Lass, you enjoy your time off."

"That I will." She tapped his hand. He touched her shoulder then exited before her. Desiree paused at the door, turned and looked at the old house. She nodded as a slight glow crept across her face. She was proud of her men, and even more so of the relationship she had finally cemented with them.

The warm, early morning blue sky greeted Desiree as she stepped out of the stationhouse and headed to the department issued red Ford Blazer. She disarmed the alarm system, opened the passenger side door, threw her nylon bag onto the seat, and then shut the door. She was startled when she turned and faced a wide chest encased in black. Her eyes trailed upward and met a pair of stern, brown eyes. Her mind clicked. She recognized him as the serious, but fine, Detective Joshua Davis.

"Didn't mean to startle you," Joshua said as he stepped closer. The acrid smell of smoke greeted him and seeped into his nostrils.

"What do you need, Detective Davis? My shift's ended. I'm on my way home."

"I need to discuss today's fire and the other fire from last week." He tilted his head as he attempted to get a better look at the woman who bested many to become the first black female station captain. A swell of pride rose in his chest. He wasn't one of those chauvinistic brothers who thought women had no place at the firehouses. Actually, some of the best firefighters he worked with had been women, and he had been proud to have them by his side whenever he fought the beast.

Desiree twisted her slightly full lips. "Can this wait until I'm back on duty? I'm too tired to talk, and I smell like smoke. All I want to do is go home."

Joshua looked at her clothes. With the exception of a pair of white gym shoes on her feet, she still had on her uniform. "It won't take but a moment. The first twenty-four hours are the most crucial. You know that." He wanted to talk to her about the fire, see if she had noticed anyone or anything out of the ordinary.

Bone tired, body aching, Desiree couldn't think clearly. She decided after she got a few hours of sleep.

She pulled a business card from her pocket, wrote her home number on the back then handed it to him. Waving her hand, she rounded her vehicle and prepared to leave. Blondie's "One Way or Another" blared from the vehicle's speakers. Moose and Tulley appeared and danced their way to their respective vehicles. Tickled by her men, she laughed as she rolled down the window.

"Detective, call me in a couple of hours. I'll be more lucid and able to give you one hundred percent of my undivided attention," she said as she placed the vehicle in drive and sped off.

The exhaust from the vehicle covered Joshua. He waved his hand slightly across his face. The last sound he heard was the refrain from the song. "Okay, Captain. Have it your way."

This was the part of the job Joshua disliked. His shift had ended at seven that morning, but because of the deaths at the fire, he needed to get as much information as possible during the first twenty-four hours.

He worked the night shift, not by force, but by choice. Since Serena's death, he hadn't been able to sleep more than five hours on any given night. The memories weren't too bad during the day—they were at their worst at night.

He rode along State Street. His eyes swept across the expansive parcels of vacant land—land that once occupied one of the most infamous housing projects in the country and was home to thousands of low-income residents.

He shook his head and continued toward the Cook County Coroner's office. Once he finished his round of interviews at the coroner's office, he headed to his office.

Joshua stepped out of his department issued sedan and nodded at several officers he knew. He grabbed his evidence case and a bag that contained the various items he retrieved from the fire, then walked through the back entrance and down a flight of stairs. He opened the door to his unit. Its once white walls turned a garish beige from the effects of cigarette smoke. His thoughts went to the couple lying down at the Cook County coroner's office, one burned beyond recognition, the other burned so badly, even if the elderly woman had survived she would have faced years of skin grafts and operations just to have a life.

According to the couple's adult children, the pair had been married for fifty years and was inseparable. Inwardly, Joshua cried for the couple. He and Serena would have celebrated their tenth wedding anniversary in a month. He had taken notes from the couple's children, then from the coroner who would be conducting the autopsy. He had returned to the examination room and said a silent prayer over the couple, whose bodies lay side by side.

He shook his head and walked to his desk. Tall file cabinets set between five additional desks, all with computers atop them, set away from one of the four walls, their occupants furiously typing on computer keyboards and talking into telephones. He waved to each, who either nodded or waved back.

Typically, he would be alone and glad for the silence his single presence brought with it. His mind returned to the elderly couple. Today, he was glad to be among the living.

After placing the evidence bag on his desk, he went to grab some coffee from the vending machine down the hall. The cup dropped and brown liquid filled to the brim. He raised the protective shield and then took a sip of the hot brew. Unfortunately, the coffee tasted like chalk. He tossed the cup and its contents into the nearby wastebasket, walked to another vending machine and bought a Pepsi. He drank down the cool beverage then returned to his office.

He took his bag of items from his desk and walked to the evidence room. After cataloguing and noting the various items from the fatal fire, he placed them in respective drawers, shut off the lights and returned to his desk to complete paperwork on a case he had just solved. He glanced at the clock. It was just past noon. He stretched his arm above his head. His body ached for just one more. One more hit to sooth the gnawing pain.

Joshua Michael Davis had been sober for nearly six years, yet every-day was a battle. His fortieth birthday was a month away. He had entered a detox program on his thirty-fourth birthday. Since then, he knew he had to remain sober—his job and his sanity depended on it. In the beginning, he had been a social drinker, drinking just enough to illicit a decent buzz, but he had begun to imbibe more often a few years before Serena's death. At her insistence, he entered the program, then joined Alcoholics Anonymous and fought daily to control the desire to drink. Ironically, Serena's death came one year after his sobriety, at the hands of a drunk driver.

Joshua opened the middle drawer of his desk, took out the framed picture and studied it. It was something he did when the pull of liquor became almost too much to bear. As he held the picture, he thought of the horrible way his wife and unborn son died.

He sniffed and wiped at the slight mist that formed at the corner of his eyes. He smiled absently at the sparkle in his late wife's eyes on their wedding day. Joshua placed the picture back in the drawer. *Another day. Yes, I can make it another day.*

He turned on his computer and began furiously typing in notes from the fire then finished a report from two other arson cases he had recently solved.

His instincts told him that an arsonist started the fire that had killed the elderly couple. *Great, now we've got another arsonist loose in Chicago.*

Joshua poured over old files of paroled convicted arsonists, searching for clues, some type of pattern that may give him insight as to who and why.

After another hour, his search came up cold. The three convicted arsonist he did find were all locked up. The remaining didn't fit the pattern.

Joshua folded his hands and bent them backward. He then pulled Desiree's business card from his pants pocket. He looked at it. He needed to talk to her he thought as he picked up the phone.

"Good afternoon, Assistant Commissioner Paglinini's office. How may I help you?"

"Hey, Marge. It's Joshua. How are you today?"

"Doing well, detective. And you?"

"Good. Look, I need a small favor."

He explained to Marge that he needed Captain Charles' address to do a follow-up on a couple of cases. He had to smile as Marge "hmm'd" at his excuse.

Joshua jotted the address on the business card, thanked Marge for the information then placed the card in his pocket. He pushed back from the desk, stood then stretched his large arms wide. He knew he should head home to get some sleep. It was now two o'clock, and he had to be back in nine hours.

He climbed into his car then headed toward the house he had once shared with his late wife. But an inexplicable pull had him take Desiree's card from his pocket. He headed to her home instead.

CHAPTER 5

Desiree heard the doorbell. Remised to move herself from her spot on her deck, she had accomplished everything she said she would. She had come in, removed her uniform, soaked in her whirlpool tub for an hour, then crawled into her bed and slept for hours. Once her body had been satisfied, she rose and headed outside to rest on the chaise lounge on her deck. She loved the way the warmth of the sun shone on her bare legs. It was July in Chicago, normally a time for searing heat, but July had been ushered in with warm temperatures, low 80's, just the kind of temps Desiree liked. The door chimes sounded again. She huffed loudly, then rose from her lounger and headed out the side gate of the backyard. She shook her head as she watched him peer into the door's window just as he began knocking on her glass screen door.

"Don't break down the door, Detective Davis," Desiree ordered. "How'd you get my address? I thought you were going to call?"

He looked away sheepishly. "Come on now. I'm a detective. I have my ways." He watched her closely as she inhaled deeply. "But let me apologize for not calling first. I was heading home. I hope you don't mind my stopping by? I promise to keep it brief. I smelled something strange along the side of the house. And I know this is one of your specialties."

Desiree tilted her head. "Fine." She motioned for him to follow her. Joshua walked behind her and noticed her attire. Cut-off jeans showed her long shapely legs, and a Chicago Fire Department T-shirt hung loosely about her body. Her hair was pulled off her face and hung just at the nape of her neck in a ponytail. He sat in the chair she pointed to, furthest away from the chaise lounge.

"Okay, Davis, what do you need?" she lay back on the chaise lounge and crossed her legs, her face pointed toward the sun.

"Please call me Joshua." The bright fuchsia paint on her toenails took him by surprise. "I want to know did you smell anything when you and your crew arrived on the scene?"

"As a matter of fact we did. We got a whiff of something that smelled like ammonia with a mix of nitrate. It was faint, but I caught it as we rounded the side of the house. I remember there was grass on that side. Did you get any samples?"

"Sure did. I smelled it too, but I wasn't sure. Did you smell anything else or the same odor when you got to the rear?"

Mouth twisted, she said, "Now that you mention it, the scent did become stronger as we got closer to the rear, but when we circled to the rear, I didn't smell it anymore."

"Did you notice if your boots slid on the grass or stuck to it?" He pulled out his note pad and began taking notes.

"Detective, we were rushing, so unfortunately I didn't notice."

"Call me Joshua," he repeated. "It could be what was used to start the fire didn't have nitrate in it. I know an arsonist who would use craft glue to start fires."

Desiree nodded her head, but never met the eyes that slowly rolled up and down her prone body. Joshua shook his head. *Focus,* his mind screamed as he tried to ignore how smooth her slightly muscular legs looked stretched out before her. He fired off another round of questions.

What began as a fifteen-minute inquiry turned into an hour of back and forth questions, answers and hypotheses.

"You'd make a good detective, Captain Charles."

She noted the seriousness in his eyes and the way his face held no emotion. "Thank you, Joshua." She smiled. "Wait! Where are my manners?" She swung her legs around so that her bare feet rested on the deck. "I haven't offered you anything to drink. Would you care for some tea, water, Pepsi or a beer?"

Joshua looked at Desiree, her eyes shielded behind a pair of dark sunglasses. He nodded his head.

"Beer?"

"No, I'll take some tea."

She headed to the rear door. "I hope you like sweet tea. It's the only kind the Charles household serves."

"That'll be fine," Joshua replied as he watched Desiree disappear into the house.

She returned several minutes later with a round glass tray topped with a pitcher of tea, two glasses filled with ice, and a bowl of pretzels. For another two hours, they discussed the case of the fatal fire and the other fire her team had just responded to a week before.

As the sun began to set, their conversation turned from the fires and became more personal. "You live here alone?"

Desiree nodded.

"How long have you lived here?" he asked as his dark eyes scanned the expansive yard.

"I bought the house two years ago. Actually, it was the yard and the upstairs master bedroom that sold me. Want a tour?"

"Sure." He rose to follow Desiree. His eyes trailed up and down her back. Her rear sat high and voluptuously round. He couldn't help eyeing the view. He found it odd that he was so interested in her.

Most times when investigating arson, he would conduct his interview and then leave, no socializing. Since noticing her name on the file, then seeing her at the recent fire, he couldn't seem to stop wondering about her. The case gave him a legitimate excuse to see her.

As Desiree outlined various parts of the house, he watched her face, now absent the sunglasses, her warm nutmeg complexion held hints of red, underlying her smooth complexion. He looked at her hands. Her slightly long nails were neatly manicured and painted the same color as her toe nails. He watched her deep brown eyes light up animatedly when she led him to her basement, which boasted a theater with real theater seats.

As they climbed the stairs that led to her bedroom, Joshua paused. Several pieces of art hung about the small enclave. One in particular stood out.

Desiree paused and followed Joshua's eyes. "My ex gave me that for my birthday."

He looked at the painting, a couple surrounded by light, their fingertips touching. Created by Merrill, it was titled "Connection."

"I've got the same painting." He thought of the time he and Serena had visited a small art gallery in Savannah, Georgia, and had purchased the painting on sight—its vibrant reds and yellows reminded them of passion, of the connection they had with each other…

"I actually like it. It's so passionate. So alive."

Joshua nodded his head, but remained silent. Desiree continued her ascent. "Here's my home office." She pointed inside. Several framed movie posters hung about the walls, which were painted a burnt orange color.

"And over here is the guest room." She entered the room. Joshua followed her and swore he had stepped back into time. The room, painted a light taupe, had an old-fashioned walnut head and footboard, with a matching walnut sitting table and highboy. He titled his head to one side.

"Something wrong with my room?" Desiree asked, feigning insult as she placed her hands on her ample hips.

"No. It just reminds me of my grandmother's room. She was born in Charleston, and I swear she had the same furniture."

"Well, my parents and I own a vacation home in Charleston. I go twice a year in September and May."

"Yeah?" he turned and faced her. "Where at?"

"Isle of Palms off Sullivan's Island. Have you heard of it?"

"Yeah, my grandmother worked not far from there on Dunes. She was a nanny. I've run all over those islands. As a kid, I spent many a summer in Charleston. I use to lie out on the beach, look out over the Atlantic and wonder what it must have been like to be a pirate." He seemed stunned at his own admission. *TMI*, he thought. *Too Much Information!* "Ahh, anyway. Nice furniture."

"Thanks," Desiree looked at him. It was the first time she had an opportunity to examine him up close. His smooth, chestnut complexion sported an even mustache, goatee and high cheekbones. His dark brown hair was cut low and laid about his round head in curly waves. And his eyes were round, brown, doe eyes, surrounded by long lashes that gave him a boyish appearance. She noted they held a hint of sadness. "When I'm in the Carolina's, I make sure I make a trip north to buy furniture. I found this at a furniture antique dealer. As a matter of fact, my entire house is furnished from North Carolina."

She stepped out of the guest room and opened a door. "This is the master suite."

Painted a stark white, the large room's central focal point was the expansive cherry wood platform bed. Joshua looked at Desiree, then back to the bed, covered in a cream chenille spread, with matching pillows and shams.

"This reminds me of a southern belle," Joshua stated.

"Well, technically I am. I was born in Alabama then came here when I was just about three. Like you, I spent many a summer with my grandparents. My mom and I even went back there for about six months after Dad joined the department."

"Why?"

"Death threats." Desiree didn't meet Joshua's eyes. She knew each time she made that statement, the knowing looks and pious pity would meet her. She shrugged her shoulders and continued the tour. "And this is the master bathroom."

Joshua whistled loudly. He guessed the bathroom, painted a creamy peach, was at least twice the size of his bathroom. He looked at the shower stall, enclosed in glass and trimmed in gold, then over at the cream-colored whirlpool tub. *Fit for two*, he thought. He shook his head. *Where did that thought come from?*

"So, that's Chateau Charles."

"This is really nice, Desiree. Umm, I can call you Desiree? That is, if you don't mind."

"I guess so, especially since you insist on my calling you Joshua. The biblical warrior."

"Sure is. Moses's right hand."

They stared at each other. Desiree caught a faint scent of cologne.

She didn't know what the scent was, but whatever it was it made him smell delectably delicious. She batted her eyes and wondered what possessed her to invite this man, one she had heard of, but didn't know, into the very intimate parts of her life: her bedroom!

In turn, Joshua wondered what had made him stay much longer than he had intended to. He broke the stare and checked his wristwatch. "It's getting late. I have to get to the office in a few, and I haven't had a dime of sleep. Thanks for the tour and the tea."

"Not a problem."

He nodded slightly as he stood close to her. The smell of eucalyptus with a hint of spearmint met him. The fragrance was both intoxicating and calming.

"Joshua."

He heard her repeat his name. The sound of it rolled from her pursed lips. The cadence of her warm voice elicited an inexplicable solace. He followed her down the stairs toward the front door. He forced his eyes from the way her hips swayed to unheard music to take in the simple decorations of the living room. The four ecru walls had abstract art on each, the muted olive color of her sofa played off the orange, rust, and olive colored winged-back chairs. Both chairs had an accent table between them.

At the door, he stopped and faced Desiree, noting that the top of her head reached the bottom of his chin. He thanked her again, then stood to the side as she unlocked and opened the door.

"Take care, Joshua."

"You, too. If I have any further questions, can I call you?"

"Sure. Not a problem. Good night." She closed the door then placed her back against it and breathed aloud. *No way*, she mused. *No way did Joshua Davis come to my house! Wait until Annette hears this.*

Desiree watched as Annette strolled into the small restaurant. The

Hilltop Grill had been one of their favorites for years. The food was good and the service fast. Though the menu changed rarely, the owners had recently added pita sandwiches.

"Girl, you won't believe who's investigating the fire I was at the other day."

Annette kissed Desiree on the cheek, sat, then picked up her menu. Her light brown eyes scanned the menu once. She set the menu down then looked upon Desiree's face. "Who?"

"Joshua Davis."

"What?! You're joking. I thought he took care of the north side. What's he doing on the south side?"

"I don't know. I saw him after the fire was contained. He came to the house."

"Came over?" Annette leaned over, her full bosom rested on the table, a wicked smile spread across her tanned, caramel face. "Des? Where did he 'come over' to?" She raised her arched eyebrows.

Desiree cleared her throat then looked at the woman who was the closest thing to a sister she had. They had been in the academy together, even stationed at the same house their first assignment. Annette was now a lieutenant who filled in for several firehouses on the southwest side of the city. Desiree was proud of her "sister" and prayed that she would obtain a promotion to captain one day soon.

"Well, Nette, he came to my house to ask me a few questions about that fire the other day. Two people died."

"My God," Annette said. "But why couldn't he talk to you at the stationhouse?" she looked at Desiree.

"Well, I didn't give him a choice. It was quitting time." She shrugged her shoulders and thought of the tall, handsome brother, with the sad but beautiful, brown doe eyes. "You know I can't keep my eyes open after all the excitement has died down."

Annette sat back; her mouth pursed and her eyes twinkled. Desiree laughed at the expression. It was like a game of cat and mouse. Annette opened her mouth, then shut it when the waitress appeared, took their order, then left.

"Okay," Desiree began once the waitress left their table. "I know you've got something to say. Might as well spit it all out." She settled in for her best friend to dish all the information she had on Joshua Davis. Typically, Desiree wasn't interested in other people's business, but Joshua Davis was a different story. She wanted to know something about him, other than what she already knew: intelligent, serious, tall, dark and handsome.

"Well, one thing's for sure. That man's no dog. But…" Annette's lips curled up as she looked over Desiree shoulders.

Desiree turned and saw two of Chicago's finest enter the restaurant. Annette had a thing for the boys in blue. Lately all of her dates had been Chicago Police officers.

"Umph, I know him. That's Officer Carl Jackson. He's cute. Don't you think?"

Desiree gave them something akin to a frown as the two officers approached their table.

"Annette, it's good to see you. Are you keeping out of trouble?" Carl took Annette's hand in his.

"Well, I can't say that I have, but you can always help me," Annette purred and placed her free hand atop his.

Desiree stifled a laugh. Her girl was too much, but she had met many a man hanging around Annette, who's creamy caramel skin; sassy, short hair cut with honey blond highlights, and light eyes drew much attention, not to mention that her girl was built like a brick.

"Hey, don't I know you?" Carl's partner asked.

"You may," Annette answered for Desiree. "She's the fire captain at Engine Company #19. My girl here is running *thangs*!"

"Congratulations. My name is Michael." He extended his right hand. "I've heard of you. The brothers say you don't take any shit."

Desiree clasped his hand halfheartedly. She didn't know whether to be flattered or insulted. The remark could mean either she's fair, but stern, or she's a ball buster, as the men liked to say. She shrugged her shoulders and offered a simple, "Thanks."

"Annette, give me a call. Hear me, baby?" Carl stated then pulled out a business card, flipped it over and wrote a number on the back. "And don't let me run up on ya and you haven't called me." He winked, nodded at Desiree, and left, his partner in tow.

"Carl's a real cutie," Annette said as she watched him walk away. "He wears the hell outta that uniform."

Desiree knew the look in her eyes. "Annette."

"Oh, yeah, where was I? Umm, that fine ass Joshua Davis." Annette exhaled. "Well, you know the brother don't take no crap. He's all about the business, both for the department and as the VP of the International Black Professional Firefighters Association. You've seen him at the AAFL meetings. But the dude has got some serious demons. You know he's a widower. Poor brother lost his wife and an unborn child some years ago in a car accident. Reliable sources say that he doesn't date. And hasn't been interested in no—"

"Enough already," Desiree interrupted. Now she wasn't so sure she wanted to know how much of the man's business had hit the skids. She knew he was a widower and had heard the rumors of his drinking. She didn't like gossip, but the stories about his not dating and turning down sex were the ones she had listened to. Upon further thought, she couldn't recall ever seeing the man smile, neither in person nor in the pictures in the IABPFFA newsletter.

"Why? You interested?"

"No… I… was. No. Just wondering."

"Umm, sure. Well let me tell you, my sister, a brother with that type of baggage isn't the one for you."

"Like Donald was?" She hadn't intended to snap, but every time Annette started in on the brothers with baggage speech, her mind instantly went to Donald. They had dated for three years, were engaged to be married. When she finally caught up with Donald after nearly a week of hunt and search, he had finally admitted that he didn't want his "woman" to lord over a bunch of men at a "raunchy stationhouse." She hadn't realized, until after speaking with her father, that Donald was solidly against her promotion to captain.

"Oh, girl, that was one of my mistakes. He seemed cool and looked to have all his marbles in one place."

"Looks are deceiving."

"Anyway, let's not drudge up the past. Besides, its' been what, seven months or more. It's time you got back out there. Did you see the way Carl's partner was sizing you up? Girl, that's the next one. Mark my words."

"Oh, no! No way, Annette! You aren't fixing me up, and we're too damn old for double dating."

"Not! It won't hurt to go out, though. You need to."

"You just want me along in case you have to make a speedy exit."

Annette's rich laughter filled the restaurant. The sparse afternoon patrons looked their way, a few even smiled at the infectious sound. When Annette laughed, everyone wanted to. The sound seemed to come from the depths of her soul.

"Okay, seriously though. Detective Davis has one too many demons. My girl Yavette told me that she practically begged him to go out. When they did, she threw everything at him, including a kitchen sink and a stove, and he out right turned her down. You know my girl is a real looker. Has a body to die for! So you know folks began to wonder about the boy, if you get my drift." Annette raised her eyebrows.

"Now why does it have to be that the brother is gay? Because he wasn't interested in the one and only Yavette? Some men don't want to engage in the hit and run," Desiree spat out.

"Hold your horses, sister. I didn't mean to ruffle your mane. I'm just telling you what I heard."

"Not what you know," Desiree finished the old cliché and found herself relieved that the man had morals and didn't engage in gratuitous sex. *Why do I care what the man does?* Desiree wondered. Yet something about the tough, no-nonsense Joshua Davis intrigued her. Though she couldn't admit it, Desiree knew she wanted to know more about him. "Annette, let's change the subject."

As they discussed incidents at their respective firehouses, their food arrived. Annette and Desiree held hands as they bowed their heads to pray over their orders of half of a chicken salad sandwich and cup of soup that sat in front of them.

The rest of the lunch went by without another mention of Joshua Davis. Desiree had been glad for the reprieve. The one thing she liked about Annette was she knew when to drop a subject. Desiree knew the next time she discussed Joshua with Annette she'd be the one broaching the subject, not Annette.

After lunch, the pair headed to Saks Fifth Avenue on Michigan Avenue to do what Annette called, "power shopping."At the end of the day, tired but satisfied at the selections she had found on sale, Desiree happily dragged her tired body onto her front porch. She paused as she opened the door and stood in the entry. She recalled how Joshua had stood in this very spot less than two days ago, his broad frame filled the entryway, the warmth of his deep, chestnut complexion. *And those full, kissable lips. Kissable?* Desiree wondered where that thought came from. She didn't know him and didn't want to get any closer than she had already. She knew it was time to reverse whatever direction they were heading. It was time Joshua went back to being Detective Davis.

CHAPTER 6

A week passed and she hadn't heard a word from Joshua. Desiree looked at her wristwatch. She and the crew hadn't had one call since their shift started at seven that morning. She shut the door to the SUV and stood back to examine her handiwork. The vehicle shined like brand new coins. At many of the other stationhouses, the captain had the crew wash the department issued SUV, but not Desiree. The vehicle was her charge and therefore her responsibility to keep up the maintenance and cleanliness. She picked up the bucket, which contained various cleaning products, walked into the stationhouse and headed to the kitchen.

"Detective Davis called," Carroll said. "He needs to meet with you. Wants you to come down to his office later tonight." He handed Desiree the message. She looked into his tanned face and noted the amused expression that danced in his green eyes.

"Don't you have some work to do, Carroll?" She stuffed the note in the breast pocket of her white uniform shirt.

"Yup. Getting to it right now." He smiled as he placed the last dish in the drainer, emptied the sink of its water, and then wiped down the counter. She eyed him as he stole several glances her way, the amused expression still danced in his eyes.

Desiree tapped her foot as he finished the kitchen detail. Finally, she wanted to say, as she watched Carroll exit the kitchen. His exit meant that she wouldn't have to watch the expressions on his face, which tempted her to smile and get all giggly. That was something she didn't want the men in her charge to see. She felt it important to have a level of professionalism.

Twenty-five years old, William Carroll had been on the force for three years and was the youngest at the stationhouse. Medium built with sandy blonde hair, he was as strong as Moose. Desiree found him to be a good firefighter, but she felt he too often followed others, which didn't bode well in her book. She wanted leaders, not aimless followers. Carroll was like many firefighters in the Chicago Fire Department. He was a third generation firefighter, following in the footsteps of his father and grandfather. She guessed it just ran in ones blood.

She placed the bucket in the storeroom then headed to her quarters upstairs and sat down on the twin bed. Her thoughts had been consumed with the image, look and smell of Joshua Davis. And she hadn't even touched the man. *What's wrong with me?*

She rose from the bed and decided to do some serious cleaning of her quarters, which included the only shower for female firefighters. She wasn't messy, but she made sure she swept and mopped each day that she was on duty.

For three hours Desiree swept, dusted and cleaned every nook and cranny of the quarters in an attempt to cleanse her mind of Joshua. She stood back and admired her handy work. The old chrome of the bathroom fixtures gleamed and the area smelled of sweet oranges, thanks to a bottle of Formula 409.

She looked around for something else to clean. So far, she hadn't done a good job of moving him from her thoughts. She gave up. The images of Joshua seemed to have impaled themselves in her mind. She thought about his message and pulled it from her pocket. He wanted to see her. He hadn't stated why, so she assumed that he just wanted to discuss the events of the fire last week.

She knocked on the door that led into the men's quarters. When she didn't get a response, she peeked inside, and then turned on the lights. She shook her head and shut off the lights. *No way.* She'd save that chore for the men that slept there.

She left the upstairs quarters and went down to the kitchen. Tulley's back was to her as he finished preparing dinner.

"What's for dinner?"

He turned when he heard her speak. "Hey, Captain. We're eating beef short ribs with homemade gravy, rice, green beans and cornbread. And I made some sweat tea for you."

"Sounds delicious. I'm starved."

"You should be. You finished cleaning everything?"

"Everything but you guys' quarters. Where is everybody?"

He handed her a stack of plates. "Heaney and Moose are playing ping-pong. Carroll is sitting in the yard reading."

She set the table, always making a point of helping around the stationhouse. She looked at the bowls and platters of steaming food Tulley arranged on the table. Out of the four men in her charge, Mikel Tulley had been the best of his class. A fierce firefighter, Tulley had been on the force for ten years. His austere grey hair and sometimes scowling, cocoa-colored face attractively set with hazel eyes, lied on his age. Tulley was only thirty-three. When she first met him, he had been distant, but after a little table incident … The siren broke into her thoughts.

Tulley and Desiree rushed to the engine. She put on her turnout gear and jumped into the cab of the fire truck at the same time as Heaney. She held on to the grip bar as she readied herself for another one of Heaney's wild rides. She checked the address of the fire, which, according to the dispatcher, was contained to a garage at the rear of a residence ten blocks from the stationhouse.

A few hours later, the team of Engine Company #19 had successfully put out the fire. They talked and joked as they headed back to the firehouse. Desiree glanced at the clock on the dashboard. It was half past nine. She knew that Joshua's shift started in two hours.

Her stomach growled. She and her men sat down and ate. After dinner, Tulley and Moose cleaned the kitchen, while Carroll checked the engine to make sure all the equipment was in its rightful places. Heaney sat at the desk, began to write down the day's activities, and created the schedule for the next week.

He looked up as Desiree stood near the desk.

"Heaney, watch the house. I'm heading over to Detective Davis's office. Phone me at his office if we get called to a fire." She wrote the office number on a post-it note then placed it on the open pages of the daily log.

He glanced at her over his reading glasses. "Will do. Be careful," he called out as she walked toward the door and exited the stationhouse.

Desiree waved her hand over her head.

She drove down the expressway, then exited at thirty-fifth Street and headed east to the Chicago Police Department's headquarters. Desiree turned into the parking lot, found a spot, parked, and then strolled across the lot. She opened the large glass, double doors and headed toward the desk sergeant.

"I'm here to see Detective Davis."

The pie face, colorless sergeant looked up at her. He looked at her uniform then the nameplate attached to the left breast pocket of her shirt. "Sure Captain Charles. He's down the stairs over there." He pointed left over his shoulder. "Make a right after you go through the doors. You can't miss it. As a matter of fact, Josh just came in."

"Thanks Sergeant," Desiree began as she peered at his nameplate, "O'Leary. Thanks a lot."

"You're welcome."

She followed the sergeant's directions. The sound of whistling accompanied by the smooth sounds of jazz could be heard as she got closer to an open door. She stepped inside the room and saw Joshua as he sat at a desk, his head bent as he looked over papers. She stood in the doorway and watched him, his round head bent, his wide back and large, muscular arms stretched the fabric of his long-sleeved dress shirt, his warm complexion was a wicked contrast to the bright shirt. She could have stood there and watched him all night long but thought better. She cleared her throat. Joshua raised his head then looked at the clock on the wall.

"Just in time. I just got here." He rose from the desk.

Poetry in full motion, Desiree thought as she watched him saunter over to where she stood. This night he was dressed in a white shirt, a gold tie, speckled with black diamond patterned accents, and black jeans that fit him as if they were painted on. The muscular outline of his thighs took her places she didn't want to go.

"I got your message. What's up?" She decided to meet him half way. She inhaled the heady fragrance he wore, musk with a touch of something she couldn't quite discern.

"Got a few ideas. But I need you to look over some files and tell me how the particular accelerants I found at the fire burn."

Desiree wanted to laugh. She knew that Joshua was on something—she hoped it wasn't dope.

Joshua eyed her. He had hoped she'd believe his little white lie. He wanted to kick himself. He wasn't a liar, but he wanted to see her every-day since he'd left her house. Several times over the past week, he had wanted to call her, just to hear her voice. When he first called the station-house, he'd hung up before anyone answered. Once he did strike up enough nerve to allow the call to connect, she had answered the phone. Her voice, slightly deep and husky, seeped into him and wrapped itself around his brain. He was tongue-tied; his voice wouldn't come. *What is wrong with me?* He couldn't seem to get her out of his system, and he knew the only way to exorcise his continued thoughts of her was to see her. And now she stood inches from him, her smooth skin, deep brown eyes, and those lips that formed the cutest pout he had ever seen. Drawn to her, he felt it was time he came clean.

"Desiree." He paused. "I'm sorry for getting you here on a ruse, but I wanted to see you again. I just didn't know how. I didn't completely lie. I do need you to look over some old files of past fires in your area, the ones that Engine 19 has responded to over the past couple of years. See if you notice a pattern."

The seriousness in his eyes, the apology on his full sensuous lips—she wanted to feel his lips on hers. She shook her head. Even though she thought the rouse was somewhat cute, she felt the need to teach him a les-son. Sure she would forgive him, but not before she turned up the heat a little. She stepped up to him.

"Let me tell you something, Davis." She narrowed her eyes. "My time is extremely valuable. I've a stationhouse to run." She tapped her right foot, clad in the regulation black, soft-soled shoe, against the floor. "See this on my chest?" She tapped her nameplate. "It says 'Captain Charles.' And as captain, I've got responsibilities."

He seemed to shrink before her very eyes. He had opened his mouth to speak several times, but quickly closed it as she went on.

"So, let's get one thing straight." She leaned into him and placed her hand on his chest. The well-formed pectoral under her hand tensed, but she didn't remove her hand. "Any time you want to see me, Joshua," her voice dropped an octave, the edge now gone. "Just call. You don't have to make up excuses."

Joshua blinked several times. His somber face slowly turned to relief. The laughter shone in his eyes as the realization of what she had said hit him. He threw his head back in laughter.

"Woman, you're too much," he said as he placed his hand over hers. He felt a jolt rush up his body. The heat permeated through his shirt down to his soul. He removed his hand and stepped back. "But, seriously, I do need you to look over the files. You mind?"

"No, I don't mind. How many are there?" Her eyes absorbed the small laugh lines around his full mouth, his slight overbite, the way his eyes nearly shut when he had laughed. She had never seen the serious Joshua Davis smile before, much less heard him laugh. *He has dimples!* Set so deep, they added a boyish charm to his handsome face. She much preferred this to the somber expression he always wore, even on the day he stopped by her home.

He nodded his head toward the desk behind his.

"Joshua!" she spat out as she looked at the large stack of files. "It'll take me all night to go through those."

His long lashed hooded his lowered eyes. *I want you here with me for the rest of the night*, his mind whispered.

She looked up into his face and wanted to reach up and feel the texture of his skin, stroke her fingers lightly across his mustache, then down his goatee. *If the rest of him was any indication of the feel of his chest...* She felt the need to rein in the run-away emotions.

"Joshua, the only way I'll be able to go over those files is if you buy me something to drink. Preferably a Pepsi. A real Pepsi."

Joshua nodded his head then left the room. He returned with a 16 oz. bottle of soda. "How's this for a real Pepsi?"

"Just fine. Let's get started."

As the night gave way to the wee hours of morning, Desiree scribbled notes as she read the files of old arsons, her attention to the causes and accelerants used. Several times her mind wandered as she stole glances at Joshua as he sat at his desk looking over files. Once she even caught him looking at her.

His mind raced. He was no stranger to attraction, but it had been a long time since he'd wanted to allow that attraction to capture him, take him in. He thought of Serena. That was the last woman to make him take pause, to make him want to throw all caution to the wind and let the attraction take its natural course. But no one could take the place of Serena, he thought as he watched Desiree, the beautiful siren that sat mere feet from him. He watched her mouth move as she wordlessly read the files in front of her. His eyebrows rose as he watched her take a sip from the bottle of soda: her lips placed at the opening, the movement of her slender neck as she bent her head back slightly to partake of the cool liquid.

The phone on his desk rang, breaking him from his observation of Desiree.

His eyes made contact with Desiree. He averted the sensual glare and picked up the receiver. "Detective Davis," he responded.

Desiree watched his head as it nodded up and down while he scribbled on a pad of paper. She sat straight when she heard him say, "We're on our way."

"Got a fire at a restaurant several blocks from the stationhouse."

Desiree was on her feet in seconds. She grabbed the piece of paper from his hand and headed quickly to the exit. She didn't realize that Joshua was right behind her until she arrived at her vehicle.

"Come on, I'll drive," Joshua stated as he rushed to his car.

Desiree held on to the door handle as Joshua whipped the car from the parking lot, the single mars light and siren imposed on the darkness. *And here I thought Heaney's driving was bad.*

In all of ten minutes, Desiree arrived at the blaze, a two-alarm fire at a local restaurant.

"Heaney," Desiree said as she jumped from the vehicle and rushed to his side. Tulley raced along side of her. He handed her the various items from her turnout gear. "How's it looking?" Her eyes took in the scene before her. The fire seemed to be contained to one area near the rear of the building.

"We're using the foam. It's a grease fire." Tulley spoke as they began to walk toward the building. "No injuries. The cook was cleaning after closing and left a vat of grease on the stove. He tried to put it out with water."

They both paused and looked at each other. In unison, they shook their heads. Water would only serve to feed the fire, make it spread.

Joshua stood back and watched. He was in awe as Desiree took over. She never missed her stride as she effortlessly donned her boots and protective jacket. She directed her team, gave orders, even backed up her men by securing a hose to the truck. She had done so in a manner that was not harsh, but stern and protective. He smiled, liking what he saw.

Shortly, the team had the fire under control. Desiree and Heaney stood by and watched as the rest of the firefighters inspected the rubble.

Desiree knew he had been watching her. She smiled inwardly as she turned to see him. His firm body rested on the car. Heaney stood next to her.

"I see we have an admirer," Heaney stated then walked away. Desiree turned to watch Heaney as he walked over to the tuck and readied it for its return trip. She called to Moose, Carroll and Tulley to assist. She looked at Joshua. The pride in his eyes was unmistakable. She walked over to him slowly. She thought of her turnout gear. *So much for being sexy.*

She was only feet from him when her boot clad feet gave way. In an instant, she felt a pair of strong arms under her, which lifted her up, then set her gently on her feet. Desiree looked up to see Joshua staring down at her.

"Be careful, it's slippery out here."

Desiree nodded. "Thank you."

Slowly he released her. "Well, I better get back. I'm still on duty." He didn't move. He wanted to take the helmet from her head, take her in his arms, and kiss the lips that dared him to. *What am I doing?* He stepped back. "I can take you back to get your vehicle."

"That's okay. I'll get one of the guys to come get it." She spoke what her heart didn't feel. More time was what she wanted, but she also need-ed to get back to the stationhouse. Duty won out.

Joshua nodded. He wanted salience, some more time to figure out if maybe she felt the attraction, felt the very thing that made him want to be with her, to protect her.

"Gotcha. I'll talk to you later." He climbed into his vehicle and drove off.

Desiree watched as the tail lights of the sedan disappeared into the night.

She turned at the feel of a tap on her shoulder. She was surprised to see the son of her Battalion Chief, Mike Callahan, at the fire.

"What are you doing here?"

Mike Callahan, Jr. smiled at her. "I'm a lieutenant and a firefighter. I can go wherever I want to. Besides, I was at a bar a few blocks away when I heard the fire over the radio and thought you guys might need a hand."

The strong smell of liquor on his breath about blew her away. She no more liked the son, than the father. To her, they were the same. She knew that he shared his father's strong dislike for all people of color, thus found it strange for him to be drinking at a neighborhood bar full of black peo-ple.

"As you can see, Mikey." Desiree purposely called him by the name he despised. "The fire is out, so why don't you go home and sleep off that hair of the dog you put on." She didn't give him time to respond as she walked to the fire truck then climbed in once her men were all seated. She glanced out of the right side view mirror at Mike Junior. She found it odd that he would be on this side of town of all places.

"Heaney?" Desiree began. "How long has Mikey been here?"

Heaney leaned over and looked out the right side view mirror. "I just noticed him when he started talking to you. What's he doing way over here? His station is on the southwest side of town."

"He said something about being at a bar a few blocks away," she responded.

Heaney shook his head, placed the engine in gear, and drove to the stationhouse. Desiree looked in the mirror one last time. Mike was still there.

At the stationhouse, Desiree instructed Tulley and Carroll to pick up the department car from Joshua's office. She then began to complete her paperwork, noting the shift's events in the daily log, followed by a thorough check of the engine's equipment. Though she knew this was Moose's job, she needed time to try to clear her head of the heated thoughts of Joshua.

As she prepared to leave, her shift over, the phone rang.

"Engine #19. Captain Charles speaking."

"Hi," Joshua said.

"Hi, yourself."

"You were something else out there."

"Thanks. I try hard."

"No need to. You're a natural," Joshua stated. "I've worked with female firefighters, but none have had the presence you do. You're good."

She didn't know how to respond. She always took her job serious, had always attempted to do and be the best. Yet, it was nice to hear his complements.

"Desiree, do you mind if I call you at home?"

"No, I don't mind. Call me in the evening. I'll be fully awake by then."

"Will do. Take care and sleep tight."

"Thank you, Joshua. Same to you." She placed the receiver on its base. She gathered her personal items then left the stationhouse. As she drove home, her body heavy as if a lead weight were attached to it, she thought of the feel of Joshua's arms around her, the soothing comfort of them. She shivered uncontrollably.

"Wicked. Just wicked," she stated aloud.

CHAPTER 7

Her hands outstretched, she came to him, a vision of warmth and security. She hugged him, her arms tight about him as she whispered into his ear, followed by a light kiss upon his lips. He laughed like a schoolboy. The sound lifted up to the heavens. She stepped out of his arms, waved goodbye then ran. Joshua ran after her, close on her heels, the sand under his feet parted. Yet, the faster he ran, the further away she became, until he could no longer see her.

Joshua sat up in bed. His heart pounded in his chest. Sweat beaded across his high brow. He breathed in deeply as he attempted to steady his run away heart. He hung his head, but the tears refused to come, refused to flow. He hadn't dreamed of Serena in months. *Why now?*

He glanced at the clock near his bed—9 p.m. After talking to Desiree, he had finished his paperwork and gone home. He thought of Desiree all the whole time: the way she had looked dressed in her uniform, her long hair pulled back into a ponytail. He thought of the way the navy pants viciously hugged her womanly curves. He hadn't been able to sleep for more than two hours at a time without waking with the same thoughts that had become his constant partner since meeting Desiree. *Is it time?*

He huffed loudly as he climbed out of bed and headed to the bathroom. He looked at his image in the mirror. The circles under his eyes told him he needed more rest. He thought about his upcoming furlough in two months. According to his rank and department, he'd be off for twenty days. *Maybe I should visit my brother*, he thought, but dismissed it. He was never comfortable with prisons and found it hard to visit his brother, Abel, who was doing a life sentence for murder. Joshua shook his head. His only sibling resigned to a ten by twelve cage. Had he only listened, but Abel had been a strong willed, hardheaded boy, and as a man was even more so.

Three years his junior, Abel had seemed to attract trouble. It was during high school when harmless pranks and broken windows gave way to the world of gangs and their unscrupulous dealings. Though Joshua had gone to jail once, for stealing an action figure from a department store when he was twelve, the four hours he spent locked in a local police district cell was more than enough. He hated that caged feeling. Still, he wondered where he and his family had gone wrong when Abel had been arrested, then later arraigned and sentenced for the murder of a rival gang leader.

Joshua winced as he recalled the stricken looks on his parents' faces as the judge read off Abel's sentence, "life with no chance of parole." They had prayed he would get twenty to thirty years, and with time off for good behavior, maybe he'd be parole after fifteen years. But due to the manner in which Abel chose to murder his rival, the judge had refused to let Abel ever roam around free to murder another soul. Abel had shot, and then slit his rival's throat. That was ten years ago.

The phone rang. He placed a robe about his body, picked up the phone near his bed, then sat down.

"Hello?"

"This is a collect call from the Illinois Pontiac Correctional Facility. An inmate from this facility is attempting to reach you. To accept . . ." the voice droned as Joshua waited until the recorded message ended before hitting the key to accept the call from his brother.

"What's up Josh?"

"I'm good, man. How are you?"

"Ninety-nine more to go," Abel deadpanned without emotion. For the past seven years, Abel had responded to his brother's general question by restating the obvious; he'd never walk out of that prison. Joshua always wondered when Able would give up the pat response and move on with the reason for his call. Joshua refused to respond.

"Mom and Dad are coming down next month. Are you coming with them?"

The last time Joshua had been down state to visit his brother was shortly after Serena's death. He had found it difficult to visit, but knew that he should at least send him a care package once a month. Eventually Joshua came to realize and accept that he was angry with his brother for choosing to live on the wrong side of the law.

"I'm not sure. My furlough isn't for another couple of months. We'll see then."

He heard his brother mumble a response. "Well, you know where I'm at. I just wanted to say hello. That I'm thinking of you. Take care and be careful out there." Abel hung up without further words.

Joshua replaced the receiver in its cradle, rose from the bed and headed back to the bathroom. He turned on the shower's water, made a mental note to call his parents, then he thought of his brother again. He needed to put aside the anger and disappointment and just be there for him.

He switched thoughts and began to make a mental task list he intended to complete during his shift. Another image of Desiree popped into his head. He thought of the whirlpool tub, just the two of them. He shook his head. *What am I doing?* He removed his boxer briefs, stepped into the shower and let the warm water bead down his body.

After his meticulous bathing ritual, which included shaving and trimming his mustache and goatee, Joshua dressed in a pair of olive colored Dockers, a matching shirt, and his signature Kangol cap, turned backwards. He waved to one of his neighbors as he stepped onto the front porch and picked up the paper from the steps. He glanced at it. *Old news.* He folded it, placed it under his arm, stepped down the steps, then climbed into the department issued sedan and headed to his office.

"That was some fire, Lass," Heaney said as he backed the large engine into the stall of the firehouse. "And it's the fourth one in the last week. All of them during our shift. That's a lot. I'm just grateful that there have been no more deaths."

Desiree nodded her head as her mind replayed the events of the last four fires they had fought. All had started approximately ten hours after their twenty-four hour shift began. And all of the fires, with the exception of the house fire where the children had been and the one that killed the elderly couple, had been contained to garages and vacant houses. Yet, at each fire, she smelled the same, acidic odor. To add to it, she received strange phone calls right before they left to fight the fires. Almost as if the obscene phone caller knew they were on their way to a fire.

The last fire came to her mind. When they arrived, the fire seemed to burn cleaner. And the absence of any odor of accelerants was noted. Still, something wasn't quite right. She had an eerie feeling and prayed that Joshua would solve this case and fast. To her, it seemed as if Engine Company #19 had been targeted. She made a mental note to mention all of this to Joshua.

Joshua. She beamed as she thought of the conversations they'd had over the past week. She had come to look forward to his calls. Each night he had contacted her by phone, either at the stationhouse when she was on duty, or at home. She thought of his voice last night, the unsure tone when he asked her out.

Joshua had called her at home. She laid in bed as they began their ritual by discussing the suspicious fires that were breaking out on the South Side of Chicago. According to Joshua, a pattern had begun to form. He was certain that the fires had been set, using a highly volatile mix of accelerants, which were supposed to burn quickly and give the impression that the fires were started by faulty electrical wiring.

"Desiree?"

"Yes, Joshua."

"Umm, I was wondering."

"What were you wondering, Joshua Davis?" She felt that he was going say something that would give her more than a hint as to what he wanted from her. She wasn't one to assume.

"I'm off day after tomorrow, and I'd like to go to the show."

"You would?" she responded. "What would you like to see?" She wasn't going to make this easy for him.

"A movie," he replied. "And I'd like for you to go with me. Are you free day after tomorrow? Around six?"

Desiree paused. This was what she wanted, an opportunity to see him outside of work. But she didn't want to appear anxious. Just as she opened her mouth, a beep interrupted them.

"You mind holding on? I've got another call coming in."

"Sure. No problem."

Desiree switched over to the incoming call. "Hello."

"Hey my sistah," Annette said. "What's up?"

"Nothing. Sitting here chatting with Joshua."

"Oh! It's Joshua now. What happened to Detective Davis?"

Desiree snickered. "Well, tonight he's Joshua."

"And tomorrow he'll be your man. Girl, don't keep him waiting too long. Call me tomorrow. I'm on my way out with Carl."

"You be careful."

Annette laughed. "No, he needs to be careful. The brother doesn't know who he's playing with. Nite-nite."

"Nite, girl. Don't hurt him."

Desiree clicked back over to Joshua. "Sorry about that. Now what were you saying?"

"Day after tomorrow. Will you go to the show with me? Around six?"

"Sure, Joshua. I'll be ready."

"Great. I'll see you at six. I'd better get to work, and you need to get some sleep. I know I've talked your ear off."

"I've enjoyed it. Good night, Joshua."

"Nite."

For the rest of that night and into the start of her shift, she felt as if the day crept along, that her shift couldn't end soon enough. She sighed as she forced her mind back to her work. She jotted notes from the recent fire in the log, then into a small notebook. She had begun keeping a journal once Joshua said he suspected that an arsonist was loose.

The rest of her shift went by without incident. She had taken the brief reprieve to ponder over what she would wear on her first date with Joshua.

"Captain Charles. Telephone," Tulley yelled.

She rushed to the only phone in the stationhouse, which sat on the corner of the desk. She placed the receiver to her ear.

"Hello."

"Hey you," Joshua greeted. "How are you?"

"Good. And you?"

"Nervous."

"Why?" she asked.

"I haven't asked a woman out in years. I'm rusty at this."

Desiree laughed. "Rusty? Sure you are. You mean to tell me that in all these years you haven't gone out?"

"I ain't gonna lie and say I haven't, but they asked me out. I didn't ask them."

"Oh."

"Wait, that don't mean I spread myself like peanut butter. It's just that it's been a while."

"I see."

"So, are we still on for tomorrow?" Joshua asked.

"Unless you've changed your mind, then we're still on. Six o'clock, right?"

"Six it is."

"What are we going to see?"

"Can I surprise you?"

She twisted her face into a scowl. She hated surprises and the way they made the giver feel bad if the receiver wasn't pleased.

"How about you don't."

"Where's your sense of adventure?" Joshua laughed. "Woman, let your hair down and just sit back for the ride."

Reluctantly, Desiree agreed. "Okay, surprise me. Don't be disappointed if I'm not thrilled. Fair warned?"

"Fair warned. But I think you'll like this movie."

She spoke into the phone for a half-hour in hushed tones. She watched as Heaney, followed by Tulley, Moose, and then Carroll each pulled up a chair to the desk and sat down. She eyed them as they sat and looked at her. She made faces at them. When that didn't move them, she pointed upward toward their quarters with her thumb. They stole quizzed glances at each other, shook their heads and remained rooted to their respective seats.

"Well, I need to get off the phone. I've got one too many pairs of ears and eyes sitting here staring into my face and listening to a one-way conversation."

"I'm going to assume that your men are sitting around you."

"You assume correctly."

Joshua laughed. He knew that he could just about say anything to her and she wouldn't be able to respond. "So, what are you going to wear, Desiree?"

"Not fair."

"What's not fair? I just wanted to know how I should dress. I don't want you to show me up. Don't want to look bad. Should I wear jeans or dress slacks? Oh, and would you like to go to dinner before or after the show?"

"Joshua!" she spat out then covered her mouth. The cat was out of the bag. Desiree had made it a point to separate her personal life from her professional one. She clinched her teeth, then raised her arched eyebrows as she watched Tulley pull a twenty-dollar bill from his pocket and hand it over to Moose.

"Okay, my bad." Joshua laughed again. "I'll let you go back to your work. Besides, I need to finish up some paperwork myself."

"Thank you," she sighed.

"You're welcome. Nite, baby. I'll see you…" He paused. "I'll see you in less than twenty-four hours."

Desiree glanced at the clock on the wall. "Will do. Good night,

Joshua."

She hung up the phone, rose and looked at her men. All but Heaney had bemused expressions on their faces.

"I'm gonna hose each and every one of you down," she warned. "Don't you guys have something to do?" They shook their heads. "Well, if that's the case, then I think I can find something for you to do." She watched as Tulley, Moose and Carroll stood and rushed from their perches. Heaney didn't move.

"Go ahead and say it, Pappa Shay."

"No. You're a grown woman."

She tilted her head to one side. Heaney had never completely stayed out of her business before. She wondered why now.

"But," he began, "just be careful. Trent and I are too old to be breaking legs."

She smiled at Heaney and tapped him on his arm. "I will."

He rose and headed to the upstairs sleeping quarters. She stared absently at the phone, allowing visual images of Joshua seep into her being. She thought of his question of what to wear and knew that whatever the brother put on would look good on him. *Damn good.*

CHAPTER 8

Despite having only slept for five hours, Desiree rose early. Normally, after she completed her shift at 7 a.m., she would sleep for at least eight hours, but today wasn't a normal day.

After a quick shower, she tossed on a pair of shorts, a T-shirt and donned a Chicago White Sox baseball cap. She rushed out the door and headed to her hair stylist. She allowed her stylist to add bronze highlights to her warm, natural sienna colored hair. Desiree liked the highlights so much that she allowed her stylist to cut her hair into layers, which framed her oval shaped face.

According to her watch, she had two hours to shower again and dress in the items she selected to wear for her date with Joshua.

She lathered her body with a scented shower gel then ended her special ritual with a matching scented lotion. She put on her lingerie, a pale pink, lace bra and matching thong, and then walked out of the bathroom into her room. At the closet, she chose a pair of hot pink capris; a striped pink and white, sleeveless blouse, and topped the summery outfit with a pair of pink, low heeled, pointy-toed shoes. Her pink cloth handbag completed her outfit. She glanced in the mirror. She liked what she saw, the soft effects her new haircut and highlights had on her deep brown eyes. She applied burnt cinnamon lipstick, then stepped back to admire the total package. She had to admit that she liked what she saw.

When the doorbell rang, she rushed down the stairs. She reached the door and opened it. She took in the tall, muscular figure as he stood on the other side of the screen door.

Joshua was dressed in blue jeans and a red polo shirt. She noted the outline of his muscular chest and the way his biceps strained the fabric of the shirt. She sucked her teeth. *Damn, this brother looks good.* She came to her senses, unlocked the screen door then held it open as Joshua stepped inside. The heady fragrance he wore rushed in and swept her up. She gripped the doorknob in an attempt to calm her runaway olfactory senses.

Joshua handed Desiree a single red rose. "You look good. Pink is definitely your color. I like it." His eyes traveled up and down her body.

Desiree blushed. "Thank you."

They stood in the vestibule for what seemed like hours as the two examined and wondered. Desiree cleared her throat.

"I guess I should put this in a vase." She tilted the rose forward. "Then we can leave."

"Sure." He shook his head as she walked toward the back of her house. The capris hugged her form, and he wiped imaginary sweat from his forehead. Up to this point, he had seen her in her uniform, then in a pair of shorts, and he thought she looked great either way. But seeing her in this outfit, he knew he definitely appreciated articles that showed off her shapely figure.

She returned with a thin vase filled with water. She set the single rose in it then placed the vase on the end table near a wingback chair.

"Ready?" she asked.

"Yes. Are you?"

Desiree looked into his warm, mahogany eyes. The double entendre wasn't missed. *I'm ready for the date, but am I ready for you, Mr. Joshua Davis?*

Joshua opened the car door to his champagne gold Lexus. Desiree slid into the passenger seat. He walked around the car, eased behind the wheel, turned over the ignition, checked his side view mirror then pulled away from the curb.

She sank into the butter soft tan leather, her body turned sideways in her seat so she could face him. Soft jazz played lowly over the car's speakers. They engaged in idle conversation, which ranged from weather to sports. When Joshua entered the Dan Ryan Expressway, Desiree wondered where they were going, but censured her desire to ask about their destination. He had said it would be a surprise.

They continued to talk. She glanced at Joshua's hands as one gripped the steering wheel and the other rested on the gearshift. She noted that his nails were short and neat. She wanted to scream out "amen," for many men didn't find it necessary to keep their nails clean, much less trimmed. She had seen too many men with nails longer than hers.

Joshua quickly looked over at her as he maneuvered onto Lake Shore Drive, then exited at Columbus Drive. Now silent, he nodded his head to the music. Desiree opened her mouth then shut it. The temptation to ask where they were going became strong.

When he pulled into a parking lot off Congress Parkway, Desiree looked at him and opened her mouth. "Joshua, where—"

"No asking," he interrupted. "I told you, it's a surprise."

Joshua parked, stepped out of the car, then came around and assisted Desiree from the car. When she opened her mouth again, Joshua shook his head and took her hand in his. He remained quite as they walked down Michigan Avenue. They stopped in front of the Fine Arts Theatre.

Desiree grinned in delight when she heard Joshua request two tickets to *Black Orpheus*. The hauntingly beautiful love story was one of her favorite movies. Set in Brazil during Rio Carnival, the 1959 film was laden with obvious sensuality, with an abundance of the supernatural belief in Voodoo. The sad ending always left Desiree sniffling. She never let men see her cry.

"We've got a few minutes before the movie starts. Want some popcorn? Something to drink?"

"Sure. I'll take a lemonade. And don't forget the extra butter."

Desiree carried the drinks while Joshua carried the large tub of popcorn and two boxes of Goobers. They settled into seats situated in the middle of the theatre. The lights dimmed. Joshua reached into the tub of popcorn, removed several buttered puffs and fed them to Desiree.

As she sat in the dark theatre, her shoulder close to Joshua's, she had to admit that this was indeed a wonderful surprise and she was glad she had chosen censorship over verbosity.

"How'd you know I'd like this movie?" she asked, her voice a low tease.

"The movie posters in your home office. *Key Largo*, *It Happened One Night*. Those are classics. So I figured you'd like *Black Orpheus*," he whispered as he looked down at her. She could make out a faint smile on his lips.

After the movie, Joshua insisted they stop at a little place in Bronzeville for a nightcap. He opened the door for her then shook the hand of the man standing nearby. Desiree looked up at him. "He's the owner," he informed her as he directed her to a small bistro table inside the Negro League Cafe.

Recently opened, the cafe's walls were adorned with every name of the Negro Leagues of the 30s and 40s, some later, and their players. Desiree smiled as she read off the names of the famous and not-so-famous Negro League baseball players. Of course she knew Satchel Paige, but she hadn't recognized others. As she looked at the names, Joshua came and sat next to her at a table for two.

"Who's Al Burrows?" she asked.

"He was once the first baseman and pitcher for the New York Black Yankees."

"You must be a big baseball fan."

"That I am. When I was a kid, I got a chance to meet some of the players of the Kansas City Monarchs. I was no more than five or six, but I remember them as if they were standing right here. From that day forward, I wanted to play baseball. So, my father bought me a glove."

"Did you play Little League?"

Joshua nodded. "Pony League, high school and college. I pitched and wasn't too bad at bat."

"What happened? Why didn't you go to the major or minor leagues?"

"I broke my arm in a motorcycle accident my senior year in college. Representatives from the Yankees, the White Sox and Seattle were coming to an upcoming game that I was to pitch. Up to that point, I had pitched two seasons straight with no injuries and with countless no hitters. In celebration of the beginning of the season, I bought myself a motorcycle. I thought I was all that on that contraption. My mother had warned me that they were dangerous. Well her words became reality when I hit an oil spot and spun out. The bike went one way and was run over by a truck. I went the other way and hit a wall. I sustained two fractures to my arm—my right arm. My pitching arm."

"Wow, that must have been hard," Desiree commented.

"It was. My career was over."

"So what made you join the department?"

"My other love as a kid was to be a fireman. You know most kids grow out of it, but I didn't. I finished college with a degree in Organizational Behavior and joined the department. And I haven't looked back since. What about you?"

For the next half hour, as they sipped on cranberry juice and nibbled on pretzels, Desiree told Joshua about her parents, her being an only child, and her decision to join the department, which was fueled by her father and the countless times she had watched firefighters raise to the call of a fire. She had admired them, their seemingly steel will and their commitment to the job. She ended by telling him that she was the only female in her entire family that was a firefighter.

At the end of the night, Joshua escorted Desiree up the steps of her porch. He took her house keys from her hand then opened her doors. He placed the keys back in her hand and stood over her. His eyes bore into hers, a hint of uncertainty shone in them. She placed her hand on his arm, then tipped on her toes and kissed him lightly on the lips.

"Thank you, Joshua. I had a really nice time."

"So did I. We must do this again." Neither moved. They stood in her doorway and stared, each in their own thoughts. Joshua bent and kissed her, his arms hung loosely about her waist. He knew that to place his hands anywhere else would not only be disrespectful to her, but also damaging to him. The wicked charge of her closeness snaked up his entire body. Without a doubt, he wanted to get to know her better, but he also had things he needed to tell her, things he had told no one.

In time, he decided as he nodded his head, mouthed "good night," then stepped off the porch to his car.

Desiree shut the door then bounded up the stairs to her bedroom. She kicked off her shoes and flopped across her queen-sized bed. She picked up the phone near the bed to call Annette. She changed her mind and placed the phone back on the nightstand. She laid on her back and thought of Joshua. There was no denying their attraction. *Am I ready to enter into another relationship?* One that could possibly end if she were to be promoted to Battalion Chief, or even Commissioner. *Will he stand in my way? Or worse, leave me because he can't deal with his woman supervising men in the department?*

She slid off the bed, disrobed, put on a nightgown, then climbed back onto the bed. She closed her eyes and thought of the one man who dared to make her re-think her stance against dating another man who worked for the department.

Joshua walked into his house. He spied the various pieces of mail that poked out of the mail slot. He grabbed the envelops and magazines then tossed them onto the sofa table. The act caused the framed picture of his late wife to fall to the floor, breaking the glass. Joshua picked up the frame. He rounded the sofa and sat down. He studied the frame, the way the broken glass snaked neatly across the middle of the picture.

"Serena, she's good people," he spoke to the photo. He shook his head. Undeniably, he was attracted to Desiree, like no other woman since Serena's death. The nagging question remained unanswered. *Is it time?*

He took the photo from the frame and carefully removed the protective glass. He placed the photo in the frame, put it back on the table, rose from the sofa and headed down the hallway to his bedroom. He looked at the phone near his bed. He wanted to call Desiree, to hear her mellifluous voice, feel the warm sensations her voice invoked. He changed his mind and settled on his thoughts of the evening he had just spent with Desiree Charles, the illustrious Captain, who'd take no stuff off anyone, but was every bit a woman, a fiery, sexy woman at that. Desiree wasn't like some of the female firefighters he'd met; their hardness remained with them long after the fire was out and they had left the stationhouse. No, she was tough when she had to be and knew how to be soft and feminine. It was something he noticed about her the day he went to her house unannounced.

Joshua took off his clothes and lay on top of the covers. He thought of Desiree and knew that whether he was ready or not, she had captured his heart.

Over the three days, two of which were her scheduled days off, Desiree and Joshua had spoken no less than five times, and she couldn't help but wonder when she'd see him again. Last night she'd listened as he revealed more of himself, almost as if he were purging his soul, as he told her that his younger brother was doing a life sentence at Pontiac, a maximum-security facility, and his parents had moved to South Carolina shortly after the sentence. She didn't respond when he told her that he hadn't seen his brother in nearly four years.

By the time Desiree realized the hour, she and Joshua had been on the phone for hours. Their conversations left her giddy and anxious, like a schoolgirl being asked to the prom by the most popular boy in school. The feelings frightened her. In all of her thirty-seven years, she had never felt this strong of an attraction to any man. This was no good, she thought. She had to get a grip on her runaway emotions and fast. She didn't want to suffer through another dead-end relationship. Sure, Joshua, up to this point, had been a pure gentleman and seemed to be generous with his time. Unfortunately, she still wasn't sure about him—Joshua Davis the man. She had yet to hear about his late wife.

Annette's words came to her, "He's got demons."

The minute Desiree arrived at the stationhouse to begin her shift they received a call. The call turned out to be a woman who claimed she was seeing people strike matches in her living room. Desiree had called the paramedics and whispered to them upon their arrival that they should take her in for a psychiatric evaluation.

"Captain Charles," she heard a voice call her name. Desiree looked through the side view mirror to see Battalion Chief Mike Callahan standing inches behind the engine. She glanced over at Heaney and rolled her eyes.

Desiree climbed from the engine and slowly began to remove her turn out gear. For this one, she'd make him come to her. She hadn't liked Callahan from the day she met him fifteen years ago as a cadet. He had been her field instructor and had tried to make each day a living hell for her.

If he treated the other cadets the same she would understand, but he had singled her out. Initially she didn't know why. After speaking with her father, then Heaney, she knew that Callahan had an ax to grind with her father. Add to it, Callahan was a hard line racist. She felt that if he were angry with her father, then he needed to take it up with Trenton Charles, the man, and not Desiree Charles, Trenton's daughter.

Desiree glanced over her shoulder. Callahan had gone from warm tan to beet red. She gloated inwardly as she continued to remove her turnout gear. She slowly slid off her boots, stretched, then placed her feet in her black shoes and walked over to the desk where she sat down and jotted down the activities of the last fire in the daily log. "This is my house," Desiree said to herself as she refused to glance in Callahan's direction.

"Captain Charles," Callahan hissed as he stomped over to the desk.

She looked up into his face. *Good! He is mad, and I don't give a damn.* He was in her house, and he would play by her rules. As Battalion Chief he could suspend her. *But for what? Not answering to him when he calls my name? It would never fly with the union.*

She closed the log then stood. "What can I do for you today, Chief Callahan?"

"I need to discuss the rash of fires. Found out that the couple who died in that fire a few weeks ago were the parents of the alderman in this area."

Desiree raised her right eyebrow. She doubted it took all this time for him to come to her to tell her this bit of information. She wondered if Joshua knew. "Aren't you talking to the wrong bunch? That's Detective Davis's job. Our job is to put out the fire."

Callahan raked his fingers through his sparsely gray hair. Desiree stifled a snicker. *He must have been a cute baby, 'cause he sure is an ugly man.*

"Charles, you teach this stuff at the academy. It's important that you become more involved with solving this case."

Desiree walked past Callahan, barely brushing his shoulder. Something wasn't quite right. She wondered why he was asking her to become involved in a case that clearly was out of her realm of responsibility. Oh, she could do it, had been assisting Joshua with her knowledge of accelerants and how they burn. Her mind continued to go over the questions as she headed to the kitchen to grab a bottle of water. She heard Callahan's feet behind her.

"Well, the word has come down, and you're going to assist with this case."

Desiree barely looked at Callahan. "Where did this order come from?" She knew that questioning Callahan's orders were running afoul, but she couldn't help it.

"The mayor's office."

She opened the refrigerator door, grabbed a bottle of water then moved to sit at the long bench with seats attached to it outside the kitchen. She smiled to herself. After the table incident, the guys brought a bench with seats attached to it.

She opened the bottle of water and took a long drink. She glanced at Callahan and saw his eyes fixed on the water. She refused to offer him a bottle. Let him starve for it. *That was mean*, she thought. She changed her mind. "Chief, would you like a bottle of water?"

Desiree didn't wait for a response. She rose from the table, went into the kitchen, grabbed a bottle from the refrigerator, then tossed it to him. She returned to her seat. "The mayor's office? The deaths at that fire was weeks ago. Davis is the investigator in charge. Why not let him continue?"

"He will. There's a need for another person on it."

Desiree could see that it was bothering him to no end to have to come to the stationhouse and request her assistance.

"What about the stationhouse?"

"What about it?" he snapped.

Desiree raised her eyebrows. "Will I still run the house?" She responded with as much attitude.

"You're expected to."

She rose from the bench, drained the bottle, then threw it into the garbage can. "So, let me get this straight." She walked over to Callahan. "I'm to do both?"

He moved a pace backward. His grey eyes, so much like his son's, met hers. She could see the disdain, the pure contempt aimed at her.

"You weren't my choice," Callahan spat. "So make it happen." He turned and walked away. She wanted to throw something at the back of his head, anything to let him know that he wasn't being fair to her. But she'd be damned if he'd best her. He couldn't when she was a cadet, and he wouldn't now that she was captain.

She stormed out of the kitchen and was halted in her tracks when she bumped into Joshua. She was glad to see him and steeled herself from throwing her arm around him.

"What was Callahan doing here?" he asked, his face taunt.

She peered at him. "To talk about that fire you're investigating. Did you know that the couple was the alderman's parents?"

Joshua nodded.

"Why didn't you say something?"

"Wasn't important. They were human beings who were killed in a fire started by some lunatic. Whose parents they were doesn't even rank on my Richter scale. End of story."

Desiree understood that, but also knew that the alderman could make unnecessary waves. "Callahan was also here to tell me I'd be investigating with you."

Joshua's face twisted in a scowl. Something was brewing, his gut told him so, but he didn't have a clue as to what. It would rest in his craw for now.

"What's the matter, Joshua, you don't want a woman working closely with you?" Desiree placed her hands on her hips, her face inches from Joshua's.

He looked at her, her brown eyes took on an almost golden blaze. *Cute, simply cute*, he thought as he watched the storm brew behind her lids, her slightly full lips as they stretched into a fierce frown. He'd risk a slap just to taste the lips who had called his name with such sweet cadence.

"That's not it, Desiree. You should know that by now," he responded, his voice low and even.

"I know no such thing." Desiree threw up her hands and began to pace. "First, you hound me for all of the information I have in my head, then Callahan shows up here out of the blue and insists. No! Orders me to work this case."

The vein in Joshua's neck began to throb. He looked into her face and saw the angry fire in her eyes. He removed the space between them, took her by the arm and without preamble, pulled her into his arms and kissed her. The electric charge from the simple, intimate act surged through his body. *Sweet, Mary, mother of Jesus.* This was pure, unadulterated fire he was handling. He released her.

Desiree blinked quickly. She knew her voice would betray her if she spoke. Instead, she walked away from him and headed to her upstairs quarters.

Joshua watched her leave and thought he'd better leave well enough alone. He had grown accustomed to talking to her everyday, enjoyed the soothing, husky sound of her voice late at night, the full richness of her laughter. *Am I ready?* He had asked himself that question a thousand times since their date. He wanted to see her again, needed to be near her to make sure that the once foregone emotions weren't a trick of his mind, a result of his just being lonely.

He turned to leave and was blocked by Heaney.

"You think that was appropriate?" Heaney leaned against the wall. "She is the captain of this ship. If it smells rotten, she'll get the brunt of it."

"I know what I'm doing, Heaney."

"Do you, Davis?" Heaney pushed off the wall and stood face to face with Joshua, his nose inches from Joshua's. "I remember when you couldn't move a day without it. Stand warned. You hurt my lass up there and you won't have to worry about Trent. He'll be the least of your worries. I'll come after ya myself." Heaney's brogue was thick as he sucked his teeth and walked past Joshua, bumping his shoulder hard.

Joshua started to respond, but thought better. He knew Heaney was Desiree's godfather and her father's best friend. Though he and Heaney were the same height, Heaney outweighed him by a solid fifty pounds. He glanced up at the stairs. He needed to get it together. He had to shake the feelings the sound of her voice invoked in him. Seeing her again had only intensified his emotions.

He walked out of the stationhouse. At the same time, his beeper went off. It was a message from his best friend, Assistant Commissioner John Paglinini. He reached his car and took his cell phone from the middle console. He dialed the number.

"Hey, John, what's up?"

"I need to talk to you, my brother, ASAP. Meet me at LaMahara's in Oak Park in half an hour."

The line went dead.

CHAPTER 9

"What's up, my brother?" John said, a large grin plastered across his face.

Joshua eyed John suspiciously. Over the phone, John seemed to be anxious, and the sound of his voice and sudden disconnect of the phone had him driving like a mad man to get to him. But seeing John in person, his bemused expression, Joshua became confused. "I should be asking you the same thing."

He sat across from John who signaled the waitress. John ordered his usual, a Corona with two wedges of lime and three steak fajitas. Joshua ordered the same, minus the Corona—he opted for a glass of ginger ale.

"Hold on to your helmet," John began, his face contorted with pride. "You are now looking at the new Commissioner of the Chicago Fire Department."

Joshua nearly choked on his own spittle. "Say what? When did this happen?"

"Today. I got a call this morning from the Mayor's office. I went to see the mayor, and he made me an offer I couldn't refuse. Of course the official word hasn't been put out yet. The mayor's press folks will do that next week."

He knew as the Assistant Commissioner that John would be in the running for the recently vacated position, but he didn't think in his wildest dreams that he would actually get the position. Oh, John was good, had been a great firefighter, was a good instructor, and seemed to have done well as Assistant Commissioner, but in the past his devil may care attitude had gotten him in trouble on more than one occasion. To Joshua's way of thinking, he just couldn't see John as the Commissioner of the Chicago Fire Department. He didn't know how to react to his best friend's news. And his face showed it.

"Man, I thought you'd be happy for me. You know I want you as my right hand man." It was more a statement.

Joshua looked at his friend. "I am happy. Congratulations."

"If I didn't know any better, I'd say you were a killjoy. What gives?"

Joshua didn't know how to tell John that his indifferent attitude wasn't what the department needed. He knew John. Back when they were first year candidates, John always remained neutral when racial or gender issues rose at the stationhouse. He believed and lived by the credo, live and let live. Joshua thought of the deaths at the fire he was investigating, the growing racial tensions at several firehouses, and not enough women or people of color being promoted to higher ranks. He just didn't think that John's way of doing business would be good for a department riffled with controversy. He decided to speak on his feelings later. Right now he'd be happy for his friend.

"Naw, man. Congratulations. I trust you'll do great."

John peered at Joshua. He tilted his head to the left as he eyed Joshua. A broad grin spread across his face. "So, you think you want to join me? Become Assistant Deputy Commissioner or Chief of Investigations?"

Joshua smirked. "I don't know about that, John. Maybe. I'd really have to think on it."

Joshua knew his position in the African American Firefighters and Paramedics League would have to go to the wayside. He knew it would be hard to balance the two. Besides, he wasn't so sure he wanted to. Yet, as a deputy he could bring the issues closer to home. It certainly was worth more than a simple thought.

"I guess we're celebrating then?"

"Sure are. Drinks and food is on me," John said loudly. The few patrons in the Mexican restaurant looked at them. "Drink much and eat heartily, my brother."

Joshua laughed.

John's tone turned serious. "Joshua, I really want you to join me. I wouldn't trust the guy the mayor's people subtly suggested I hire as

Deputy Assistant Commissioner. They mentioned Mike Callahan, Senior."

Joshua's eyebrows rose. Callahan had been he and John's nemesis from day one, when they both first set foot into the academy as cadets. Callahan had made no bones about his feelings of women and "you folks of color," joining the fire department. Then it hit him. Callahan's visit to Desiree. If Callahan could get Desiree out of the way, by assigning her a case that could cost her a demotion if the assailant wasn't captured soon, or worse a forced resignation, then his son Mike Junior, a lieutenant, would be a shoe in to captain. And what better than to put her on a high-profile case that's sure to incite a lot of controversy.

"You've got to be joking!" Joshua spat. "The mayor's people have got to know what a racist Callahan is. Does the mayor even know?"

"Not yet. But you can't deny that he's good. Knows his stuff. If I had absolutely no choice, I'd take…"

"John, let's not go there. I'll think about your offer."

John looked Joshua in the eye then resigned to accept Joshua's response—for now.

"Okay, so what else is up? How's the investigation going?" John asked as he forked a piece of steak.

"This one is crazed. John, these are not your garden-variety fires. They're different."

"How so?" John looked up from his plate.

"First off, they're all within a two-mile radius of Engine 19. And second, the same accelerants have been found at each scene."

"And only that one had fatalities?"

"Yeah, you know that."

"Just going over the facts. Okay, Detective Davis, then how's Desiree?"

Joshua squinted his eyes. "How do you know about Desiree?"

"Folks talk. I heard about you calling the stationhouse, showing up, and taking her out."

"Where'd you get your information from?"

"The man who prides himself on knowing everything that goes on at his stationhouses. Callahan."

"Callahan? What, y'all best friends now?" Joshua snapped

"Not hardly, but he mentioned it when I saw him." John wasn't ready to tell of the impromptu meeting he'd had with Callahan. He looked away before he spoke. "Do you think it's wise to be involved with her? I mean if she gets the Battalion Chief's job and you two got a fling going on."

"It's not a fling!" Joshua defended. "I really care about her. Even though she's not talking to me right now." Joshua tossed his napkin onto the plate. "But I didn't know she was being considered for another promotion. Why's it so important to you?"

"I told you I want you to be my right hand. If she gets the promotion to Battalion Chief, which is contingent on the outcome of this investigation…"

Joshua rose and leaned across the table, his nose inches from John's. "What the hell do you mean 'depending on this case?' Desiree's qualified, even though she's only been captain for a little over a year."

"Calm down and sit down, please." He watched as Joshua returned to his seat, his eyes dark. John didn't want his best friend angry, but he had to be straight with him. "All I'm saying is that if the outcome is favorable, she gets the position. If you agree to one of my offers, it'll give the impression that you pulled strings."

Joshua's eyebrows rose. Several patrons in the restaurant stared at them. He lowered his voice. "Since when have you cared how things look?"

John raked his hands over his coal black hair. His eyes begged Joshua not ask any more questions. "Look, all I'm saying is that I don't want that type of thing to mar my appointment. The slightest implication of impropriety will set the press off. The mayor has made it clear that he wants no more bad press from the department."

Joshua snarled. "He can no more control those vultures, than either you or I. But tell me this, are you going to stand in her way?"

John looked away.

"Answer me, John. Are you?"

"Not if I can help it." He took a long gulp of beer.

Joshua stood again, his back straight. His eyes dark with rage, he looked dead into John's face. "If you make it hard for her in anyway, or allow that crazy-assed racist Callahan anywhere near her, you will both rule the day you ever laid eyes on me."

Joshua walked to the exit.

John rushed to his side. "Josh, man, don't let her come between us."

He looked at his friend, the man who called himself his brother. "She already has."

"In Chicago, there are over fifteen thousand fires a year," Joshua stated. "Most of them occur during the winter months and are started by improper wiring and space heaters. In these fifteen thousand fires, approximately two percent are intentional. Some are for profit, while others are intended to feed the proclivities of an individual who's fascinated with fire. In other words, ladies and gentlemen, an arsonist is loose. And that's where my unit comes in." Joshua stood in front of the cadets. His face gave no hint of emotion as he went through his session on arson. "As a detective, it is my job to find the causes, research old files of known arsonists, and find the perpetrator."

As the first part of his session neared the end, Joshua heard the door at the rear of the classroom open. He looked up to see Desiree, in dress blues, step into the class. She stood, her hat in her hand, at the rear. Joshua became fixated, his train of thought lost as he looked at the woman who made him wonder, made his emotions ramble out of control. He looked at his notes in an attempt to gain control over the feelings. He had thought a lot about her the last two days: their date to the movies, his overwhelming desire to kiss her, once after their date, then the abrupt kiss at the stationhouse, and Heaney's words. He purposely hadn't called her. He needed time. Besides, she hadn't called him either, and he still smarted over her insinuation that he had a problem working with or for women.

Gathering his thoughts, he closed his session by asking for questions. When none came, he granted the seated cadets a fifteen-minute break.

"Hey, what are you doing here?" he asked Desiree.

"I'm filling in for Paglinini"

Joshua nodded. He and John had been conducting this class on arson and causes and types of fires once a month for nearly five years. He thought of their last conversation. He hadn't expected to see John, but he also hadn't expected him to get Desiree to replace him either.

"Did John tell you how this goes?"

"No, but he did say to follow your lead and to lend my expertise in accelerants where I thought best fit."

"Umm, I see. Okay, let's do it."

Once the cadets returned, Desiree and Joshua, much to both of their surprises, played off each other, as Joshua moved effortlessly into the types of arson fires and Desiree described the various accelerants typically chosen by arsonists and the methods the department employed to douse those fires.

"Well, we've been at it for nearly three hours. How about we dismiss early?"

The cadets cheered as Desiree dismissed the class.

"Detective Davis, that was great."

Joshua titled his head. She called him Detective Davis. *That's cool—for now.*

"That it was, *Captain Charles*." He eyed her, wanted to see her response to formal use of her given name.

They stared at each other. Again, a strange feeling enveloped them as they stood in front of each other. Desiree broke the stare first. She gathered her papers and headed toward the exit. She stopped then turned. "It's been a real pleasure. Have a good day." She disappeared out the door.

Joshua stared at the vacant space, raked his hand over his close-cropped hair, then gathered his own things and exited the classroom. He arrived outside just in time to see Desiree drive off in the Ford Blazer. He thought of one of the dreams he had of Serena and wondered if in deed it was time; time for him to move past the woman he once loved and toward the woman he knew he was falling in love with.

"This is over. Not by a long shot, Desiree," he spoke aloud as he climbed into his own department issued sedan.

A full week had passed since they had taught the class together. Since then all Desiree had heard from Detective Joshua Davis were faxed notes on the case. Sure, she reasoned, he was giving her space and she knew her outburst had been childish at best. *Why am I afraid of him, of what we could have?* He had held her hand during the walk to the theatre, had fed her popcorn throughout the movie, and had treated her with all the kindness and respect she deserved. When he dropped her off at home, he had kissed her, respectably keeping his hands at her waist. *No rushin' hands or roamin' fingers.* The brother was all about control. Add to it all, the flaming hot emotions she felt when he kissed her at the stationhouse. She found herself wanting him more and more with urgency, a scary longing of sorts.

All the better they weren't talking, she mused, she wasn't interested in dating anyway. Besides, Donald's words still rang fresh in her mind, even though the pain of his betrayal had ebbed to a dull nuisance.

Desiree stepped into Plumber's Hall. She had allowed Annette to persuade her to attend the monthly meeting of the Chicago Chapter of the IABPFFA, the African American Firefighters and Paramedics League. She had just finished her shift some eleven hours prior. She was tired and Annette had come by and awakened her. After several minutes of ongoing insistence, Annette told her it was her duty to support the Association, Desiree gave in.

She nodded her head as she walked with Annette, seeing faces of fellow firefighters she hadn't seen in some time. She stopped several times, once to speak to Timmons, then Tulley, before she and Annette found seats near the front of the hall. Desiree read over the minutes from the last meeting, then scanned the evening's agenda. Her head snapped up when she head his voice—the rich deep timbre as it called the meeting to order. Joshua stood at the podium, set high on the stage. He was dressed in a navy, NYFD T-shirt and jeans, each article hugged every muscle in his body. Their eyes met. He nodded his head in her direction. Desiree returned the gesture as her stare was broken by a poke to her side.

"Hey!" she whispered excitedly. "What's that for?"

Annette chuckled. "Your husband is here."

Desiree looked back at Joshua.

"Des, I was talking about Donald."

Desiree gave Annette a feigned evil glare then followed her eyes to where Donald sat across from them in the next row. He nodded his head at them. Annette waved, while Desiree ignored his presence. She focused her attention on Joshua. She watched his lips move, and she remembered the soft feel of them upon hers. If she didn't know any better, she'd swear that her body threatened to go up in an incinerated flame, turning her into ashes. *That kiss was too hot*, she told herself.

For over an hour, Joshua conducted the meeting. Several times during the meeting, Joshua turned the podium over to the various officers who gave their respective reports. She watched him watch her from his seat. They had an unobstructed view of each other.

At the end of the meeting, Desiree stood to leave. She tried to will her eyes not to search the sea of faces for Joshua. They betrayed her. She wanted to get at least of glimpse of the man who'd burned her insides and heated her from head to toe. Disappointment crept into her. He was nowhere to be found.

As she exited, Annette and Tulley by her side, she felt a tap to her shoulder. She turned and instantly frowned.

"It's good to see you again," Donald said as he stepped closer to her, their bodies forced together by a bump from someone moving past

Donald. Desiree's frown deepened. At one time, she welcomed his close contact—not anymore.

"I wish I could say the same," she responded and began to walk away. Donald grabbed her arm.

"Don't you ever walk away from me, Desiree," he said angrily. "Just because you rule those patsies at the stationhouse, doesn't mean you can rule me."

Desiree opened her mouth to speak, but was cut off.

Tulley stepped forward. His brown face contorted. "Man if you ever—" he was interrupted by a tap on his shoulder.

"Tulley, I got this." Joshua appeared. Tulley stepped to the side. "Brother Anderson, how's life?" Joshua asked, standing at least five inches over Donald, his face mere inches from his. "Someone told me that you're getting married soon? Is that true?"

Desiree looked at Donald, then back to Joshua. Donald began to stammer. Joshua held up his hand. Donald shut up quickly.

"Give my regards. But before you go, let me tell you something. It's extremely impolite to manhandle a woman. No matter what the rank. Please don't ever let me see you manhandle Desiree again. Agreed?" Joshua squinted his eyes and tilted his head to one side. "Are we in agreement or not?" Joshua spoke evenly through clenched teeth. Donald nodded, cast an angry glare at Desiree and began to walk away. Joshua called him back. "And you owe Captain Charles an apology."

"My apologies, Captain Charles," Donald mumbled, then hurried away.

Desiree looked up into Joshua's face. The pulse at his temple throbbed double-time. She touched his arm and felt the muscles in them tense before they relaxed.

"Thank you," was the only thing she could muster. She had always fought her own battles, even when unevenly matched. She had never had anyone fight for her. Her father and Heaney had let her fight her battles. Even Donald had let her fight alone. The times she had cried on his shoulders, he always ended it with, "You'll get over it." To have Joshua defend her honor, stand up for her as a woman, stunned

Desiree. A foreign emotion swirled inside of her.

"Hey, what are you doing tonight?"

Desiree snapped out of her emotional trance. Before she could help it she had quickly replied, "Nothing."

"I know this nice little cafe. Care to have a cup a coffee with me?" He asked her. She could see the uncertainty in his round eyes.

"Sure. Don't you have to work tonight?" she asked as her anger slowly ebbed to a mere flicker. She decided not to read into his request. Besides, it was just coffee, nothing else.

"No, this is my day off. Give me a minute to wrap up one more thing, then we'll get out of here. Besides we need to talk."

Desiree nodded and watched as Joshua walked back down the aisle and began to speak to one of the officers.

"Hot damn!" Annette said. "Now, if I ever need rescuing, I'd take that one."

Desiree smiled at Annette. "Girl, you're reading too much into it."

"Well, call me crazy, but didn't he just get up in Donald's face. Looked like he was staking his territory."

"He was doing no such thing. He saved Donald from a verbal beat down from me."

"And a serious ass kicking from me," Tulley said as came up beside Desiree. "But Captain, my man Davis was on point. Gotta give that brother some props."

Desiree looked up into Tulley's hazel brown eyes. They twinkled. She wondered what was going on behind those light eyes of his.

"Not a word of this at the stationhouse, Tulley. You hear me?"

"Aye-aye, Capp-ee-ton!" Tulley clicked his heels together, saluted Desiree, then marched away.

Annette laughed at the scene, then turned to Desiree.

"Yeah, right. This is me. Your bestest friend. I've got eyes and I say other, but you go ahead and hold on to that thought." Annette paused, looked down at her cell phone, which was vibrating at her hip. She pulled the phone from her hip, looked at the caller-ID, then smiled. "That's my date for tonight," she responded to Desiree's raised eyebrows. Annette began talking into the phone. She batted her eyes and spoke lowly. At the end of the conversation, she turned to Desiree.

"Well, sister, gotta go. Come on, so I can drop you off." Annette turned to leave, then stopped. "Aren't you ready?"

Desiree twisted her mouth. "Joshua and I are going to go and get a cup of coffee."

Annette squealed. "Told you! Call me tomorrow. *Ciao, bella.* Have a great time."

Desiree watched Annette walk out of the hall. She wished that her best friend could find a nice guy to settle down with, but at thirty-seven, Annette wasn't having any talk of marriage and babies. She said that one heartache was enough to last her a lifetime. That heartache came in the form of her ex-husband—who had shown her how not to treat a woman. The first time he hit Annette she had been stunned, the second time, he had nearly drew back a nub. Since then Annette had kept men close enough for them to think she was interested, but far enough for them not to be able to penetrate her heart.

"Ready?" Joshua's deep voice whispered close to her ear.

She turned and looked up into his deep brown eyes. If she didn't know any better, she'd sworn that his simple question held a double entendre. "Ready, if you are."

CHAPTER 10

Desiree nodded and allowed Joshua to escort her from the hall. Eyes watched them as they walked, his hand at her elbow. When a group blocked Desiree's path, Joshua casually placed his hand around her waist and effortlessly moved her around the group.

He kept his hand placed possessively at the small of her back, inches above her behind. They walked in tandem as he nodded to several people who had congregated outside the union hall. They came to stop at a midnight black BMW, its windows tinted the same dark color. Joshua pressed the remote then opened the passenger door for Desiree. Suddenly, Desiree became very self-conscious about her appearance. Her hair was hanging about her shoulders, with just a hint of curl. Black jeans and a short-sleeved, white blouse clad her body. White gym shoes covered her feet. She fussed with her mother's voice ringing inside her head as she had admonished her to, "always look your best."

She watched as Joshua slid into the seat beside her. He glanced at her, put the key in the ignition, put the car in gear, then sped away from the curb.

They spoke at the same time.

"No, ladies first."

"Where's the Lexus?" Desiree wanted to kick herself. Why ask about a car, when she really wanted to know why he hadn't called her. In reality, she was angry, not so much over his lack of phone calls, but because he raised a foreign emotion in her—one so strong she wanted to forego all senses and decorum and reach out and pull him to her, covering his mouth with hers. Anger was an emotion she could understand and control.

"I just got it yesterday. I bought it with the settlement."

"Settlement?"

"The wrongful death suit," Joshua replied matter-of-factly.

Desiree watched as his hands gripped the steering wheel. The same pulse at his temples throbbed. This was the first time he had made any mention of his late wife. Annette had told her that his wife and unborn child died in an auto accident.

"Oh, that settlement. That's heavy." Desiree didn't want to say, "I'm sorry" for she was sure he had heard it countless times.

He looked back at her and saw the sympathy, but not pity in her eyes. He was relieved. When most people heard you lost a loved one, they always said they were sorry. But were they really—how could they actually be sorry when they had no clue as to the magnitude of his loss? At one point after his wife's death, he avoided people all together. The word "sorry" seemed to cut through him like a knife. Yeah, sure, he got over that, but he still thought about the emptiness of the word itself.

"Thank you," he said and noted that the sympathy had been replaced with curiosity. "I'll explain later. Okay?"

Desiree nodded and they fell into an easy conversation that surrounded their respective jobs. Desiree told him the story of the dog food in her boots and she laughed at the incident, describing to Joshua the funny, wet, squishy feeling she had to endure for three hours as she fought a fire. She looked over at him. He was laughing, hard. She noticed his eyes squinched when he laughed. She was warmed by the rich bass of it and was glad to see the boyish glint his face held.

By the end of her story, they both had tears in their eyes as Joshua brought the vehicle to a stop in front of Cafe Luna. Desiree decided then that she much preferred this Joshua to the serious, no-nonsense one. She placed her hand on his forearm and looked into his eyes.

"You know, I really like it when you smile. You should do so more often."

He faced her. How could he tell her that it was she who made him smile, who made him hope that after all these years he could connect to a special person, feel emotions that had laid dormant for so many years. He stroked the side of her face. "I'll try. For you, I'll try."

Joshua got out of the car, came around to the passenger side, and opened the door. He put his hand out to her and grasped it lightly as she swung her legs around then stepped out of the car. He watched the demure act and chuckled to himself.

They walked into the small cafe and found a seat near the window. They ordered two mocha java latte's, with a dab of whip cream and two beignets.

They watched each other over the rims of their coffee cups. Desiree sensed a growing easiness about Joshua. He was definitely not the pent up brother she had seen at the fire. She listened to his voice, the rich deepness, as he told of his life as a firefighter, then as an arson investigator.

"Joshua." She tapped his hand, which rested on the small round table. "I need to apologize for snapping at you last week. I was wrong."

"Apology accepted. And for the record, Desiree, I have no problems, pent up issues or anything resembling, when it comes to working with women. Some of the best firefighters I've worked with have been women. But we do need to talk."

"I know."

"Where do we start?"

Desiree's pulse raced. She wanted to ask the question, wanted to know, but she didn't want to force him to speak on it, not until he was ready to do so.

"How about we start out light and let it roll from there," she responded.

Joshua smiled. "Okay, that's fair. How about you tell me something about you that most folks don't know."

Desiree smiled at the challenge. She placed both hands flat on the table and leaned over. Joshua moved toward her. "I used to play football."

Joshua narrowed his eyes, smiled, then shook his head. "No way." His dimples deepened as he laughed. "You stand no more than 5'5" right now. And you can't weigh anymore than a buck-o-five soaking wet." He rang his hands together as if wringing out a wet towel.

Desiree widened her eyes, her brows raised. She sat back in her seat and crossed her arms in front of her. She let him continue.

"What? They let you toss the ball around? Let you be in charge of Gatorade?" His laughter eased as he spied the incredulous expression on her face. "My aplogies. You're serious."

"As a heirtbeat. And for your information, I am five-foot-five and 135 pounds of soid woman."

Joshua rised his hands in surrender. "I'm sorry. I was only joking. I just couldn't picture you playing football."

"I did and I played up until I was thirteen. Played Pop Warner."

Joshua's mouth hung open. "What position?"

"At first I was a wide receiver, then I got moved to defensive line. I'd knock those little boys on their behinds." She poked her chin out. She could still feel the pinch her mother would give her when as a youngster she would challenge boys to a quick game. The unsuspecting boys never had a clue as to her speed and agility, must less her blocking ability. Her nickname on the team was "Assassin."

Joshua raised his eyebrows as he watched the woman sitting across from him and wondered who she really was.

"Why'd you quit?"

Desiree shrugged her shoulders. "The officials found out I was a girl. By thirteen it became quite obvious."

Joshua looked at the swell of her breasts that sweetly filled out the front of her sleeveless blouse. He shook his head. "I'll bet." He cleared his throat.

He thought of how nicely she filled out those shorts she had on the day he dropped by her house and those capris that hugged all the right places. For some reason, he could see her running down that field and hitting a receiver. He laughed at the image. "Tell me, how did you get away with it for so long? And what did your parents say?"

Desiree chuckled. "Dad knew all about it, I think he wanted a boy. I'd braid my hair, then Dad would put a stocking cap over my head and my helmet on me before we'd get to the games. But when my mom found out, she lost it. I'm her baby, her one and only. She reamed my dad something terrible. In fact, it was one of the few arguments I remember my parents ever having. But her insistence that I stop playing fell on deaf ears. I snuck and played for a full year until I was forced to stop playing because of puberty."

A new sense of respect gripped Joshua. He knew this sister had moxie, knew it when he saw her at the restaurant fire, but he also knew she was kind and sweet, and had a good heart that could be touched. That was evident at the movie as she sniffed during the sad scene. He had sampled the soft side of her, and he aimed to find out just how much softer this siren sitting across from him could get.

"Okay, Detective Davis."

"No, we're not going back to that, Desiree. My name is Joshua. Joshua Michael Davis; and, if you call me Detective Davis one more time, I'm going to ignore you."

"Like you've been," Desiree spat out without warning.

Joshua's chest rose and fell. "No, you've been ignoring me. I've called you. You haven't called me back."

"You think that faxing over notes is a replacement for a phone call?" She raised her eyebrows. "Anyway, we're just investigating an arson case that resulted in two deaths. What else is there really to talk about?" Desiree turned up the corners of her mouth.

"How about the kiss? This attraction? My wanting to see you again."

"What about it?" she tried to sound nonchalant. Yet truth be told, the simple, intimate act melded to her, seared a brand on her that would forever remain.

Joshua inhaled deeply. "Look, Desiree. I'm attracted to you. I'm not sure if you see that as a good thing or a bad thing, but it is what it is. The question is, can we work on this case and see each other at the same time? I want to see you outside of this case."

"We can work with each other."

"Woman, I'm talking about spending quality time together," he stated. "Desiree, I know I can see you anytime, but to sit next to you, feed you popcorn, hold your hand. That's what I'm talking about."

Desiree leaned over the table and peered at him. She wanted to see it in his eyes. She stared at him. He didn't bat an eye. She averted her gaze. She wanted the same thing.

"Can we really start over?" she whispered.

"Baby, we haven't even begun." He was attracted to her, wanted to get to know her better, and his emotions and heart told him to go for it. He held out his hand to her. She looked at his hand, then into his face. She could see he was sincere. She placed her hand in his and noted how his large hand swallowed her hand.

"Thank you, Desiree."

"You're welcome, Joshua," she said. "Alright, now, it's your turn. Tell me something very few people know."

He looked out onto the street, watched a couple stroll by. He wanted to avoid her eyes as the urge to tell her his story, share an intimate part of himself, grew strong. He wanted to be straight with her. Didn't want to tell half lies, whole lies, white lies. To him, a lie was a lie. Besides, she had granted him a chance to make things right.

"I'm a recovering alcoholic," He blurted out then waited—waited for the gasp or the words the few women he'd dated had spoken that signaled either he would never hear from them again, or they would become his savior. He wanted neither from Desiree. He wasn't sure what he had hoped to gain from the admission. The one thing he did know was that he wanted to get to know her better. Much better.

"So how are you dealing with your sobriety?" she asked.

He met her eyes. There was no saving, no pity, no indication that he would never hear from her again. What he saw was something in her he hadn't seen since his wife's death, understanding. He cleared his throat. "One day at a time. I'll admit it has been a struggle."

She wanted to tell him she could empathize. No, she wouldn't feel sorry for him. To drink had been his choice, but she did understand, more than he may ever know. Her godfather, her second dad, Heaney, had battled the bottle for nearly ten years before a trip to the emergency room following his wrapping a car around a utility pole after a night of heavy drinking forced him into sobriety. He narrowly missed hitting a family as they crossed the street. it was during his years as an alcoholic when she found him obnoxious and unbearable. At one point, Desiree, her parents, Heaney's wife, Mave, and their three children, banded together and confronted him with his drinking. They each vowed to leave him if he didn't stop. The accident, as fate would have it, came one week after their meeting with him.

"How long have you been sober?"

"Four years and   counting." He smiled ruefully.

They shared a comfortable silence as they stole glances at each other. She felt funny, almost light, as if she were levitating as her eyes swept across the handsome man sitting across from her. Out of all the things she had heard about the secretive, yet reclusive Joshua Davis, that was one of the things she hadn't heard. She knew that fellow firefighters rarely, if ever, discussed situations as deep as this. She had a newfound respect for the man who sat across from her and bared a part of what made him the man he was.

She shook her head subtly. If you had told her yesterday that she would be sitting across from Joshua Davis, the man Annette described as one walking with "demons," agreeing to a relationship, she would have placed money against it all. Yet, she didn't feel threatened, didn't feel as if she should run, didn't feel the need to save him.

Joshua drained the last of his coffee. He studied the woman across from him. He liked what he saw and didn't want to stop talking to her. She didn't seem to judge, just seemed to be interested in him. He looked at his wristwatch.

"Desiree, it's close to ten. Are you ready to leave?" He hoped she'd say "no."

"Actually," she began, "I'm a little tired. Besides, I don't think I could digest another beignet or drink a second cup of coffee. I'd be awake all night." She had wanted the night to go on, but she didn't want to appear desperate. Admittedly, she wanted to go out with him again, wanted to know more, see more. Joshua had listened to her, hadn't patronized her, or chided her for the decision she had made to work in the crazed, male dominated world of firefighting—where women were few and people of color even fewer.

Joshua was quite impressed with her. He knew she had come into her own, knew when to turn on and off the switch that would take her from a hard line leader at work to a sultry siren poised to burn him to a cinder.

"Are you off tomorrow?"

"Yeah."

"Want to get together?"

Desiree paused, but before she could accept or decline his offer, he began to speak.

"I've had my shots. I don't bite. I'm house broken. I don't drink, as you know. I don't do drugs and I'm HIV negative. I've had very few women in my life and have slept with even fewer. I'm harmless and a lot of fun once you get to know me." He grinned at her.

Desiree laughed. *How could I resist such a tempting offer from such a handsome man?*

She pulled her bottom lip inward. She had to be sure. "To talk about the case?" She'd hoped not.

"Not hardly."

"I see."

"No, I'll show you. How about we go to the DuSable Museum? I'll pick you up at 11 a.m."

Desiree looked at him and nodded. She didn't dare say a word. Now she was not only physically tired, but also emotionally tired as well. The man sitting across from her, with the beautiful complexion, smooth voice, and tight body was wrecking havoc with her senses.

Without preamble, they both rose. Joshua pulled several bills from his pocket and placed them on the table. He came to her side, placed his hand at the small of her back and led her to the car.

At her house, he got out of the car, opened her door and escorted her up the steps. He waited as she unlocked the screen door, then the service door. She turned to face him.

"Thank you, Joshua."

"My pleasure. I'll be here at eleven to get you. Sleep tight." He quickly bent and kissed her lightly on the lips. He turned and strolled down the steps. At his car, he waved, then got in and sped around the block, out of sight.

Desiree closed the doors and stood still. She touched her lips, sealing the searing act into her memory banks. She wanted to kiss him repeatedly.

CHAPTER 11

Joshua climbed the front steps to his home, opened the door then stepped inside. He walked into the living room and looked at the picture of Serena sitting on the sofa table.

"It's time, isn't it, honey," he said to the picture, more a statement than a question. He studied the beautiful gleam in his late wife's eyes.

He turned then headed into the kitchen. He opened one of the cabinet doors and retrieved a package of Chips Ahoy cookies. He took the bag of cookies with him as he entered his bedroom and undressed down to his boxer briefs.

He climbed in bed, cookies in tow. He looked around the room. Serena had decorated it, its warm pastel colors not overly feminine. The poster bed they had shared was covered in the spread she had chosen. He thought of the rest of the one-story, brick Georgian. Most of its furnishings and decorations had been completed by Serena. No wonder he hadn't been able to get past it all—everything in this house had her touch. He hadn't complained. He had actually thought it quite tasteful. But because it all had her touch, her spirit, he hadn't been able to move past her, past the love they had shared.

He knew that for the rest of his life he would love Serena, but having met Desiree, he also knew that his love for Serena would have to be placed in its own, rightful place in his mind and heart.

He munched on a cookie. As a crumb fell onto the bed covers, he remembered the times Serena would chide him for eating in bed. He climbed out of the bed, took his pillow, package of cookies, and a blanket at the foot of the bed and went to the den. He stretched out on the overstuffed couch and grabbed the remote control. He flicked on the television then turned the volume down low.

He looked at the clock of the VCR. It was past eleven in South

Carolina, but he needed to speak to his parents. He'd only gotten a chance to speak to them briefly a few times following the last phone call from Abel.

He picked up the receiver that rested on the base of the cordless unit then dialed his parents' number and listened as the line rang. After the third ring, he heard the familiar voice.

"Hello, Mom. It's Josh."

"Is anything wrong, baby?" Carrie Davis asked her son.

He smiled. No matter how old, he'd always be his mother's baby. He was just glad that she didn't call him "baby" in front of folks outside of their immediate family. He had to smile at the thought of his parents. Both seventy-eight years old, Carrie and Richard Davis had taken early retirements following their youngest son's sentencing. Since then, the couple traveled often, coming to Chicago several times a year to check up on Joshua and to visit Abel in prison. "No, Mom. Nothing's wrong. Just wanted to call you back. I've been busy with this arson case."

He spoke with his mother, followed by his father, then back to his mother. As he started to end the call, his mother stopped him.

"Are you going with us to see Abel?" she asked, her voice low, almost a whisper.

He shook his head. Abel had been locked up for years, it was no secret. "I'm thinking on it. I'll let you know."

"Okay, baby. We'll be there the middle of August. I think your father made reservations for the twentieth. We're flying into Midway."

"Will do. I'll pick you up. You guys are staying here. I've more than enough room."

He thought of when his parents had visited him last Thanksgiving. His mother talked about how the house was decorated. Gently, she had admonished her son to re-decorate, to start fresh. He winced. He hadn't been ready. He looked around the one room that Serena hadn't decorated. She had told him it was his room, to do with it as he pleased. And he had. He had painted the walls a deep olive, with the ceiling painted a shade lighter, placed shelves along one side, which held all his trophies and plaques. Along another wall rested a 42" television that sported six speakers and an X-box. The only pieces of furniture were an old tan nightstand that belonged to his late grandmother and an over-stuffed emerald green leather sofa.

His mother hesitated. "I'll tell your father." He could tell she had more to say. And whether he wanted to hear it or not, she'd speak her mind. He braced himself.

"Have you bought any new furniture?"

"No, Mother. I haven't."

"I see. Well, it's late. You take care and be careful out there. We'll see you soon."

"I will. Nite, Mom."

"Nite, baby."

Joshua placed the receiver on its base. He wanted to tell his mother about Desiree, but thought better. He stretched out on his back, sleep coming slow, he thought of Desiree—the fire in her eyes, the way she felt in his arms.

For the first time since Serena's death he had wanted to explore the possibilities, wanted the feel of a sensuous, passionate woman beneath him. His member stirred to life. He started to touch himself, do what he found himself doing lately to satiate the primal need, to ease the hardness. He hadn't been intimate with a woman in over a year. The last woman he had slept with rightly accused him of holding on to his "dead wife." But Joshua knew that only one woman could put out the embers, or raise the flame a notch. And that woman was Desiree.

He thought of Desiree and the siren she was. As he allowed sleep to claim him he dreamed, of Serena. She hugged him, kissed him gently on the lips, then waved at him as she turned to leave. He waved back and watched her disappear into a plume of fog.

Desiree flopped onto the sofa and looked absently around the liv-

ng room. She looked at her wristwatch. The digital dial read 2230
ours. She stood, walked to the kitchen and picked up the phone on
e wall. The tree tones she heard indicated she had messages. She
tered her password and listened as the messages played. She laughed
Annette's message to be a "good girl." The next message was from her
f her. His soft voice reminded her of their standing morning ritual of
w king out followed by breakfast. She had forgotten all about it when
sh agreed to go out with Joshua. Normally, Desiree and her father
w ld hang out all morning. She would just have to call Joshua and ask
hi could they get together later. She listened to the final message. She
fro ed as her father told of the incident at the Union Hall between
she d Donald, and her leaving in a black BMW with "that crazy
Josh Davis dude."

siree laughed as she erased the message, pressed the button, then
dialec er parent's phone number. She decided that she would cut their
standi date short. She listened as her parents line extension rang. Her
moth nswered.

"   Mom."

"H   sweetie. How are you? You didn't call me this morning when
you got   ?"

"I'm   rry. We had a fire a few hours before quitting time. I was
beat and   nt to bed the minute I hit the door. Then Annette came
by." Desir   frowned. She felt like a ten-year-old child, not the thirty-
seven year-   d woman she was.

"I hear   , sweetie. Your father is looking for you. Something about
a Joshua be ing his chest before he grabbed you by your hair and
dragged you   ut of the union hall." Her mother laughed. Desiree was
grateful that   er mother took the stance she did about her daughter's
dating life. N w if her dad could do the same.

"Great. W o called Dad?"

"I don't k ow. One of them folks that belong to the Association.
You know the n. You're Charles's baby girl. Wait, your father just
walked into the room. Sooth the savage beast, or else I won't get any
sleep tonight."

Desiree chuckled as she heard her father cuss and fuss in the background.

"What were you doing hanging out with that Joshua Davis? The man's crazy!"

"Daddy, you trippin'. He actually got up in Donald's face after Donald grabbed me. Did your spies tell you that?" she said as calmly as she could. "We went for coffee, Father. And we will be going out tomorrow." She had every intention of calling Joshua and pushing the time of their date back a few hours, but after her father's accusation, she knew she wouldn't feel much like hanging out without her telling her father off. Ever since her father left the department, he'd become more and more protective. Hell, he wasn't that protective when she was playing football.

"Don't get involved with him. He's got some serious issues."

"No more than you do right now," Desiree spat, then regretted the outburst upon hearing her father suck in air.

"Wait a minute now, little girl. I'm still your father."

"I'm sorry, Dad. But I'm also a grown woman," she defended. "When Donald and I first got together, you didn't like him. Now that we've split, he's the best thing since sliced bread, a toaster and butter to spread."

"I just don't want my baby hurt. That's all."

"I hear ya. But I'm a grown woman and I think I can take care of myself."

She heard her father inhale deeply. "I know. I'm sorry. But I've heard things about Joshua Davis. I just don't want you mixed up with him. He could hurt your career."

"How so? I know about his being an alcoholic."

"Who told you that?"

"He did, Daddy."

"Well, I worked with him. He's some piece of work. That's all I'm a say about it."

Desiree laughed in spite of herself. She remembered his praise and glory of Joshua when he was a young firefighter and had hung on

Trenton Charles's every word. Now, he was no good. Well, she wasn't surprised. She knew what her father was trying to do and he'd been doing it since she started dating at seventeen.

"Gotcha. Don't worry, okay? Are we on in the morning or what?"

"That's if you have time for an old man like me."

Desiree shook her head. She had checked him and he hadn't liked it. Now he was ready to kiss and make up by pulling out the old pity card. What the hell. Might as well play along.

"You know you're my heart, Dad. But let's do something different tomorrow. Let's just go to breakfast at eight. How's that?" She calculated the time. Two hours for breakfast. That would take her to 10, 10:30 at the latest. She'd be home by 11. Ready and waiting for Joshua.

"Okay, puddin'," he responded, using the nickname he had given her as a child. Desiree knew that meant all was well between them.

"Good. I'll be by at 7:30 to get you. Be dressed."

"Will do. Nite, Puddin'."

"Nite, Dad. Let me say goodnight to Mom."

She waited as her mother got on the extension. "Thank you. Chile, I wouldn't have gotten one ounce of sleep. Are we still on for lunch Wednesday? I want to go to BJ's Market."

"Sure. I'll pick you up around noon. Is that okay."

"Perfect. I'll see you in the morning."

"Nite, Mom."

"Goodnight, baby."

Desiree placed the receiver in its base. She shook her head, realizing that she had just committed to having her parents occupy her scheduled two days off. *Not good*, she thought. She normally spent one day with them both. *Oh, well. At least Joshua will provide a nice respite.*

CHAPTER 12

Desiree paced as the hands on the clock in her living room, situated over the fireplace mantel, struck eleven. At the same time, the doorbell rang. She paused. She didn't want to run to the door, make it seem like she had been waiting with bated breath for his arrival. She took her time as she walked slowly to the door. She peered out of the door's peephole. She had to look again. Damn, this man looks good, even through a peephole.

She unlocked the service door, followed by the screen door. She pushed the screen door open and smiled as Joshua stepped in. He smiled back, showing off his deep-set dimples.

"Right on time. I'm ready if you are?"

He nodded; his intense stare bore a hole through her. She began to fidget and wondered if something was wrong. "Are you okay?"

Joshua closed his eyes as he slowly shook his head then opened them. "Woman, you look good in that outfit. I'm not sure I want to take you outside." He stepped closer to her. "And that perfume. What is it?" He stepped even closer. She inhaled his masculine fragrance; the heady scent surrounded them. He pulled her to his chest and looked into her eyes. He placed his lips upon hers then gently pried them apart with his tongue. Desiree complied, lost in the masterful way his tongue explored the inside of her mouth. Against better judgment, her arms came to rest as the nape of his neck. She held him, pushing his mouth closer to hers. She heard a groan, but didn't know which one of them made the sensuous cacophony that reverberated through them both.

Reluctantly, Joshua pulled away. His eyes bore embarrassment at his physical state. "I ... I... don't know what came over me. Please forgive me."

Desiree pulled him back to her and kissed him. Her tongue now parted his lips, conveying the message that she had wanted the kiss. She released his lips, but not his body, as she held him. "No reason to apologize. But I do think we need to get a move on it."

Joshua smiled. "I agree." He stepped out of her embrace, opened the door then put his hand out to Desiree. She looked at his large hand then placed hers in his. "Desiree, I do plan to hold your hand today, but I want you to give me your door keys first."

"Oh." She handed over her keys and watched as he locked the doors. He placed the keys in the side pocket of her purse then took her hand. They walked down the steps, got in the car and headed to the museum.

The trip to the museum lasted longer than either expected. They strolled, hand in hand, from exhibit to exhibit, speaking in hushed tones.

Joshua paused as his eyes came upon a sketch of a man standing in between a heart and a pair of jail cell bars. The man's dark eyes seemed to glance in the direction of the heart. Joshua thought about his brother, Abel.

"That's a deep piece," Desiree said. "The brother can't decide if he wants to go to the heart of his issues, which are pulling him, or toward the negative ones that would lead him to a prison cell."

He nodded then led her to the other exhibits.

Desiree was surprised at his vast knowledge of African and Black History. He explained each exhibit. Following the museum, they went to the local bookstore, where for hours the two sat on a settee, hip to hip, and read to each other from the books they had selected. Joshua was blown away by the soothing sound of her voice as she read a poem "Black Love," by Shangè, to him. He heard the intonation, the cadence of her words, the meaning behind each inflection. When she reached the part that read: "I have eaten bitter words and sour dreams . . ." he knew she was telling him that she had tasted heartache and disappointment. When she finished reading, he looked at her, took the book from her hand and put his arm around her. No words were necessary. The poem told all.

He purchased the book, and several others. They ended their date at his home, where he cooked a southern meal of oven baked fried chicken, fried corn, corn bread and string beans mixed with white potatoes. He ended the meal with a small helping of peach cobbler, of which he admitted that his mother had prepared.

At the end of dinner, he escorted Desiree to the living room.

"You know, Joshua, I had a great time today." She sat on the love seat.

"So did I." He sat next to her. His mind visualized the picture of the man torn between the heart and the jail cell.

"Joshua, are you okay?" She placed her hand on his forearm.

He looked at Desiree. "The picture at the museum. It reminded me of my brother, Abel."

"When's the last time you saw him?"

"It's been almost five years," he responded.

She rubbed his arm. "That's a long time."

He forcefully blew out his breath. "Yeah. I do need to go see him. I just don't like the whole operation, being patted down, going from one area to the next being watched like you're about to steal something from them."

Desiree was at a loss for words. She had never had a family member in jail nor did she know anyone who had ever been to prison, so she had no frame of reference. She began to look around the living room, painted a warm pistachio. The open room was furnished with mahogany tables, situated on each side of the sofa and love seat. A large pale green area rug was the focal point of the room, with the wooden feet of a cream winged back chair and matching sofa resting at the edges of the round rug. She turned her head, and was taken aback by the photo of the beautiful woman sitting on the sofa table. Joshua's eyes followed hers.

"That's my late wife, Serena."

"She's quite pretty."

An uncomfortable silence enveloped them. He didn't want her to run. Didn't want her to think she had to compete. He saw the uneasiness in her eyes. He knew he had to assuage her impending fears. He decided to tell her about Serena and once again hope for the best.

He told her how he had been sober for one year when he found out she was expecting their first child. They had been married for five years, and Serena had admitted that she had purposely taken birth control pills, for she didn't want to bring a child into the house of an alcoholic. Joshua admitted that he was happier than he had ever been. He had left for work, he was at a firehouse at the time, and kissed her goodbye as he always did. Later, he received a call at 2 a.m. for him to go to a local hospital, for his wife had been seriously injured in a car accident. Paglinini drove him to the hospital. He said he remembered a strange feeling creep across his entire body and knew in that very instance Serena had died. Once he arrived at the hospital and asked for her by name, the nurse pointed him to a waiting room. For what seemed like hours, which were only minutes, he waited for someone to confirm what he already knew—Serena was dead, as was the child she carried.

He buried Serena and his unborn son, and fought the never-ending pull toward the bottle.

"The ironic thing was that she was killed by a drunken driver. That's where the money came from. It was a settlement for the suit I filed against him and his insurance company who kept insuring him after he had received two DUI's."

Joshua had never told the entire story to anyone outside his mother. He looked at Desiree expectantly—waited for her to bolt. She didn't move.

"That's a hard loss, Joshua." Desiree rose from the couch and stood by the large picture window.

He came to stand by her side. He turned her to face him. He lifted her face by her chin and kissed her eyelids followed by her lips. He inhaled her fragrance, the undeniable scent that had become her. He wrapped his arms around her. The tightness in his groin was telling. He continued the kiss, deepening the act with his tongue as it darted in and out of her mouth. He signed heavily as she began to suckle on his tongue, intimating an act he hadn't engaged in for some time. They both moaned as her hands trailed up his back, then down his taunt behind.

Slowly, they backed up to the couch. Sitting, Desiree looked up into Joshua's eyes. The desire in them stoked a fire that was sure to blaze out of control unless it was fed with the passion that had swelled in them both. Wordlessly, Joshua put his hand out to Desiree. She placed her hand in his, grabbed her purse, and allowed him to lead her upstairs.

Briefly her eyes flickered around the room, the feminine touches evident, a warm glow cast about the room from a single lamp. Joshua sat on the side of the bed and pulled Desiree to him. He raked his hands through her hair as he motioned her closer. His lips found hers as the passion ignited. He wanted her, needed to feel her weight upon him, her body near his. He broke the kiss and saw the apprehension in her eyes.

Desiree shut her eyes as she felt Joshua's hands slide under her silk tank, then up and around her full breasts. She dropped her purse at her feet as the ministrations intensified, threatened to make her loose all control. She grasped Joshua's hands.

"Let me make love to you, Desiree."

The simple words wound themselves around Desiree. She released his hands then pulled the top over her head. Joshua buried his face in her cleavage, brushing his face in the sweet swell of them. He reached behind her, searching for the clasp. Desiree pulled his hands to the front. She watched the slight smile cross his lips as he undid the front clasp, freeing her to experience the light flick of his tongue as it laved over her pert nipples. She gasped as he continued to lightly pull and suck on the engorged peaks. Her legs threatened to give way.

Joshua paused long enough to unbutton the wrap skirt from her. His hands made their way around her. The thong became his undoing as he stood suddenly, picked Desiree up into his arms then laid her on his bed. He watched the unbridled fire dance in her eyes. She wanted him, and he would put out the fire and start another.

Desiree watched as his hands slowly undid the buttons to his shirt, showing inch by teasingly inch the curly hairs that covered his muscular chest. She wanted to snatch the articles from his body. Finally, she breathed in. He did away with his pants and stood near the bed in only a pair of white boxer briefs, the heaviness in them quite evident, strained for release. She reached out to touch him. He shuddered at the feel of her warm hand caressing him. She looped her fingers in the band of his briefs and tugged them downward. To say she was pleased with the exquisite build of his entire body was putting it mildly. He was muscular. His broad, hairy chest boasted rigid pecs. His waist tapered into strong, muscular thighs and legs. And his thick member swayed in the glow.

She leaned over the bed, grabbed her purse from the floor then quickly found the square package and placed it on the pillow near her head. She then leaned back onto the bed and opened her arms to him.

He came to her. He quivered upon feeling the heat of her body mixed with the intoxicating scent of her arousal. He wanted to feel her: to join her body with his, to brand her, to be seared by the heat of her essence. He pulled the thong from her and tossed it over his back. His fingers slid down her body and danced over her bud. He stroked her; plied her with his fingers. Desiree closed her eyes and moaned.

"Yes, baby. Come for me."

He increased his assault as he ravaged her body, made the heat from her ignite into a combustion that would surely overtake her. Desiree's hips crashed into his fingers as she began a wicked climax. Her legs trembled. As the fire began to ebb, a new one began. She wanted to feel the full hardness inside of her. She opened her eyes then pulled Joshua atop her. He shook his head.

"Tell me. What do you want?" he asked, his voice raspy with need.

"I . . ." Desiree stammered as he brushed the length of his hardness across her opening. She grabbed at him about his shoulders.

"Tell me," he demanded softly. "Tell me what you want, and I will give it to you."

"Joshua," she whispered. "I want you. Please. I want you."

"Then take me," he dared. Desiree blindly reached over to the pillow. She took the condom in her hand, carefully tore the small plastic pouch then sheathed him. She looked into his eyes, the tip of his hardness rested teasingly at the core of what made her woman. She wrapped her arms around him, followed by her legs around his waist, pulling him in, capturing him inside her.

Joshua groaned loudly as the warmth mixed with the tight sweetness of her made his head spin. He closed his eyes. Flashes of light roamed behind his lids. He could barely control the heavy emotions pounding in his chest.

He grabbed her toned legs and joined her body in the dance. The tempo played out in the in and out motions. Joshua tried to fight the feeling, his mind nearly mush as he felt himself become harder.

"That's it, Joshua. That's it," Desiree whispered in his ear as she held on to him, matching him stroke for stroke. Her mind blanked as the sensuous dance took over and bubbled forth. She tightened her legs around him. Suddenly, he rolled them over. Desiree sat astride him and began to ride him long and hard. His thumbs played with her nipples as her essence tightened around him. He knew he would not last much longer if he allowed her to continue. He stilled her.

"Not yet," he breathed, and then eased out of her sweetness. He rolled her to her side and gently pulled her to him. Her full, round behind settled against his groin. He entered her slowly, until he could go no further. He placed his hands around her and began teasing her nipples into hardened peaks as he moved inside her.

"Baby, you feel so good," he moaned, his deep voice low.

Desiree began to move her hips, grounding them into his as another orgasm threatened. She moaned softly as their bodies moved fluidly.

He needed to see her face. He sat up, turned her to face him and was pleased with the wanton look in her eyes. Not since Serena, had he wanted a woman so fully, so completely. He smiled at her. She didn't return the gesture, instead she began to raise then lower, raise then lower. Joshua grabbed her hips and joined her. They moaned and allowed themselves to be swept up by the passion, the fire, they felt and knew could only be extinguished in the other's arms.

"Desireee," Joshua called out through clinched teeth as he throbbed inside of her, spilling his seed in the protective sheath. Moments later, she joined him, milking them both.

Joshua put his head to her breasts. Desiree stroked the smooth hair at the nape of his neck.

"Woman," he breathed out. "What did you just do to me?" He chuckled. "No, don't answer that."

Reluctantly, he removed himself from the warmth and security of her body and discarded the condom. He pulled her to rest on top his body. His hand trailed up and down her back, lingering long at the roundness of her derriere.

"Mr. Davis, you shouldn't do that."

"Shouldn't do what?" He continued to feel her soft, firm roundness.

"That, sir, will get you into trouble." She gasped as his fingers kneaded and plied the supple skin. Desiree moaned as he dipped his finger between her legs. Her hips began to move. And, once again, they fell into the heated dance, loving, hoping that the fire could be satiated, but fully knowing that they were far from over.

Desiree stirred. Her entire form tingled as her eyes opened. She glanced at the man who had awakened a passion, a fire she had never had extinguished—not even with Donald. She watched Joshua's face and frowned. From his expression, he seemed to be dreaming, his eyebrows knotted. She gasped.

"Serena, thank you" he called out in his sleep.

Desiree became still. He wasn't over his late wife. A pang so deep entwined itself around her heart. She had fallen for and spent the night with a man who still loved his wife so much that she haunted his dreams.

Desiree quietly rose from the bed. She refused to cry. She hadn't shed a tear since she broke her arm playing football. He father had told her back then to "suck it up," and suck it up she would.

After dressing quietly, she tried to tip from the room.

"Leaving so soon?" Joshua's husky voice sounded behind her.

Desiree faced him. She looked at the man lying in the bed they had just made love in hours before. She wanted to kick herself for not asking the one question that would have made all the difference. But that was lost, for she had let the feelings he stirred in her override her senses. She had never been this gone before.

"Ah, I've got to go."

Joshua climbed out of bed. Desiree averted her eyes. She didn't want to see the man, the object of her emotions, the one who dared to make her dream of the possibilities.

"So soon? I thought we'd at least have breakfast in bed." Joshua noted the change in her, the way she avoided his eyes. He didn't know where the sudden change had come from. Just hours ago they had made love and he had just short of told her that he had fallen in love with her, that he wanted her in his life. Now, he just stood and looked at the pained expression creased onto her beautiful face.

"Sorry, but I've got a few things to do this morning," Desiree lied and was instantly ashamed. She had never been a liar. Why now? Her inner voice responded, "You really don't want to know, now do you?"

"Well, at least let me get dressed and take you home."

"That won't be necessary. Besides, I called Annette." Lie number two. This wasn't how it was suppose to be.

Joshua walked over to her. "Baby," he turned her to face him. "What's wrong?"

She faced him and saw the look of concern in his eyes. She didn't want to tell another lie, but she was also afraid of the answer to her question. The one she should have asked him from day one. But she had to. She met his gaze head on. "Are you over the death of your wife?"

It was a simple question to a difficult answer. Joshua saw the look in her eyes. He didn't want to lie to her, but he didn't want to end the feelings he was having for her.

"I think so. Let me tell you . . ."

Desiree held up her hand to silence him. She didn't want to hear the rest. She knew he wasn't over his wife; he had called out her name in his sleep. A lump formed in her throat. She looked away. Had she asked that question long before making love to him, she wouldn't feel like such a fool. She had to get out of the house, out of his presence. She ran from the bedroom. She heard his footsteps behind her. She didn't want him to follow her, didn't want to sit down and discuss this like two rational adults—she felt far from rational. The doorknob turned easily as the clouds of her tears blurred her path. She heard Joshua's voice behind her fade as she got further from him. Her short-heeled shoes made an angry click-clack sound on the pavement.

Joshua stood on the porch clad in the only thing he could get his hands on quickly—his briefs. He called out to Desiree as she strode quickly down the street. He lost sight of her as she rounded the corner.

He stepped back into the house and quietly shut the door. He leaned against the door and breathed deeply. He wondered what had made her ask him about his late wife. He looked at the picture frame then remembered he had been dreaming of Serena. He wondered had he called out her name. In the dream, he and Serena had talked. She had wished him well as she pushed him toward a door. When he awoke, he felt free and he wanted to tell Desiree all about the dream and its subsequent meaning. Instead, she had asked him was he over Serena; and instead of allowing him to explain, she had run from him. "Damn!" he spat then sat on the couch. "I've got to make her understand."

Joshua rushed up the steps, jumped in the shower and quickly dressed. He needed her to understand. As he came to his front door, he glanced around the room: the furniture, the color of the walls, the picture of Serena. She was all around him. All of the things Serena had purchased, touched, were here. Instantly it came to him. If Desiree was going to believe that he was ready to move past his late wife, then he knew he had to show her.

He crossed over to the sofa table and picked up his late wife's picture then walked to the basement and retrieved several boxes. He placed each picture and personal memento into a box. After sealing the boxes, he stored them in the basement. Next, he grabbed the Yellow Pages from the kitchen pantry and contacted a painter. When he hung up, he went to the bedroom he had shared with Serena. He removed the bedding then looked at the bed itself. *Got to go*, his mind informed him.

For the next several hours, he cleaned the house of all traces of his wife. He knew that Serena rested in that part of him that would never forget her, but would also allow him to move forward with Desiree.

"Desiree." Her name came to his lips. He sat down on the floor in the middle of the now empty bedroom. He knew what he had to do.

CHAPTER 13

Joshua rubbed his eyes with the backs of his hands. For the past three days, he had either directed painters or shopped for furniture when he should have been sleeping. Each morning when he got off, he shopped. He wanted to change the entire look and feel of his house. He yawned loudly. He had stayed up the entire day directing the delivery of his new bedroom furniture. All that he had left was to purchase living room furniture. He pulled a fabric book from his desk drawer and began thumbing through the countless samples. He thought of Desiree.

"Why not just get some leather?" the voice behind him stated.

"Why don't you mind your own business?" Joshua spat as he slammed the book closed and moved it to the right side of his desk. "What are you doing here?"

John sat down across from Joshua. He looked at his best friend and noted the change, admittedly for the better. Finally, John thought, he had moved past Serena's death, but he still wasn't so sure if he should be doing so with Desiree.

"I came to apologize," John stated, his hands rested on the desk. He thought about the meeting with Callahan. He should have told Joshua. He looked at the man who had fought fire and men beside him. He breathed in deep then told Joshua how Callahan had come to him and all but told him that Desiree Charles, "that simple little colored gal," was not to become the next Battalion Chief for the South Side district. He said he didn't care who it was, but he did want his son, Mike Junior, to be elevated to captain. John told how he had grabbed Callahan, anger in his light eyes, as he informed Callahan that the decision was not his to make. Upon releasing Callahan, he shoved him out of his office.

"I wanted to kick his ass. That's for sure," John said. "I made my decision right then."

John went on to tell how the mayor's people had been given a list of possible candidates for the position once the mayor informed John that he would become the new Commissioner. Out of the four names, only one name really stood out, and he knew that Captain Desiree Charles would be the one. Even though the mayor's people insinuated that the appointment would be made after the outcome of the fatal fire investigation, John had made up his mind and submitted his choices, knowing that Desiree would be perfect for the South Side.

He thought of Callahan's son and winced.

Joshua opened his mouth to speak.

"No, there's more." John shook his head as he shared Mike Junior's secret. "Now, everybody who knows me knows I love black women. But I had no idea that Mike Junior shared my love."

Joshua's eyes widened. "You lying, man."

"No, I'm not." John went on to tell how he came upon Mike at a local bar. He was shocked to see him lip locked with a black woman. Upon seeing John, Mike had rushed over to him; Mike's breath reeked of whatever he had been drinking.

"You didn't see me," Mike had sputtered as his body waved from side to side. He held on to John's arm for support. "Please. Don't. My father would have a stroke." Mike laughed; the sound was demonic. "Maybe that wouldn't be so bad after all."

John had looked over his shoulder to see the bland women with caramel skin and a slight build. Her dark eyes looked him up and down. He knew it wasn't a look of attraction, but more of contempt. John shook it off and pulled Mike outside.

"Okay, Mike. But isn't it a little dangerous for you? You know your father is all over this side of town."

"Fuck him!" Mike yelled. "I'm tired of him controlling my life. He's the reason I'm a firefighter. I never wanted it. He forced me to join the department. Now he's talking some madness about my becoming chief. I didn't even want to be a lieutenant." Mike sat on the curb, chest heaving in and out.

John stepped back. He knew the signs. He sighed as Mike began to empty the contents of his stomach. The stench rose up and greeted him. John frowned, watching as he finished. "Mike, you okay?"

"Yeah. Go get my girl. It's time we went home." Mike swayed as he tried to rise. John grabbed his arm and helped him up. "I'm okay. Get my girl, will ya?"

He did as Mike requested, then watched the couple as she helped him into the passenger side of a gold Mercedes. The woman motioned for John to come over to the vehicle. The passenger side window slid down.

"John, not a word. Okay?" Mike Junior implored.

John nodded his head, then righted. He looked at the woman who stood in the driver's side doorway. Something about her was familiar. He had always been good at remembering faces, yet he couldn't place hers. The woman narrowed her dark eyes at him then climbed into the car and sped off.

John looked at Joshua. "Deep." He stood and faced Joshua. "I'm sorry. I never should have said that you and Desiree shouldn't see each other. Are you gonna forgive me, or do I have to grovel? "

Joshua looked up into his friend's eyes. "Yeah, I guess so."

"You've got to. Who else is going to put up with this poor Dego boy from Little Italy? You're my brother."

Joshua laughed. "Okay, apology accepted. So, what's got you up at this bewitching hour?"

"The press conference for my appointment is Monday. I really need to know by this Thursday what your decision is. Actually, I'd like for you to take the Assistant Deputy's position, but I'll be happy if you accept the Chief of Investigations position."

Between thoughts of Desiree and re-decorating his home, he hadn't given much thought to John's request. Either position, he knew, would allow him to begin to address the racial issues that plagued the last administration.

"Give me two days to think on it," Joshua ended that line of conversation. "And Desiree? She's actually going to be the South Side's next Battalion Chief?"

John mentally recalled his meeting with Callahan. Desiree would replace Callahan, he knew this, especially after Callahan's implied threat. To add to it, was his seeing Mike Junior in his drunken stupor. He knew that both had to go. He knew he'd let Callahan retire; he had over thirty years with the department. As for Mike Junior, he needed help. In the few times he had interacted with Mike Junior, John always smelt traces of alcohol on his breath.

John raked his hand over his coal black hair. "Yes. And no matter the outcome of the case, I'll be fighting for her to get the position."

Joshua nodded his head. "I'm glad to hear you've had a change of heart."

"Well, after I saw Callahan, I submitted my choices. Your name is on that list as well. That's why you have until Thursday to make up your mind."

Joshua looked at the calendar on his desk. It was Tuesday. He had twenty-four hours to make up his mind.

"How's the case coming along?"

"There are some missing pieces." Joshua went on to tell him how the fires started, the accelerants used and how the fires were always during Desiree's shift.

"Seems as if this nut case starting these fires knows them. You think it's an inside job?"

"Could be. But I haven't a clue as to where to begin."

John grabbed several files and began flipping through them. He then looked over Joshua's notes. He agreed with Joshua, there was something missing. He also knew that eventually something would raise its ugly head and give him the missing pieces.

Joshua and John bantered back and forth over the evidence of the fire for hours. Both men jumped at the sound of the phone on his desk as it rang. He hoped it was Desiree.

"Arson. Detective Davis speaking," he responded into the receiver.

"Look at the logs of the ladders on the southwest side," an unfamiliar faint voice said just before the line went dead.

Joshua glanced at the Caller ID attached to the base of the phone.

The unit read "private call." He replaced the receiver.

"That was strange."

"Who was it?"

"A voice… I'm not sure if it belonged to a man or a woman, but it said to check the southwest side ladder company logs."

"There are a lot of ladder companies on the southwest side."

"I know." Joshua tapped his pen on the desk. "Wait, get that book over there. It's got the addresses of all the stationhouses."

John walked to where Joshua pointed. He pulled the thick book from atop the file cabinet and brought it back to the desk. "What am I looking for?"

"The ones that are closest to Engine #19."

John flipped through several pages. His eyes scanned the addresses. He grabbed a pen and a piece of paper. "Found three."

Joshua stood. "Well, what are we waiting for? The missing pieces may be in those logs."

An hour later, Joshua and John pulled up outside of Ladder #12, the third and final one on John's list. John looked up at the newly constructed firehouse as they walked inside.

Memories flooded them both. For John the memories tasted bad. The old building that housed Ladder #12 had been he and Joshua's first assigned station. The crew hadn't been kind to either of them. At the time, Callahan had been captain, and he made it hard for both of them. Once the guys at the station found out that John was married to a black woman, crude, vile pictures of naked black women began to show up in his locker. Many a time, following a bar room brawl that was the result of a fellow firefighter insulting his wife, it had been Joshua who had kept John from completely losing his cool.

For Joshua, the memories were both bitter and sweet. For his first six months as a candidate, Callahan had made it difficult at best for him. Joshua had refused to be bested by some racist redneck. At fires, Callahan would make him take point, sending him first into whatever inferno they were fighting. He had been angry, for he knew what Callahan was up too. If anything awry would happen, Joshua would be blamed, hurt, or killed.

But he knew firefighting, was tops in his class, and he vowed that he would never let the likes of Callahan, or anyone of his kind, get the best of him. He also held great memories. After Desiree's father and godfather were assigned to the house, he had two allies, even though Trent Charles had been hard on him.

"Mike," Joshua said as Callahan's son appeared before them. Joshua watched as Mike and John exchanged brief nods.

"Lieutenant Callahan to you."

"Yeah, right. I need a copy of your logs for the past two months," Joshua said. It was more a demand than a request. Joshua had never liked Mike. They had been cadets at the same time. Joshua found him to be an exact replica of his father. Both were mindless asses to him.

"What do you need them for?" Mike stepped closer to Joshua.

Joshua looked at him; Mike's pale face held an ugly red hue. The stench of liquor assaulted Joshua's senses, thus he stepped back.

"I'm investigating that arson fire that Engine #19 fought last month."

"Who says it was arson?"

Joshua noticed his hands were balled into fists as they rested by his sides.

John raised a questioning brow. "Accelerants were found at the fire. The same was found at several of the fires 19 fought. Go get them, boy. Don't make me pull rank!" John barked.

Joshua watched as Mike's pale grey eyes roved from his to John's then back again. Joshua thought he saw panic in them.

"Wait right here," Mike said as he disappeared into an office. Joshua ignored his request and began to walk around the modern station. He whistled at the gleaming engines and cleanliness of the floor. He walked toward the back and eyed the large, state-of-art kitchen. Its chrome shone like a brand new quarter.

"John, man, get a look at this." Joshua stepped back. He saw John stare at a female firefighter. She wasn't his type, Joshua thought, as he sized up the tall, slender woman, her light complexion and short hair. *No, not his type at all.* John liked his women brown with some meat on their bones. He laughed. It was no dark fantasy for John. He truly loved black women. John's first wife had been a sister, and his last flame was as such.

"John," Joshua called out. He frowned at the odd look on John's face.

John walked backwards into the kitchen. "Why are two lieutenants on duty here?" He asked and continued to watch the woman. "Wait, she's the—" his words were interrupted by the shrill sound of the overhead siren.

They watched as several firefighters rushed from points unknown toward the large engine. Joshua looked up to see Mike motion to him. He tossed several sheets in Joshua's direction; the pages hit the floor haphazardly. Joshua swore.

John walked over to the sheets and picked them up. He looked up as the woman began putting on her turn-out gear. The acknowledgment registered in both of their eyes. She was the woman John had seen with Mike at the bar. John finished picking up the sheets. He handed them to Joshua just as the engine roared to life then sped out of the station.

"Come on," Joshua said as he walked to the other side of the station. He climbed the stairs. At the top, he looked around at the large workout room, three treadmills, two crunch machines and two stair masters lined the large window, which gave a view of the street below. Opposite the machines stood two workout benches with weights upon them.

"We never had anything like this," Joshua said as he left the workout room and walked into the living quarters. The door was clearly marked "MEN." He poked his head inside. The highly polished tiled floor gleamed in the airy space. A total of ten beds lined both sides of the walls, a large locker sat next to each near the head of the bed.

Joshua called out to John. When he didn't respond, Joshua left the men's quarters. He found John in the women's quarters.

"It's her, Josh," John said as he searched through one of six lockers. The room was the same size as the men's, but with fewer beds. "She's the woman I saw Mike Junior with that night."

"Okay. So, what are you looking for?"

"I don't know. But there's something odd about Mike and his lady friend." He crouched low and pulled out an open folder. "Look at this."

John rose then handed Joshua two pictures. One of a baby, dressed in an azure blue, his extremely light complexion giving a hint to his parentage. The other was of Mike Junior and the female firefighter he had seen moments before. They were locked in a warm embrace.

"Wow!" Joshua shook his head. "I wonder does Callahan know about this?"

"I'd give my paycheck and this appointment that he doesn't. Hell, Callahan would give birth to a cinder brick if he knew."

Joshua looked around. This was too much. But he couldn't fathom the connection to the rash of fires. "What's the name?"

John peered around the locker door and spied the name written on tape attached to the locker. "J. Timmons. You know her?"

"Heard of her. Nothing crazed our outstanding. She and Desiree were considered for captain at the same. And we know who got it," Joshua replied. "Hey, we need to get out of here before they come back. Where'd you get these pictures from?"

John took the pictures from Joshua and placed them back in the locker. He shut the door and snapped the pad lock shut. As they descended the stairs, the ladder truck was backing into the stall. John looked at Timmons as she stood behind the engine and guided it into its place. Their eyes locked as John walked past her. She narrowed her eyes and twisted her lips into what John considered a snarl. John refused to respond to the nasty glare.

Joshua and John left the stationhouse and headed back to Joshua's office. They both became still when the dispatchers voice crackled from the radio speaker.

"All available units. All available units. 10-51 to Eighty-third & Stewart ASAP. Four alarm blaze."

Joshua leapt from his seat. "That's Desiree's area!"

CHAPTER 14

The heat was intense as Desiree followed Tulley into the burning vacant warehouse. She prayed as the heat felt as if it was burning her skin. She crawled along the floor, past several offices, touching Tulley's feet as she did. He had insisted on taking the lead, and she had reluctantly agreed; if he were ever to raise the ranks, she would have to stifle her over protectiveness and allow each of her men to take the lead.

"Tulley," Desiree spoke into the mouthpiece inside her oxygen mask. "Do you have the heat seeker?"

Tulley didn't respond. She was going to kill him when they got out of here. She reached out to feel for his feet. Nothing. She swept her hand violently across the floor. Still nothing. She crawled quicker. Her feet propelled her forward as the flames raged yards from her body. The thick black smoke impaired her vision.

"Tulley!" she yelled into the mouthpiece. She tried to calm herself, knew that if she didn't the oxygen would be used up that much quicker. She closed her eyes briefly and said a quick prayer "God be with us," as her instincts pushed her forward.

Desiree stopped suddenly as the top of her helmet met an obstruction. She reached out her right hand and felt feet. Her hand moved up, feeling the outline of legs. She tapped them, but felt no movement. She knew it was Tulley. Her hands began to roam further up, as her body inched up. She felt the raised numbers on the back of his protective coat. Engine 19.

"Heaney, where are you?" Desiree spoke calmly but harshly into her mouthpiece.

"On my way, lass," was the only response she received as she checked the oxygen indicator on Tulley's tank. The indicator didn't make a sound. Tulley's tank was empty. She inched her body alongside his and felt around his face. His mask was gone.

Despite the flames, Desiree scrambled upward, her hands her guide, as she rolled Tulley over, then took a deep breath of oxygen. She held her breath, snatched her mask from her face then placed it over Tulley's. She frantically sought out the additional line she carried on her utility belt. She attached the line to her tank, forcing herself to inhale through the line and exhale through her nose.

She had to get them out of there. With her mask over Tulley's face, she couldn't hear her fellow firefighters. She began rolling Tulley's limp body across the floor. Her mind went blank as she tried to remember where the entrance to the burning warehouse was. She continued to roll Tulley as she heard faint voices screaming from the earpiece.

She saw the flash of light. She looked over her head. Burning embers fell around her. She had to get them out. Now! Desiree inhaled again then drew Tulley's limp body across her back. She wobbled as she lifted her and Tulley's weight, both shackled with equipment. She thought that if they made it out of the fire alive, she would kill Tulley with her bare hands for not following her orders. She had told him twice to take some time off to be with his wife and newborn daughter, yet when she came to the stationhouse that morning, there he was sitting and ready for his shift. When she questioned him, he said his wife had told him he was on her nerves and to go to work. The reality of it all sunk in. If it hadn't been Tulley, it could have very well been one of the other men.

Several times, Desiree's legs threatened to give out, but the light drew her forward, gave her the strength she needed to get them outside to fresh air.

Desiree squatted and placed Tulley on the floor. The light was coming from a window, at least five feet above the floor. She felt around her waist and pulled the hammer from her belt. She rolled Tulley onto his stomach then began to hammer out the small panes of glass. She knew the sudden force of air would feed the beast, but she had no choice. They were trapped.

The cool night air hit her face. She dropped quickly onto Tulley's body, face down. The swoosh of heat crept across her back. She bit back a scream. The searing heat licked at her neck. She wiped frantically at the intense pain as it shot across her entire body. She closed her eyes; her small body shielded Tulley's larger one. She thought of Joshua and fought to steady the rapid beat of her heart, struggled to breath through the tube and not through her nose. She began to cough, her lungs burned. She thought of Joshua again, the way his intense eyes looked at her the day she left him. She had avoided all his calls, both at the stationhouse and at home. If he called about the case, she had Tulley or Moose act as their intermediary. When he showed up at the door to her home, she refused to answer it. Even the note he had written her was still encased in its envelope unopened.

She coughed again. She could no longer see the light from the window. She looked up one last time before she closed her eyes.

"Two trapped! Two trapped!" the voice screamed out.

Joshua punched the accelerator. The single mars light flashed across the buildings. A sudden image of Desiree popped into his head. His stomach cramped, followed by a sharp pain to his chest. He pulled over just as the words screamed out of the radio.

"Two from Engine #19. In the process of excavation."

He knew that was Heaney's voice.

"Let me drive," John said as Joshua slid over to the passenger seat. His head snapped up as John peeled from the curb, his hands placed ten and two on the steering wheel as he whipped the sedan down the quiet street.

At the fire, John had barley put the car in park when Joshua jumped out and raced past the barricades set up to keep the onlookers away from the fire. Joshua looked up and saw the large warehouse fully engulfed. Flames shot at least fifty feet into the air. His eyes searched for Desiree among the faces of several firefighters. He didn't see her. He searched for Heaney. No sign. He saw one of her men running to the truck. Joshua grabbed him.

"Where's Desiree?"

Moose looked over his shoulder at the warehouse. Joshua pushed him back and began to run toward the fire. As he ran, he grabbed a protective coat, helmet, oxygen tank and mask, and an ax from a compartment of another engine. He placed the articles on and paused only long enough to check the gage of the oxygen tank.

Joshua looked up to see Heaney begin to climb a ladder to the roof of the large warehouse. He pushed John and Carroll to the side, grabbed his safety line and began to climb the ladder behind Heaney. Heaney turned to see Joshua behind him.

"They're trapped," Heaney called back and kept climbing.

At the top of the warehouse roof, Joshua attached his safety line to Heaney. If Heaney went, so would Joshua. That's the way it was.

"Gotta get this roof hacked up. They should be right down here." Heaney pointed downward. "The block glass is too thick, and it was taking too long. We can't get any communication from them."

"Them," Joshua asked as he hacked away at the thick tarp covering the roof.

"Tulley and Desiree."

Upon hearing the sound of her name, Joshua raised the ax and brought it to the roof with a force that caused Heaney to pause. Heaney joined as his ax made way of the thick tarp as if it were tissue paper. Heaney and Joshua nodded to each, gave one final blow to the roof, then stepped to the side. The air would cause the flame to shoot out momentarily then return to its origin, yet it would only give them a few minutes reprieve, ten minutes at the most, to get down there and get them out.

Joshua peered through the hole. He was greeted by bright flames and darkness below. He fingered the medallion he wore around his neck and pushed it under his shirt. He placed his mask over his face, checked the safety line, then tapped Heaney on his helmet. Heaney braced himself to hold Joshua's weight as he began to lower Joshua into the dark hole.

Joshua could see the flames running rampant some twenty feet away. As he finally reached the ground, his foot stepped on something. He used his hands to feel the hard object. It was a hand. He felt further and came upon a small shoulder. *Desiree.*

Joshua spoke into the microphone connected to the earpiece. "Have those stretchers and oxygen ready. We're coming out."

As he knelt beside Desiree, his knee bumped another object. He felt around her and instantly knew she was lying prone atop another body. Tulley. Joshua brought his hand to feel her face. Her mask was missing. He leaned down, pulled his mask from his face then whispered in her ear. "I'm here, baby. I'm here." He placed his mask on her face then took her in his arms. Her head rested on his chest. He then tugged quickly on the line by lowering his body several times. He coughed several times as they began to ascend. The opening slowly came into sight. Joshua reached the top of the hole and handed Desiree to Heaney, who passed her limp body to Moose.

"Got to get Tulley out. Lower me back in."

Heaney tapped Joshua on his shoulder. He handed Joshua his mask. Joshua took the mask from Heaney and nodded his head as Heaney lowered him back through the hole. He noted that the fire had spread closer. He had to get to Tulley and fast if they were both going to make it.

On the floor, his foot came across Tulley's body. Joshua rolled him over then squatted. He pulled Tulley's heavy frame across his back then stood. He tugged the line again and felt himself and Tulley slowly rise toward the open roof. Joshua eyed the fire as the flames got closer and closer to the roof's opening. Just as his feet cleared the opening, a flame shot out of the roof and roared across it. Joshua didn't bother handing Tulley over. He quickly climbed backward down the ladder. One hand held Tulley around his waist, while the other guided himself down the ladder.

On the ground, several firefighters took Tulley's limp body from Joshua's back. Joshua ran to the waiting ambulance. He looked at Desiree. Her face covered in dark soot. He took a tissue from a nearby holder gently removed the dark grit. She stirred.

"Shhh, its okay, baby. You're okay."

Desiree raised her hand and opened her eyes. She looked at Joshua.

She didn't say a word as her eyes shut. Joshua took her hand in his as the paramedics announced that they would be heading to the hospital.

At the emergency room, Joshua rushed along side the gurney. He watched as the paramedics moved Desiree's unconscious body from the gurney to the small hospital bed. The tubes in her arms were replaced with new ones, a pressure gage attached to her finger. The plastic brace was removed from her neck as the triage team cut her clothes from her.

"Sir, you're going to have to leave," the nurse announced as she pushed Joshua out of the bay and snatched the curtain closed.

Joshua walked out to the waiting room where he saw the soot-covered, grim faces of two of Desiree's men. Moose looked up as Desiree's parents rushed into the waiting room, with Heaney and another woman, Joshua guessed was his wife. They came to Joshua.

"How is she?" Desiree's father asked him.

"I don't know. She's unconscious. They're working on her."

"Oh, my God, Trent," Desiree's mother said as she held onto her husband's hand.

Joshua walked away and sat in a corner near John. *This cannot be happening. No.* He wouldn't lose the one woman who'd made him laugh, brought hope to his mundane life. The one who'd made him love again. He loved her. The admission was clear. He had fallen for Desiree. The when wasn't important, but she didn't know how he felt. The last time he saw her she had a pained look in her eyes. It hurt him to know that he had been the cause of it. He had answered her question honestly, but didn't get a chance to finish. He swore that if she made it out of this alive, he would spend his every waking moment proving to her that he indeed was ready to move forward—with her.

He felt John's hand rub his back as he stood. He watched John's feet replaced by another pair. Joshua looked up into the face of Seamus Heaney.

"Come with me, lad."

Without a word, Joshua followed Heaney outside. He watched as Heaney lit a large cigar. "My wife says I should give these up. She says they stink. But it is the one vice I have. I have no others." Joshua watched as Heaney pulled in the smoke and let it out in a ring. "You know that was something else back there. We'll forever be grateful to you."

"No gratitude needed. I'd a done it for anyone."

Heaney peered at Joshua and nodded his head. He tapped Joshua on the arm and pointed over to a bench. "Let's sit." Heaney placed his foot on the bench as Joshua sat down heavily.

"So you're in love with my lass."

Joshua looked up. "Is it that evident?"

Heaney sat next to Joshua. "Well, seeing as how you muscled your way past the line, stole equipment, then put your life on the line for her, and one of her men . . . Yeah, I'd say so. But Davis, here it is. She's very important to my family, her parents, and me. We don't take too kindly to anyone hurting her. I know you've at least disappointed her. That we can all handle. It's the heartbreak we don't like. That Donald character was up to no good. I saw that, but she didn't. It's hard for her being a woman, a black woman at that. She doesn't need some pantywaist trying to keep her back. That child, my godchild, needs someone who's gonna be by her side, not try and tear her down. Hear me?"

Joshua nodded. He understood the duplicity in his words, the full meaning of being with Desiree. It was hard for women in male domi-nated jobs. He had heard the countless stories of how they were treated at stationhouses. To add to it, it became more difficult when women assumed a role of authority. But Joshua didn't care about all of that. He had made up his mind, and it was time to tell Desiree.

He looked at Heaney. "That's not what I'm here for, Heaney. I'm not here to tear her down or stand in her way."

"Then what are you hear for? We all's got things from our past. You and I share a common bond—alcohol. I nearly lost all that's dear to me. You lost what was dear to you. That's tough. In many respects, we've found our way. But she's still finding hers. I need you to know that I, nor her father, will allow you or anyone else to stand in her way. If you mean her no good—if the past still rules the present—then leave and we won't mention a word of this. Period."

"I'm here because I want to be with her. Need to. I love her."

Heaney extended his hand. Joshua took the offered hand and shook it. Heaney stood then pulled Joshua to stand on his feet. "Glad to hear it, lad. Come on, we need to get an update."

As the hours passed, Joshua sat with Heaney and his wife, Mave, Desiree's family, and the firefighters of Engine Company #19. Other firefighters from surrounding stationhouses filtered in and out of the emergency's waiting room. There was even a visit from the Battalion Chief, Mike Callahan.

Desiree's father came to sit next to Joshua. They looked at each other. The words both wanted to say remained unspoken. Joshua noticed the gratitude in Trent's eyes. He nodded at Trent and remained silent. They both looked up as an attractive woman, dressed in a lab coat, approached.

"I'm Doctor Moon, the attending physician for Charles and Tulley. They will both be fine. Charles can be released with supervision. Tulley will be here a couple of days. He's sustained some intense smoke inhalation. Now, I know you guys have been here a while. Tulley's in ICU, and his wife is with him. I can only let you guys in one at a time, five minutes max. He's on a breathing machine to help heal the damage to his lungs. As for Charles, she'll be released in couple of hours."

"Thank you, doc," Desiree's father said as he rose and shook the doctor's hand. He thanked the firefighters who surrounded them. He looked up and faced Joshua. "Umm, Detective Davis…Joshua… how can I?"

Joshua watched as Trent choked back the emotion. Joshua held up his hand then nodded his head. He watched Trent walk away, his wife beside him as they headed toward the bank of elevators at the end of the hallway. Heaney loudly cleared his throat. Joshua looked to him as he motioned with his head for Joshua to follow them.

Joshua felt like a teenage boy, unsure and apprehensive. He knew that if he was truly going to be a part of Desiree's life, he needed to step up to the plate.

At the elevators, Joshua noted that the Charles's held hands. Mrs. Charles's free hand rubbed her husband's shoulder. They didn't speak and only turned around and glanced at him as he stood a few feet behind them. When the elevator doors opened, the couple stepped in. Joshua paused.

"Come on, son," Trent said. "She's waiting for us."

At the room, Joshua waited outside. He insisted that her parents go in first. He'd visit once they were finished. For the first time since his arrival, he noticed the black soot on his hands and that he was clad in the protective firefighting gear. He knew he must have looked a mess, but he could care less. He nodded a greeting at several women who passed and smiled flirtatiously at him. *No offense*, he thought, *but there is only one woman I want a smile from.*

He looked up to see an attractive woman, dressed in a fire department uniform, run down the hall. Joshua watched as Annette stopped in front of him.

"Is she okay?" she said.

"The doctor is going to release her soon. Her parents are in with her right now," Joshua replied, then slightly smiled. "I don't think we've formally met. I'm Joshua." He put his hand out to her. Annette shook the offered hand.

"Annette Simmons."

"I know. Lt. Simmons. It's nice to meet you."

"Same here. And I heard what you did. All I can say…" Annette choked back the emotions; her eyes watered.

"No. Don't. I'd a done it for anyone of the firefighters." He gave the patent response, but knew that the firefighter lying on the other side of the door wasn't just anyone.

They both looked up as Desiree's mother stepped out of the room. She opened her arms to Annette. "Baby, she's going to be okay." She rubbed Annette's back. She looked up into Joshua's face. "Annette, go in and see her. She's awake."

Annette nodded her head, stepped out of the embrace, then walked into the room.

Cora faced Joshua. "I don't believe we've met." She took Joshua's hand in hers. "I'm Desiree's mother, Cora Lee Charles. I hear you saved our daughter."

Joshua rubbed his hand over his face. "Ma'am, no need to thank me. It's all in a day's work."

Cora snickered. "That's not what Seamus tells us. But that's okay. I'm just glad you arrived when you did. Seamus is too old for all of that. He claims he's retiring once Des makes Battalion Chief."

The word was out on the street. Everyone knew. The conversation with John came rushing back to his mind. He knew that John had no intention of suggesting Callahan be appointed as assistant commissioner. But what about Callahan's son? He didn't doubt that Callahan would fight to ensure that his son would get a promotion to captain. In addition, seeing as how there were no positions open and Desiree was the only woman, it stood to reason that Callahan wanted Desiree out of the picture. He made a mental note to tell John.

"Well, she's awake, Detective Davis."

"Call me Joshua or Josh."

"Joshua. The warrior."

He smiled. Desiree had said the same thing to him.

"I have something for you." Cora opened her purse and pulled out a small, velvet pouch. "I never thought… never dreamed I'd need to give this to anyone. The last one I gave away was to Seamus for saving Trent. Now I'm giving this to you." Cora pulled out a small, gold medallion. "It's St. Jude, patron saint of lost and hopeless causes. Take this and keep it with you always. It has protected the Heaney and Charles clans for more than twenty years."

Joshua accepted the medallion as Cora handed it to him and wrapped her small hand around his. He looked down into the face so like Desiree's.

"Again, my full thanks. I'm sure we're going to be seeing a lot of you." Cora kissed Joshua on the cheek, lightly ran her small hand down his broad shoulder then took his hand in hers again. She released his hand then turned and went back into the room. Thirty minutes later, Trent and Cora, followed by Annette, stepped out of the room.

"Go see her. We're going to take her to our home. You're welcome to come by and visit." Trent faced Joshua. Without warning, Trent pulled

Joshua into an embrace. Upon releasing Joshua, he walked down the hallway with Cora by his side. Annette walked behind them. He watched as her father stopped and placed his head onto his wife's chest. Cora's arms went around Trent's shoulders as he sobbed. Joshua heard him as he said, "She's got to give this job up. I can't go through this every time she's on duty. She's got to quit."

Joshua wiped his hand across his face and turned from the scene between Desiree's parents. *Quit!* He knew that Desiree loved her job and would never quit. She wasn't that kind of woman. *Or is she?* Never on her job, but she had quit on him. *That will never happen again.* He'd make sure that she'd never leave him of her own volition.

He squared his shoulders then knocked on the door. Hearing a faint response, he opened the door and peered around it.

"Hi," Desiree said, her voice raspy.

"How are you feeling?"

"My chest hurts and I've got a nasty burn on the back of my neck. How's Tulley? I need to see him before I leave."

"He's going to be okay. He's on a respirator to help him breath while his lungs heal. You should wait 'til you're feeling better before visiting."

"I'm not leaving this hospital without seeing him," she rasped.

"If you say so." He pulled up a chair and sat next to her bed.

"The smell was at the fire!" Her brown eyes shone with fear and urgency. "And just before we left to respond to the fire, I got a strange call. A muffled voice telling me 'got to go.'" It's happened almost every time we've gotten a call." She sat up and grabbed his arm. "Joshua, you've got to get to the bottom of this. Somebody's trying to off Engine Company #19!"

"Shhh, baby. I will," he said as he gently pushed her to lie back on the bed. "But first you have to get better. I can't very well have an ailing partner, now can I?" He smiled at her, but knew the minute she was secured at her parents home, he'd be at his office to kick this investigation into overdrive. "What time are you going home?"

She frowned. "I've got no clothes. The bunch in ER liked them better. Mom and Dad are on their way to my house–" A sudden, violet fit of coughs replaced her words. Joshua rushed to the door and called for help. A nurse rushed in and supported Desiree's back as she sat up and began to sputter. After coughing up darkly colored black phlegm, Desiree settled back.

"She'll be doing that for a day or so," the nurse responded to Joshua's stunned expression. "She should limit the amount of talking and exertion for a few days."

The nurse retreated and Joshua sat on the edge of Desiree's bed. He looked at her as she began to chuckle.

"What's so funny?" he asked. Desiree pointed at him. He stood up and walked to the bathroom. He flicked on the light switch and looked at his reflection in the mirror. He began to laugh at the dark soot smudged across his face. He looked down at the protective coat. He hadn't a clue as to where the other equipment went. Behind him, he heard the squeaking wheels of the mobile IV unit. He felt her presence before he saw her.

"You shouldn't be out of bed." He turned and faced her. He lifted her into his arms. "Back to bed." He carried her to the bed and gently laid her down. He placed the covers over her then kissed her softly upon her lips.

"Thank you, Joshua. My warrior."

"You need to be quiet. We'll discuss that and a lot of other things later."

He smiled as she yawned loudly, nodded her head then closed her eyes. A soft snore escaped her mouth as she fell fast asleep.

"I'll be here when you wake. I'll always be here." He sat down in the chair next to the bed.

After her parents arrived and she dressed, Joshua wheeled Desiree to the ICU to see Tulley. She rose from the wheel chair and walked over to his bedside. She touched his hand. His eyes fluttered open. He mouthed, "I'm sorry," just as his eyes closed again. She patted his hand then turned to leave. Joshua could see the tears in her eyes. She cared for the men in her charge and took it quite personal when one was hurt.

"Give me a minute," she said, voice low. She sat down in the wheelchair and shook her head. Joshua knelt in front of her.

"You saved him, Des. You did." He took her hands in his. "He's alive because of you."

"I shouldn't have let him take the lead. He wasn't ready."

"When are we ever ready? This is our job. Good or bad, we do what we have to do." He wrapped her in his arms, soothing her hair about her shoulders. "Let it out, baby. Let it all out."

Hot tears streamed down her face as Desiree cried. She cried for the times she had fought the beast and lost. She cried for the child she hadn't been able to save. But most of all, she cried because she had been given the gift to save lives from the unforgiving rage of fire and felt she had in some way failed. She raised her head and looked into Joshua's eyes. He smiled at her. No pity. No sorrow. Just understanding.

"I want to go home," she said.

Joshua wiped the tears from her cheeks with the pads of his thumbs. He kissed the side of her face, close to her temple, stood then wheeled the chair out of the room. At the entrance, he swept her up from the chair, and, followed by her parents, carried her out of the hospital. As they stepped to the curb, the men of Engine Company #19 all cheered. Desiree looked at her men, minus Tulley, and smiled at them. She looked up into Joshua's face. He showed no emotion, but his eyes held a warmth and love she hadn't seen in them before. For once, since becoming a grown woman, she felt safe, a sense of protection she had never experienced before.

Joshua settled Desiree in the back seat of the sedan next to her mother then drove them to her parents' house. After assuring they were all settled, he left, insisting that her parents call him if they needed anything. He stated he would see them tomorrow.

As Joshua drove toward his office, fatigue and aches began to claim his body, but he had to fight it. There was an arsonist loose, and he was hell bent on finding out who it was. He thought of the fire. He decided to return to the warehouse.

When he had first arrived on the scene, he hadn't smelled anything, but he hadn't been aware either. His only thoughts at the time were of getting Desiree out of that burning warehouse. He made a mental note to ask Desiree if she noted anything, had there been any other strange occurrences outside of the phone calls, before, during or after each of the fires.

Joshua walked though the now burnt out warehouse. The shell was peppered by black soot. He picked up and examined the charred rubble. He placed a few pieces of the burnt wood, shards of glass, and warped pieces of steel in plastic evidence bags. Mind clouded, he sighed heavily. After an hour, he decided to return to the office.

Stopped at a traffic light, he felt in his pants pocket and retrieved the medal Desiree's mother had given him. He fingered the inlay of the portrait of St. Jude then fingered the one around his neck. Yes, he had once been a lost and hopeless cause himself a time or two. He rubbed the medallion again then placed it back in his pocket.

He climbed slowly out of the sedan, retrieved the evidence from the fire then headed to the doors leading to his office. He thought of the logs. Joshua rushed back to the car, grabbed the logs and held them in his hands. He looked them over briefly then placed them in the pocket of the protective coat.

As he walked slowly down the steps, he thought of the evil glare the firefighter named Timmons had given John as they exited Ladder #12 stationhouse.

He removed the protective coat and placed it on the chair beside his desk then pulled the logs from the large pocket and set them on the desk. He rubbed his face. The stress of the day wore heavily, but he couldn't think of the aches. His only concern was solving the case. As it currently stood, someone was sending a message to Desiree and the men at Engine Company #19.

He picked up the coat. The raised letters on the back read Ladder #12.

❧

CHAPTER 15

For twelve straight hours, Joshua combed through the mounds of paperwork and evidence he and Desiree had collected over the past month. He looked at the logs from the three ladder companies, but his attention always returned to Ladder #12 and the protective coat that rested on the chair.

He looked at the coat, then back to the logs. Something about Ladder #12's logs and this coat held the key to solving not only the fatal fire, but all of the fires. He thought of all the firefighters at the scene of the warehouse fire. Ladder #12 was not within Desiree's district. They were too far away to be required to respond.

His eyes burned as he tried to focus on the pages. But he was tired and he knew that the longer he stared at those pages, the more the answer would continue to evade him.

He looked at his wristwatch—3 a.m. He needed to hear Desiree's voice before he laid his head down.

He climbed into the sedan and punched in Desiree's parents' home number on his cell phone as he drove. He smiled when he heard her voice.

"Sorry I'm calling so late. How're you feeling?"

"Better. I just woke up when the phone began to ring. Where are you?"

"Just leaving the office."

"Well I see you've had a full day. Have you gotten any sleep?"

"No, but I'm heading home to do just that."

"Good. You know my father came to me and demanded that I leave firefighting. Said some craziness about my finding a nice desk job, maybe become an instructor full time. I can only take so much of this. I want to go home."

Joshua wasn't surprised. He had overheard Trent say he wanted her out of the firefighting business.

"When?" he asked.

"Day after tomorrow. I'm won't have him cornering me every day with his ranting and ravings. This is what I do. What I love."

"Well?"

"Well what? I'm not quitting, and I certainly won't sit behind some desk everyday bored out of my mind."

"I hear ya."

"So how's the case coming along?"

"I'm close, Desiree. I can feel it."

"What do you need me to do?"

"Nothing for now. Just get better. I'll be over after I get some sleep. Okay?"

Joshua didn't know he had been holding his breath. He wanted to talk to her, wanted to wipe away her doubts and fears about him. "Desiree? Is that okay?"

"Yes, Joshua. I'll see you later."

"You can count on it. Nite. Sleep well."

"Thank you. Same to you."

Joshua ended the call. His head swam with the evidence of the case. He knew the accelerants, a volatile mixture of ammonia and glue, and he knew that all the fires were set on a Tuesday, one day before Desiree and her crew's scheduled off days. Joshua also knew, according to Desiree, that she had been receiving odd phone calls minutes before the fires. She had even gotten one just before the fire at the warehouse.

He parked the sedan then heavily climbed the steps to his home. He frowned at the smell of paint upon opening the door, but he liked the job the painters had accomplished in changing the entire color scheme of the house. He took the mail from the slot and fingered through the magazines and letters. He paused at one in particular, which didn't have a return address. He turned the envelope over. Nothing. The ringing of the phone drew his attention. He walked into the kitchen and picked up the receiver from the wall. He placed the envelope on the counter.

"Yeah," he answered, his deep voice heavy.

"Josh, its me, John. How's Desiree?"

"She's at her parents' house. She'll be off for about a month or so."

"Good, and how are you? I've been waiting for you to call."

"My bad, dude. I've been meaning to call you. I think those logs are the key, John. And the coat I wore at the fire came from Ladder #12."

"What?" John spat out. "They're over thirty miles outside of Engine 19's area of responsibility."

"I know. How did that coat get there?"

"Is there a name inside?"

Joshua picked up the coat. He knew he was tired but damn, he wondered why he didn't think to look inside the coat before now. He turned the coat inside out. He blew out his breath.

"Callahan."

"Callahan's name is in the coat?"

"Yes. John, you don't think he's starting these fires, do you?" Joshua didn't want to believe that one of their own could be the arsonist, but then again stranger things have happened. "Well, we'll just have to return the coat to Mikey, won't we?"

"I'll go with you," John said.

"Sounds good, but I'm bone tired, and I need to get some sleep. I'll call you back after I rest for a few hours."

"Bet. Won't Mikey be shocked when we show up with his coat?"

"Into a coronary. I'll talk to you later." Joshua laughed.

"Will do. We're gonna crack this, Josh. We're gonna do it."

"You with me?"

"I'm with you all the way."

"Thanks, John. Later."

"Later, my brother."

Joshua hung up the phone. His body ached from the mental and physical events of the day. He thought of Desiree and her brush with the beast. He had always been a praying man, but after his wife's death, he had ceased to call on the higher power. Now, he was grateful, relieved that Desiree and Tulley, had made it out of the fire alive. His mind went to how he had held her close to him as he waited for Heaney to pull them to the top of the roof. Admittedly, he hadn't thought of how the fire had started, his only priority was to get to Desiree and bring her out safely.

His legs felt like lead as he walked the short distance down the hall to his bedroom. He eyed the large, contemporary king-sized bed, with the ornate wrought iron headboard and matching footboard.

Disrobing quickly, he climbed into the large bed. He yawned loudly. He knew he needed to go back to the scene of the fire. He thought of the envelope then climbed out of bed. He tried to remember where he'd had set the mail. He retraced his steps and padded barefoot into the kitchen. He spied the letter on top of the kitchen counter, picked it up, returned to his bedroom and placed it on the night stand. The sound of the ringing phone captured his attention.

"Yeah," he replied groggily.

"Hey, handsome. Are you in bed?"

Joshua smiled. "Sure am, beautiful. I thought you were going back to sleep?"

"I am. I just wanted to make sure you got home."

"Thank you. Now go to sleep. I'll see you later."

"Okay. Goodnight, Joshua."

"Nite, Desiree."

He placed the received on its base, turned off the light, then rolled over on his side. He wondered if she would listen to him, hear him out. With her confined to her parents house, she would have no choice but to listen to him explain how he felt, how he wanted to be with her, and how the dreams he had been having of his late wife signaled that it was time for him to move forward with his life. And he wanted to do so with Desiree.

He yawned again then began to drift as *no return address* began to plague his mind. He reached behind him to the night stand. Light from the beginnings of daylight began to filter through the room's open blinds. He opened it slowly then pulled out a folded piece of paper. He focused his eyes on the words. They seemed odd. Joshua rubbed his eyes, then refocused on the words. He bolted upright, turned on the lamp and read the crudely written words.

"*She'll die. Desiree Charles will die at the next fire.*"

He picked up the phone and dialed John.

"Man, wake up. I got a letter in the mail."

"We all get letters," John replied groggily. "I got one today from the sweepstakes folks."

"Dammit, John. This is serious. Wake up. The letter said that Desiree will die at the next fire."

"What did you just say?!" John's voice was clearer.

"You heard me. What am I going to do?"

"Where's she at again?"

"At her parents'," he bellowed into the phone.

"Easy, man. Call her father and Heaney. She'll be safe with her parents."

"But she wants to go to her own home in a couple of days."

"Let her, but don't tell her about the note. Whoever sent it knows we are close. Was there a post mark or a return address?"

Joshua studied the envelope again. "Nothing."

"Somebody dropped that in your slot. Look, make the calls then get some sleep."

"How can I sleep?"

"You won't be any good to Desiree or this investigation if you don't. Got any sleeping pills?"

Joshua twisted his face into a scowl. "What the hell do I need sleeping pills for?"

"Come on Josh, you and I both know you aren't gonna get a dime of sleep. Take one or two of the pills and get some rest. Call me later on, and I'll meet you at your office."

Joshua's frown smoothed. He knew John was right and though his mind was twirling a million miles a second, his body betrayed him. "You've got a point. I think I've got some here."

"Good, take some, and I'll talk to you later today. Don't worry. Didn't I tell you we're going to get to the bottom of this?"

"Yeah, man, you did. Thanks. I'll talk to you later."

Joshua hung up the phone, climbed back out of bed and went to the bathroom. He opened the medicine cabinet and looked at the various bottles of prescribed and over-the counter medications. He moved several around and found a bottle of pain relievers laced with a sleep aid. He opened the bottle, popped two into his mouth, turned on the faucet, cupped his hands under the running water and sucked up a mouthful. He swallowed the water and pills, then headed back to bed.

He laid on his back and stared at the ceiling. If he had to give his life, he would to make sure that no harm came to Desiree. In spite of his worry, he yawned. His lids became heavy, and before he knew it, he was fast asleep.

"There's no way that bitch is going to be Battalion Chief. I'll see to it!" the image voiced as it wandered around the small room. The image looked at the news paper clippings that told of the rash of fires. Only one mentioned the death of the elderly couple, parents to the local alderman. The image sneered.

"She's going to be the new chief, and there's nothing you can do about it," another voice stated sweetly.

The image rushed to the mirror.

"Shut up! I'm going to make sure that she'll never fight another fire again."

The image in the mirror laughed back. "How you gonna do that? You royally fucked up the fire at the warehouse. And her dark knight rescued her. You're worthless. Had it not been for Mike you'd never have made it this far."

"Liar! I'll show them. I'll show them all. She'll never be Battalion Chief. Never!"

"How are you going to do that, genius?"

"You'll see!"

Desiree glanced at the clock sitting beside the bed. She smiled when she heard the door chimes, followed by voices. She knew without a doubt that the deeper one belonged to Joshua. She winced. Not from pain, but from embarrassment. She had run from him and yet when she came to briefly in the ambulance, she knew he was there.

A soft knock came to the door. She turned her head in time to see Joshua peer around it.

"How are you doing this morning?" He looked at his watch. "I mean, this afternoon?"

Desiree sat up, scooted over then patted the side of the bed. Joshua sat down.

"I'm feeling better. My body feels as if I've been run over by a truck, and my neck is stinging. Other than that, the Vicodin vex had me sleeping like a baby." She reached out and took his hand in hers. "Joshua…," she began, but was interrupted by his finger placed gently upon her lips. He replaced his finger with his lips.

"Shhh," he said once he broke the kiss. "I need you to get better. We'll discuss our relationship then. Until that time, you need to rest. When's your appointment with your doctor?"

"Tomorrow. Mom's going to take me."

"No, tell her I'll take you."

"You don't have to do that, Joshua."

"I do and I'm going to." His eyes bored into hers. She gave up and gave in. She had never felt so protected or loved. She wondered if he truly loved her.

"Come here," he ordered as he opened his arms to her. He pulled her flush against his broad chest and held her. His hands rubbed her back in a soothing motion. She closed her eyes and felt her body lower to the bed. He kicked off his shoes and climbed in beside her. He held her to him, careful to avoid the large bandage at the nape of her neck. She snuggled closer to him. If she lived to be one hundred, she'd never get enough of Joshua Davis. Never.

He remembered the feel of her body close to his, the way she loved him. He wanted her, but now was not the time. They'd have time for that. He wanted to tell her so, but that too would have to wait. For now, he was satisfied to hold her in his arms.

"Joshua," Desiree raised her head slightly and looked up into his face.

"Umm?"

"Thank you."

He opened his eyes and looked at her. This woman, this tough woman with the soft burning touch. His woman. He patted her shoulder and placed his hand about her head, signaling for her to lay her head down.

Neither wanted to move. They just wanted to be with each other, savor the warmth and security they found in each others arms. He kissed the top of Desiree's head. He silently promised to never let any harm come to her. He'd always be there to protect her.

As promised, Joshua took her to the follow-up appointment with her primary care physician, then to a local ice cream shop for cones. He watched as she sumptuously ate her chocolate sundae. The next day, he came to her parents' house and, with their approval, took her to her own home. On the way to her house, he made an unannounced stop.

He glanced at her as he pulled up in front of his house. He opened the car door and extended his hand to Desiree. She paused and looked up at him.

"It's okay." He led her up the steps then opened the door. He stepped to the side and let Desiree enter first. He shut the door behind them.

The first thing Desiree noticed was that the picture of Joshua's late wife was missing. She looked around and saw that the entire house had been re-painted and re-furnished. She faced Joshua.

"The day you left here, I looked around me and saw what you saw. Everything was Serena. Even my mother said I needed to redecorate. But there hadn't been any reason to." Joshua raked his hand over his dark brown, close cut hair. "I had been having dreams of Serena, and each one had me moving closer to acceptance. The last one I had, she told me to move forward. I saw that as an indication, a sign that it was time I move on with my life. That I share my life with another woman."

"What does that have to do with me, Joshua?"

"Desiree." He pulled her close. "That woman is you. It's you. I want to be with you, Des. I want to wake up with you in my arms. I want to protect and love you."

Desiree remained stiff in his arms. She wanted to believe, but she wasn't sure. True, he had replaced all traces of his late wife, but she didn't want to replace her, she just wanted to be with him.

"Look at me, Desiree."

Slowly she lifted her face and met his eyes.

"I won't lie to you and tell you that Serena is out of my heart or my mind completely. She won't ever be. But she *is* in a place that allows me to move on. And I need to know if you'll move forward with me. I don't want to without you, unless you force me to."

She looked at the man who had brought a passion and a depth of understanding with him she had never known. Her heart and mind spoke to her as one.

"I don't want to replace your late wife, Joshua."

"I'm not expecting you to."

"But I don't want to start something that will leave me hurt, either."

"Desiree, what makes you think I'll ever hurt you." He pulled her into his large arms. "Didn't you hear me? I want to be with you. But I also need to know, want to hear the words from your lips, that you feel the same way. Otherwise, this is all for naught."

Desiree slipped from his embrace. She stepped back and looked into his face. Images of him as they made love, as he fed her popcorn during her favorite movie, the feel of his protective arms around her as she left the hospital. She'd be a fool if she walked away, and she knew it.

"I care, Joshua. A lot more than I'm willing to admit. But if you can put up with me and my controlling ways, then I guess I can be your girlfriend." She chuckled when a thought popped into her head.

"What's so funny?" He smiled at her.

"I haven't said that since I was in grammar school."

"Wait." Joshua rushed from the room. He returned moments later with a piece of paper held in his right hand. He passed the note to her. Desiree took the note and began to laugh heartily. Joshua had written "will you be my girlfriend?" on the slip of paper and then had drawn two boxes, one with "yes" under it and the other with the word "no" under it. She looked around for a pen. Joshua handed her a pen. She raised her eyebrows and tapped the pen against her lips as if in deep thought. She spied a glance at him, then turned her back to him. She checked a box then handed back the note.

Joshua took the note and read it. He stepped to her, took her face in his hands then kissed her lightly on the lips.

"It's official. You are now my girlfriend."

Desiree couldn't help but smile broadly at the beauty of the sincerity.

"I can't make you any promises, but I'll be here for you. I'll be here until God has me drawing my last breath," he said as he kissed her forehead, then wrapped her in his arms.

She wrapped her arms about him and laid her head on his chest. His heart sounded like a runaway train as it beat double time. She was sure that her heart was doing the same.

"Hey, its time I got you home. Let me grab some things and we'll be on our way. Okay?"

She nodded as she slid from his arms. He walked quickly toward the back of the house then reappeared carrying a leather duffle bag slung over his shoulder.

"Ready?"

"When you are."

"Then, if all's mine is satisfied, let's be on our way."

Desiree smiled at him. "Where'd you get that saying from?" she asked as locked the door.

"My father use to say that right before we'd go on vacation."

He took her hand, led her to the car, opened the door, then shut it once he made sure she was settled. They made another stop, this time at Baskin Robins to get some ice cream. She tried to protest as Joshua bought four quarts of ice cream: vanilla, almond mocha fudge, rocky road and butter pecan. He said, "I don't want you to do anything but rest".

He looked at her. His heart had finally healed from Serena's death, thanks to Desiree. And Desiree was here with him. He knew that he never wanted her to be anywhere but by his side. And though they'd known each other less than two months, he wanted her to be in his life for good. He knew she wouldn't go for living together. No, she was too independent for that. Marriage was more both of their speeds, and he knew that when the time was right he'd ask her. For now, he would settle for her being in his life.

CHAPTER 16

Joshua carried Desiree her up the stairs to her bedroom. She watched him as he went about her room.

"Where's your pajamas?" he had asked.

"Joshua, you don't have to do this. I'm fine."

"The doctor said you needed to rest. And I'm here to make sure you do just that."

"Don't you have to work tonight?"

He pointed to the leather duffle bag that sat at the door which led to her bedroom.

"Yes, and I hope you don't mind. But I brought a few changes of clothes."

"Joshua," she began to protest, but was quieted when he held up his hand.

"Enough." He smiled. "Now, where are your pajamas?"

She pointed to the chest of drawers. He strolled over, opened a drawer and pulled out a pink, short chemise. He showed it to her and shook his head.

"Another time." He continued his search. He wondered if this woman had anything that wouldn't incite a sexual riot. He found a pair of silk pajamas, top and shorts, in fire-engine red. He placed them at the foot of her bed then headed into her bathroom.

Desiree lay back among the mound of pillows. She listened as he began to whistle. She raised her eyebrows when she heard the sound of running water. She looked up just as Joshua returned to her bedroom.

"A nice hot bath, some good food, and you'll be set for the night." He put his hand out to her. She took it and allowed him to lead her to the bathroom. "Get in, and I'll be back with your dinner in an hour."

He smiled then stepped from the bathroom, shutting the door

behind him.

Desiree removed her clothes, pinned her hair up, then stepped into the whirlpool tub. She secured the bath pillow on one side of the tub, then sank into the warm, fragrant water. She lifted her head slightly as the sounds of classical music came from the other side of the door. She smiled and wondered how he knew she loved to listen to music as she soaked in the tub. Soon a peaceful doze claimed her.

A soft rap came to the door.

"Baby, Annette's on the phone."

She opened her eyes and looked toward the door, which was slightly ajar. Joshua's arm appeared through the crack.

"Joshua, its okay for you to bring me the phone." She wanted to chuckle. Besides, he couldn't see anything—she was covered up to her neck in fragrant suds.

She watched him step into the bathroom as he grabbed a towel from the rack. She took the offered towel, dried her hands, then took the phone from him. He rushed from the bathroom.

"Hello," Desiree spoke into the cordless phone.

"Girl, I called your parents' house, and they told me Joshua came to take you home. I guess you don't need me after all."

"You're my girl. I'll always need you."

Annette laughed. "Not for what you and Mr. Davis is gonna do."

"Girl, shut up. You're too much." They laughed and talked, their conversation light with shop talk. Finally, Annette turned serious.

"Desiree, that man truly loves you. And you know I can recognize bull when I smell it, but Davis is different. I know I said he had some demons, but to tell the truth and shame the devil, we all do. It's just how much do we let those demons get in the way of finding true happiness and love."

"I know," Desiree stated. Her mind had come to the conclusion that Joshua loved her. She thought of how he had changed his entire home and how he had put his very life on the line to save her. She knew, without a doubt, that Joshua Michael Davis loved her, and she loved him as well.

She then thought about her best friend's dating habits. No, Annette wasn't a loose woman. In fact, Annette had been celibate for over two years. Still, Desiree mused internally, Annette was allowing demons to keep her from true love.

"Sometimes we have to let those demons go. You know what I mean?" Desiree hoped her friend caught the double entendre.

Annette chuckled. "I know what cha mean."

"So, what's up with that cop. Umm, what's his name?"

"Carl. Oh, that brother is a zero. You know I'm looking for a hero."

"You can't find a hero when you're wearing a full metal jacket."

They each became silent. Their words circled them, enveloped them in the harsh, yet sincere truth. After what seemed an eternity, Annette finally spoke.

"I meet men, just about everyday, but they either are into head games as a means of soothing bruised egos, or they're looking for a quick fix."

Desiree bit her tongue. She wanted to tell her best friend that it was she who played the head games by allowing brother to get only so close, then shutting them down completely when it looked as if they were getting too close for her comfort. "Don't give up, sweetie. He's out there. You never know, he might just be under your nose."

Annette sniffed exaggeratedly. "Umm, I don't smell him. " She huffed. "Look, I'm gonna let you go. I'll stop by tomorrow."

Desiree smiled. "Phone first."

They both laughed "Alright, sistah. Will do. Take care, girl. I love you."

"I love you, too." Desiree disconnected, placed the phone on the floor, sank further into the tub and began to doze.

"Desiree?" Joshua called from the other side of the door. "Are you okay?"

Desiree opened her eyes. She pictured him standing there, sans clothes, his muscular body calling out to her. No, she thought, she wasn't all right and hadn't been since he had branded her with his body. Though the water was tepid, her body heated up, the place where her essence hid tightened at the mere thought of his hands on her bareness.

"Joshua?"

"Yes."

"Open the door and come in here."

Joshua peeked around the bathroom door. He smiled wirily as he stepped into the bathroom. He cleared his throat.

"What do you need, baby? Has the water gotten cold?"

She shook her head.

"Is your neck bothering you? Are you tired? You've had a long day."

She shook her head "no" again.

His eyes met hers. The brash fire in them was unmistakable. His loins tightened. "Umm, want me to wash your back?"

She nodded her head 'yes.'

He walked slowly over to the edge of the tub, knelt beside the tub and watched as Desiree held out a bath sponge. He rolled up his sleeves, took the sponge from her hands, then dipped the sponge in the warm water. She turned her back to him.

He began to stroke the sponge gently across her back. He inhaled deeply as he attempted to steel himself against the hot, searing sensations touching her had created within him. He wanted her more than he had wanted anything or anyone in his life. He dropped the sponge then gingerly slid his hands around her back as his thumbs kneaded and plied her the soft skin on her back. His hands dipped further into the water as he rubbed the spot just above, round behind. He dipped further and began to massage her, his hands full of one of the many beauties of this woman, who he'd spend the rest of his life showing just what she meant to him.

"Joshua." Desiree turned to face him. "I haven't thanked you."

"You don't have to thank me."

"Yes I do. Thank you for being there when I needed you."

"Baby, I don't want to be anywhere else. You have to believe that."

He looked into her eyes and gently stole his hands over her stomach and up to her breasts. Slowly he kneaded her nipples until they turned into torrid, hard peaks. When he heard a moan escape from deep inside her, the sound became Joshua's undoing.

He rose suddenly and quickly removed his clothes. Desiree didn't turn away. She watched as the passion, the need burning in his eyes, seeped from his pores to hang thickly in the air like a funnel cloud. She slid her body over in the tub as he joined her. She groaned as she felt his body against hers, then laid her head on his chest. She felt the unmistakable heat his body emitted. She slid her body back further into his, molding her entire being to him, her round, voluptuous behind settled into the center of his groin.

Joshua closed his eyes and shook his head slightly.

"Woman, I'm scared of you."

She turned to face him then cupped his face in her hands and brought it to meet her slightly parted lips. She placed pliant kisses all along his face, pausing to taste the full lips that begged for her. "There's nothing to be scared of, Joshua."

She kissed him long and hard, willing the love and passion she had for him to soak into him, this man who had lost so much. Her fear of being hurt yielded to the call from her heart. She wouldn't run from him or the possibilities his very presence brought with it. She would have him—anyway he was willing to give himself to her.

Joshua kissed her back as he took her into his arms, her breasts against his bare chest. He became lost in a free fall as the emotions enveloped him. He felt as if he could remain right where he was, rooted to this safe haven in her arms. He thought of their discussion at his house. It had freed him and rightly placed the last of his past out of the way so that he could begin anew—with her.

He sighed loudly as Desiree straddled him, her essence dangerously close to his now hard member. She began to gyrate her ample hips slowly; the ministrations threatened to bring him to the precipice long before he wanted to.

Her breasts against his chest, her stomach flush against his, he couldn't stand the sweet torture another second. He raised Desiree from the water and stepped out of the tub. She wrapped her legs around his waist, the tip of his hardness pressed against her stomach.

He held her with one hand as he grabbed a towel. Effortlessly, he placed the towel on her bed, then placed her on it. He watched her eyes as he moved over her body. He positioned his hardness at her apex and began to slide, centimeter by centimeter, into her blazing cavern. His mind whirled at the heady sensation. He began to move inside of her, her strong legs wrapped around his waist and pulled him in further, her hands gripped his taunt behind. They moaned, the simple, beautiful act endeared one to the other.

Desiree knew that she wanted the sensation to last for as long as it could. She removed her legs from his waist and twisted her body from under his. She put her back to him and bent over slightly. She shivered as his hands strolled up her thighs, across her stomach, to land on her breasts. She moaned loudly as he entered her, his fingers kneaded and tugged at the now engorged nipples. She ground her hips into his, moved with him, then against him, as she taunted him toward the release she felt was close, oh so close.

"Yes, baby. That's it. That's it," he growled out, his deep voice rasped in her ear. He kissed the side of her neck as they moved in unison. The powerful scent of their lovemaking permeated the air around them. It was like an aphrodisiac. "Come with me, baby. Come with me."

Desiree let out a loud shrill as she felt his member become harder, thicker, as he pumped in and out of her with reckless abandonment. She tightened her cavern upon the feel of him throb inside of her and took them both over the edge. The heat from their bodies seared them.

He held onto her as his seed spilled inside of her. He held her that way as his breathing began to regulate. Gently, he rolled over, laid on his back and pulled her with him. He brought the covers over them both and held her close to his chest. He closed his eyes, kissed her hair and rested his arm protectively about her.

His eyes popped open. He hadn't protected her. They hadn't used any form of birth control. *My God*, he thought, *what had he done?*

"Desiree?"

"Ummm" she moaned.

"We didn't use anything."

"I know, but that's okay. I'm on the pill," she informed him, then thought about it. She'd been at her parents house for three days and hadn't had them with her. She needed to tell him.

He raised his body and looked down at her. "Why?"

"To regulate my periods." She looked at him. And though the concern was now erased, she sensed something else. "Joshua, you are the first man I've ever truly made love to. You are the first I've allowed to love me without a condom. But I have to admit something to you." She paused. "I haven't taken them regularly since the accident."

He saw the warmth in her eyes and knew that if she had become pregnant with his child, he would marry her without question. He pulled her into his arms.

"That's okay. If you're pregnant, then we'll get married."

"Joshua, why would you want to marry me?"

"Because I would want our child to grow up like we did."

Desiree remained silent. She hadn't thought that far.

"Hey, don't worry. We'll cross that bridge if we have to. But you got to know that I'm a jealous lover. I'll have no other man come between us."

Desiree raised to rest on her elbows. Her fingers played in the curly hairs on his chest. "No man?"

"No man. Besides, you agreed to be my girlfriend." He laughed. Desiree laughed with him as she reached over him and took the note from the night stand. She looked at it then handed it to him.

"You didn't sign it in blood."

"I don't think so, woman. No bloodletting. How about I seal it with a kiss?" He wrapped his fingers in her hair and pulled her face to his. He placed his lips upon hers and plied her lips open with his tongue.

She moved on top of Joshua, her body fit onto his. She stroked the side of his smooth face. She loved this man. *My man.* It would be a long time before either was finished.

Joshua broke the kiss. "Better than blood, don't you think?"

She nodded then laid her head on his chest. She drifted in and out as she listened to the sound of his steady heartbeat.

They stirred at the sound of their growling stomachs.

"The food!" Joshua rose. "I put the food on the plates and was about to bring you dinner when you attacked me."

Desiree swatted at his arms. "Lie. You attacked me." She picked up the pillow and playfully hit Joshua about the head. He grabbed the pillow from then tackled her. He wrapped his legs and arms around her.

"No fair!" She laughed out loud. "You're bigger than me."

"All's fair in love and war, darling," he said as they tussled playfully. He switched positions and sat astride Desiree, his large legs lightly pinned her beneath him, his hands held hers above her head. She looked up into his face.

"This ain't love, man. This is war."

Joshua's eyes traveled slowly down her naked form. He released her hands and stroked her face. "No. This is love," he said as he bent to kiss her lightly on the lips. "Desiree, I love you."

Moisture grew in the corners of her eyes. She looked away.

"Look at me."

She faced him. In his eyes she saw it, the passion, the love and the intensity. She felt all of her fears slip away. She began to cry. "I love you, too, Joshua."

He stood and pulled her into his arms. "That's what I needed to hear. Thank you, baby." He rubbed her back then brushed the tears from her face.

"It's time to eat. I've got to be at work in a couple of hours."

Desiree reluctantly fell from his embrace. He smiled at her then took the pajamas at the foot of the bed and dressed her. "We don't need another temptation." He dressed himself in a pair of loose fitting jogging shorts and a white T-shirt he retrieved from his leather bag.

"How about we eat downstairs? You feel up to it?"

"Yes. I'm starving."

"Wait right here. I'll come and get you after I've heated up the food."

She nodded then laid back on the bed. After several minutes, she looked up to see Joshua as he stood in the doorway.

"Ready to eat?"

"Yes," she responded as he walked over to the bed. He put his hand out to her. She followed him down the stairs and into her dining room. She batted her eyes at the lit candles and place settings on the table.

"Come and sit." Joshua held her chair. Once seated, he placed a napkin in her lap. He placed spoon full of mashed potatoes with gravy, asparagus, creamed spinach, two pork loins and a small cornbread loaf on her plate. He finished by filing his plate then sat across from her.

"When did you cook all of this?" Desiree asked as she cut into the succulent pork and placed a piece into her mouth.

He tisked. "I didn't. I got this from BJ's Market before I picked you up."

"It's good. Seeing as how you've cooked for me before, what else can you cook?"

"Oh, fried cornflakes and a serious bowl of CoCo Puffs."

She laughed. "No, seriously, what else?"

"I fry some serious chicken and my steaks aren't so bad."

"Never knew a man who could cook. A lot of men say us modern, working women have forgotten how to cook and serve their men take out."

"Wait. You talking about me. Can *you* cook?"

Desiree turned her lips up and rolled her eyes. "Baby, I'm a southerner. All southern women know how to cook."

"Allrighty now. When you get back on your feet good, I want to see just how well you cook."

"I didn't say it'd be edible. So, bring a bottle of Pepto-Bismol with ya."

"I'll remember that."

Their conversation continued. The back and forth banter was light and easy. Joshua's tone turned serious when he mentioned the fire at the warehouse. "If you don't want to talk about it, we can some other time."

"Can we do it some other time?"

"Sure, baby. No pressure. Are you ready for dessert?"

"Dessert? Joshua, you're trying to get me fat. I haven't worked out in over a week."

"A little peach cobbler won't hurt you. Let me get it."

He removed their plates and disappeared into the kitchen. He returned with two bowls of peach cobbler topped with vanilla ice cream.

"Umm, this is good. It tastes as good as my mom's," she said.

"It is."

"My mom made this? I don't remember her cooking peach cobbler. I don't even remember smelling it in the house. When did she cook it?"

"The night of the accident. You were pretty much out of it. But when I told her that I'd make sure you rest once you got home, she said it was your favorite and she would put it in your refrigerator."

Desiree placed another spoonful into her mouth. A dribble of juice ran down the side of her mouth. Joshua rose quickly from his seat, went over to her and licked the nectar from her mouth.

"Sweet." He raised one eyebrow then returned to his seat and finished his desert as he watched Desiree eat hers. He looked at the clock on the wall. "I've got about three more hours before I have to leave. John's coming over to stay the night until I get back in the morning."

"Your boy, Paglinini?"

"The one and only."

"Why, Joshua?" her voice came out rushed. "What's going on?"

He dragged his hand down his face. He didn't want to tell her, didn't want her alarmed until he found out who had started the fires and why. But he also never wanted to lie to her.

"Tell me. Tell me!"

Joshua inhaled deeply. "The day after the warehouse fire, I got a note at my house threatening your life."

Desiree knocked over the chair and rushed from the dining room. She was angry. She spun to face Joshua.

"Why are you just now telling me this?"

"I didn't want you to worry until John and I had more evidence. We're close, baby. Real close."

"The hell with close, Joshua Davis. This is my life we're talking about. You just can't play God with me. What else haven't you told me? What other little secrets are you hiding from me?!"

"Wait a good-got-damn minute! I know you're mad and you have every right to be, but you tell me how you would have handled it had the tables been turned?" He took her by her arm and held it. "Tell me, Desiree. It's okay for you isn't it? But the shoes don't fit so well do they?" He released her.

Desiree looked down at her floor. Okay, so he had a point, but still, her mind reasoned, didn't she have a right to know?

"Baby," he took her hand in his. "do you trust me?" He touched her chin and tilted her head up to meet his eyes. "Do you?" She nodded. "Then know that I wouldn't have kept it from you had I not known for sure that I could and would keep you safe. I'll be here for as long as it takes."

"What about when I return to work?"

"That's not for another month."

"No, Joshua, I'm going back next week."

"That's too soon. We need more time," he barked then noted the startled expression on her face. "Sorry. But John and I need some more time. We're too close now. Your presence will only complicate matters."

"No, Joshua, I won't hide. I have a stationhouse to run, and I'll be damned to hell if I let some cowardly ass keep me from doing it!"

"You're being unreasonable."

"And you're being ridiculous if you think I'm gonna sit idly by and twiddle my thumbs while you and John play cops." She turned from him and walked to the kitchen. She turned on the faucet, squeezed gobs of dish detergent in the sink, then began to throw forks and spoons into the sink. The loud clatter covered the sound of Joshua's footsteps. She nearly jumped out of her skin when he touched her.

"Don't do this." He held her shaking hands. "Don't do this to me. I need you to at least listen to me."

Desiree faced him, her eyes flamed with unchecked anger. "Who else knows about the letter?"

Joshua blew out his breath. Why was this woman being so doggone difficult. "Your father and Heaney."

"Does my mother know?"

"I don't think so. I don't really know. But let me and John handle this. I want you safe." He held her arms. "Don't you understand! I won't be able to make it this time if I lose you!" Joshua looked into her eyes. Desiree could see the angry, frightened bluster cloud his eyes. He released her, took two steps back, then turned his back and stormed from the kitchen.

Desiree turned off the faucet then leaned her body heavily against the sink. It was all too clear. At least they agreed on one thing: her life was important. But then again so was his. Who was to say that this fire-starting maniac wasn't after Joshua as well. She walked over to the wall phone and made several calls. After the final call, she walked from the kitchen and searched for Joshua.

CHAPTER 17

Desiree stood in the doorway to her bedroom and watched as Joshua dressed for work. She wanted to say something, sooth the brewing storm in his eyes, smooth the furrow of his eyebrows. But what do you say to a man who though had rested one demon, had another one to slay. Yes, she felt safe and protected when she was with him, but it was impossible to be together every minute of the day.

She walked over to him and touched his arm. He faced her then took her in his arms and rested his head alongside hers.

"Joshua, I understand."

He pulled back. "Then you'll wait at least a month before returning to work?"

Desiree shook her head. "I can't do that. Don't you see, that's what this lunatic wants. Besides, if I stay hidden, locked up in my own home, then what's to say this same lunatic won't find me and maybe burn down my home. If I go about my routine, that may flush him out and we'll be able to catch him sooner than later."

"I don't know about that, Des."

"Look, you've got John, my dad, and Heaney all in this. And I'm sure by now Heaney has told the entire crew. So see, I'll be protected wherever I go. And you've bought over enough clothes to live here for six months." She pointed to the mound of folded clothes that peeked out of Joshua's bag. "Let's try it. What do we have to loose?"

"Everything, Desiree."

"No baby. Not this time. I'm here to stay and you'll have one helluva time getting rid of me," she said then she placed a kiss on his lips. "We are either in this together or not all. Agreed?"

Reluctantly, Joshua nodded in agreement. He trusted her and wanted the same. And he knew that it had to begin, here and now.

Besides, she was right. She couldn't hide forever. Maybe, just maybe, the arsonist would rear his head. There hadn't been a fire in the two weeks since Desiree had been off. And he and John hadn't returned the coat to Mike, Junior at Ladder #12 in hopes that he'd come looking for it himself.

"Okay, we'll try it your way, but if anything, and I mean anything, goes wrong you're home until this case is solved. Deal?"

"Deal."

Desiree wrapped her arm around his waist and held him. He placed his arm about her shoulders and looked down into her face. He raised his head at the sound of the doorbell. He looked at his watch. "John's early." He left the bedroom and walked down to answer the door. He was surprised to see Desiree's father, followed by Heaney, Moose, Carroll, John and Annette. They each walked past him and went into the living room. Trent went to the dining room and returned with additional chairs.

Joshua turned to see Desiree come down the stairs dressed in white sweat pants and a navy Chicago Fire Department T-shirt.

"Glad you all could make it on such short notice."

They all nodded and looked at Joshua.

"As you now know, some crazed lunatic is out there starting fires as a means of getting rid of me. And you know me. There is no way in hell I'm going to let that happen. So, for starters, I'll be back to work on Tuesday, my normal day to work. We'll all be on guard, though, but I expect us to go about our jobs. John and Joshua will continue to investigate the case that started all of this. And I'll help where I can. So until this is solved, we need to make sure we're on point at all times. Understood?" She looked into the faces of the men and her best friend who sat before her. She was relieved to see a bemused expression on Joshua's face, versus the angry one she thought she'd get from gathering her team, her support system.

"And one more thing." Desiree faced her father. "Dad, I asked you to come because I wanted you to see that with this team," she walked over to Joshua and took his hand in hers, "I can handle it. I don't want you to worry, and I most certainly don't want you to tell Mom unless its absolutely necessary."

Heaney stood. "Trent, I'll take care of her at the stationhouse, like I've always done."

Moose and Carroll stood next to Heaney. Moose spoke. "So will we." Carroll nodded in agreement.

"And I'll keep my eyes and ears open. Ladder #12 is one of the stations under my jurisdiction," Annette said.

"Now that that's settled, who'd like some homemade peach cobbler?" Desiree pointed to the kitchen. She stopped at her father's hand on her arm.

"I know this is what you do. What you love. And," he paused. "I'll support you. No more trying to get you to quit."

Desiree kissed her father's cheek. "Thank you, Daddy."

"Come on, sweetie, let's go get some of your mom's cobbler."

For the rest of the week, Desiree lounged around her house. The wound at her neck had begun to heal nicely with the help of Joshua placing aloe vera on it twice daily. She sighed dreamily at the thought of Joshua—her very own dark knight. She couldn't believe that he had risked his own life to save her. And she didn't feel obligated to him, like a stranger would to a person who rescued them. No, Desiree felt a deep, comfortable, yet passionately intense love for the man who showed her just what she meant to him.

And Joshua saw to it that she was never alone. Her mornings were spent in Joshua's arms, and the nights he worked, she either sat up and talked with Annette or played cards with John.

One night both John and Annette stayed over. For the entire night, the three played cards and talked. Desiree watched as John and Annette bantered playfully back and forth, with Annette tapping John's hand and John lightly rubbing Annette's back.

When Desiree announced she was going to retire for the night, they both mumbled a hasty good night and continued to talk.

Desiree liked John. The first night he stayed with her, she was amazed at how down to earth he was. She thought that if she had to date a man outside of her race, then the easy laughing, good looking John Paglinini would be it.

The night after he met Annette, he was full of questions concerning her current martial and dating status. They ended their conversation of Annette with Desiree promising to put in a good word on his behalf.

The following week, on the night before her return to work, she and John played cards and talked. She listened and laughed with him as he told story after story of he and Joshua's friendship. She liked John and knew that he'd make a good commissioner. He was surprised when she told him so.

"How'd you know?"

"Please, John, everybody knows. I even heard that you want Joshua to be the assistant commissioner."

"So much for secrets."

"There are few secrets, especially as juicy as this one." She slapped her cards on the table. "Gin. So, when will your appointment be official?"

John blinked and placed his cards down slowly. This was the fifth time that night. "After Josh and I solve this case. So, am I to assume that you also heard the other news?"

"What other news?"

"I submitted your name for Battalion Chief."

Desiree grew still. She had never given thought to being a Battalion Chief. With each of her promotions, she just went in and gave it her best, first for Lieutenant, than as Captain. "I don't know what to say."

John smiled. "Don't say anything. All promotions are off, including my appointment, until we solve this case. I went to the mayor and asked him to hold off a week or so while we solved this case. And seeing as your accident made the news, he agreed."

"So, how close are you guys?"

"There's a missing component. We've combed those logs a thousand times, and still nothing stands out."

"You guys are good. It'll come to you." Desiree covered her mouth as she yawned. "Well, I'm getting sleepy. I guess its time I went to bed."

"I hear ya, Des. Besides, I can't take another butt-kicking tonight."

Desiree laughed and stood. She stretched her body, then headed for the stairs.

"Des," John called to her.

"Yeah?"

"You're all right. I like you for Josh. At first I was a little concerned. But now? I'm glad he's got you in his life. You know that man loves you?"

"That I do," Desiree said. "And for the record John, I like you, too." She embraced him.

"Hey, what's going on here? Release my woman, man." Joshua laughed as he entered the house. Desiree had given him a set of keys once she realized that he'd had no intention of leaving her side. "Glad I took the night off."

"She's just trying to soothe me. This woman has whipped my behind every hand. I'm sore."

Joshua walked over to Desiree and pulled her in his arms then kissed her lightly on the lips.

"Okay, I get it. It's a changing of the guards." John stood to leave. "I'll see yall later. Nite."

"Will do. I'll call you tomorrow," Joshua replied absently.

Desiree walked John to the door. She stood on the tips of her toes and kissed him on the cheek. "Thank you for everything."

John raked his hand through his dark hair, blushed then nodded his head. "No problem. Just don't forget me." He hugged her quickly, turned then stepped out of the door.

Desiree smiled. "I won't. Nite." She closed the door.

"Forget what?" Joshua asked.

"He likes Annette and wants me to put in a good word for him."

Joshua laughed. "That's my brother. He loves women of color. His ex-wife is black and ever since I've known him, he's only dated sisters."

"Annette seemed interested, but the last time we talked she barely mentioned him. I'll have to nudge her a little."

Desiree walked over to the couch. She placed the cards in the box then picked up the two glasses she and John had drunk from. She straightened. "Wait, why didn't you go to work?"

Joshua walked to her. "Because I wanted to be here with you." He took the glasses from her, placed them back on the table, then picked her up and carried her upstairs.

Desiree shivered as he placed her on the bed. The reckless fire in his eyes swarmed unchecked as he lowered himself into her arms.

They loved for what seemed like hours, the wicked blaze that surrounded them seemed to be unquenchable.

As they lay in each other's arms, the reality of the next day hit them both. Desiree tightened her grasp.

"I know, baby. But, I think we've got all the bases covered," Joshua responded. He didn't want to add that he hoped all the bases were covered. But the reality was, whoever had intended to harm Desiree was still roaming around the city of Chicago, and for all of Joshua's efforts, he hadn't found out exactly who that person was and that bothered him.

Desiree bolted from the bed. Her arms flailed about her as she waved them frantically in front of her, and she ran to the corner of the room.

"Tulley!" she screamed as she crouched down.

"Baby, wake up," Joshua whispered as he grabbed Desiree and gently took her hands in his. "Wake up. You're dreaming."

Her eyes popped open. The tears streamed down her face. Joshua lifted her from the floor and guided her to the bed. He turned on the lamp near the bed, left the room then returned with a glass of water.

"Here, drink this." He placed the glass to her lips. She drained the glass. "Better?" She nodded. "Must have been some dream. Want to tell me about it?" Desiree shook her head. "You know what the old folks down south say. If you tell the dream, it won't come true."

"I've never heard that," Desiree said.

"Want to call my mom? She's full of those old southern sayings."

Desiree laughed. "At one in the morning? She'll think we've both lost our minds."

"No, my mom is a night owl. Besides, I haven't talked to her since your accident. They're supposed to be coming to town next week." He picked up his cell phone placed near the bed. Desiree watched him as he dialed his parents' number.

"You could have used my phone."

"They got Caller ID. Mom would think something is wrong," he said. "Hey, Mom. It's me. Joshua. You weren't sleep yet, were you?"

Desiree listened to the one-way conversation. Her eyes perked up when she heard him mention her name.

"So, can you tell Desiree that if you tell a nightmare, that it won't come true. Here. Tell her." He handed her the phone. Desiree shook her head. He put the phone to her ear.

"Hello, Mrs. Davis. How are you?"

"Fine, dear. And how are you feeling?"

"Doing a lot better. Joshua's been great."

"That he is. Out of my two boys, Joshua's the one with all the compassion. That boy's got a heart the size of a whale. He just doesn't show it to everyone. Know what I mean?"

"Yes, ma'am. I do." Desiree knew exactly what the veiled statement meant. She was special to Joshua and his mother wanted to make sure she knew that.

"So, you've had a nightmare?"

"Yes, ma'am."

"Baby, don't call me ma'am. It sounds so old." Joshua's mother chuckled. "Call me Momma Carrie. I'd like that."

"Will do, Momma Carrie. So, I've got to tell this dream or otherwise it'll come true."

"Sure will. Especially bad ones. But the old sages used to say that dreams take on special meaning. Like death means birth. That sort of thing. So you've got to tell it. Don't matter to who. Just get it out."

"Will do."

"Good. Well, I'm finally heading to bed. Tell Joshua good night for me, and I'm looking forward to meeting you."

"Same here."

"Nite, sweetie."

"Nite, Mrs. Davis. I mean, Momma Carrie. Sleep well." Desiree handed Joshua the phone. He took it from her, placed it back on the nightstand then lay down. Desiree laid her head on his chest, her leg wrapped around his.

"Okay, spill it."

Desiree inhaled deeply. "We were at the fire, but I couldn't feel Tulley's legs. Then all of a sudden, Tulley appeared before me. He was on fire and I couldn't reach him. My arms were out, but I couldn't reach him. I tried and I tried. But I just couldn't get to him. And then I woke up."

"You know Tulley's okay. He's home. This is the first time you've had the dream?"

"Yes, it is."

"It could be that you're having some apprehensions about going back to work. I know I am."

"We aren't going to have that conversation again, are we?"

"No. I'm not going to say a thing. But I am worried. And so should you."

Desiree shut her eyes. She didn't want to admit that over the past week she had begun to have second thoughts about returning to work. But she knew that the only way to flush out the arsonist was to return to work. According to Heaney, Engine Company #19 hadn't had a strange fire since the accident two weeks ago.

"I can't let this stop me, Joshua. I just can't." She squeezed her eyes in an attempt to keep the moisture in them from becoming an all out watershed.

Joshua didn't know what to say that would make her change her mind. Still, he felt they were taking a great risk in allowing Desiree to return to work and become a pawn in this runaway arsonist's game.

"I understand." He exhaled loudly. "Let's try and get some sleep. The sun will be up before you know it."

He felt her nod her head then listened for her breathing to regulate. He shut off the lamp and allowed his mind to tumble over the events, the countless leads that led to dead ends, the fact that not one suspicious fire had broken out since she'd been off. Joshua became angry. He knew the arsonist would strike. The note said he would. The when would he strike was the issue that gnawed at his insides.

He rubbed her bare back and prayed for her safety. He fingered the medallion Desiree's mother had given him. If there ever was a lost and hopeless cause, this was it.

Joshua lay on his back, Desiree securely in his arms. He watched absently as the shadows of the trees danced off the ceiling. If he knew when the arsonist would strike, he'd know how to handle it. But he didn't. His only resolve was to be on his toes when the arsonists decided to strike. Besides, he reasoned, she has plenty of folks watching out for her. *She'll be all right*, he said to himself. *Lord, please let her be all right.*

CHAPTER 18

"Welcome back, Captain!" Moose yelled then swept Desiree from her feet. He kissed her cheek as he placed her on the ground.

"Yeah, good to have you back," Carroll chimed in. "Besides, no one can run a stationhouse quite like you."

"Thanks guys." Desiree smiled. "And I've missed you, too. I haven't been gone that long."

"One day without our captain is one day too much," Moose said. "Besides, we've been driven to near insanity." Moose motioned over his shoulder. Desiree followed his eyes then smiled brightly.

"Heaney, what haven't you told me?"

Heaney rolled his eyes upward and shrugged his large shoulders.

"What hasn't he done? He's run this ship just as tight as you do," Carroll said then folded his arms across his chest.

Desiree looked into the faces of her men, glad to be back, but more important, glad they had remained in tact. She thought about Tulley. She had spoken to him several times over the past two weeks since his release from the hospital four days after the accident. Their conversations had been brief and focused on his healing.

"Hey, where is everybody?"

Desiree turned toward the entry. "Tulley!" She rushed to his side and threw her arms around him. For a moment, Desiree had forgotten that she was head of the house—she was glad to see him up and about. She released him. "What are you doing out of the house?"

"Tired of being cooped up. The four walls are beginning to close in on me. Besides, I heard about the letter Davis got."

Desiree opened her mouth to protest, but was interrupted by Tulley. "We're a team. Aren't we?"

She looked at Tulley as he stood in front of her. She knew that for the rest of her career she would view her team as just that—a team. She glanced around at the faces before her.

"That we are. And a hell of a team at that."

"Good, now let's get some food. I'm starving." Heaney escorted Desiree to the kitchen.

"Who's been cooking since Tulley's been off?"

Desiree stepped into the kitchen to see Lena Timmons standing at the stove. "Hey, Captain. Welcome home. Sit down. I've prepared a special breakfast for us all."

"Hey, Timmons. Good to see you. What are you doing here today?"

"I'm filling in for Tulley," she responded. Her voice trailed off as she disappeared into the kitchen's walk in pantry.

"I didn't know that. How're the guys treating you?"

Timmons reappeared with a white casserole dish in her hands. "This is a great bunch to work with. I'm glad I got the opportunity. That group I work with is a bunch of knuckleheads."

"I feel ya. But other than that, you've been okay?"

"Everything's great. With the exception of Janice."

"How's Janice doing?"

"Crazy. I don't get her. She rides me like nobody's business, telling me how I'm a disgrace to the family."

"Disgrace?"

"You didn't hear, did you?"

Desiree took the dish from her hands then leaned her body against the counter. "No. You want to tell me how you disgraced your sister?"

Timmons looked away. She busied herself as she took a plastic carton of orange juice from the large, chrome, industrial refrigerator, followed by two dozen eggs and a stick of margarine.

"There was a fire last week at a car dealership. I was on point. It was my first four-alarm blaze. We went in, like we always do, but this time I was on point. When that ugly beast reared it head in front of me, I swear to you, I froze. I couldn't move. Then I started hyperventilating. One of the guys pushed me to the side and another one carried me outside."

Desiree cringed. She knew that fear. Knew it well, had felt the same numbing fear her first fire, but she had also come to control it, make it work for her.

"When I got outside, my sister was standing there watching."

Desiree thought it odd that Janice Timmons would be way over on the far south side of Chicago when she not only worked southwest at Ladder #12, but also lived near the stationhouse as well. She remained silent as Timmons continued.

"At first she seemed surprised to see me. I work the B shift. But it was my first day filling in for Tulley. Then she got angry. The anger in her eyes nearly gave me a heart attack. I'd never seen her so angry. I couldn't talk, and she just stood over me as the paramedics gave me more oxygen. Then she snapped." Timmons lowered her head. Desiree saw a tear roll down her cheek. She reached out and rubbed Timmons' back.

"She cursed me, Captain Charles. She cursed me like I was nobody to her."

"Janice was just afraid, that's all."

Timmons sniffled. "Well, you could have fooled me." She wiped her face with the back of her long-sleeved uniform shirt, grabbed a large cast iron skillet and dumped the margarine in. Desiree watched as Timmons cracked one egg after another until the skillet was filled with yokes and whites.

"Have you talked to her?" Desiree asked.

"No. And I don't have any plans on talking to her either. She was wrong. Anyway, let's change the subject. How are you feeling? Ready to fight the beast again?"

Desiree thought of the last time she had been in the stationhouse—right before the fire that injured her and Tulley. "I'm feeling good. Glad to be back and more than ready to fight the beast." She glanced at Timmons and wondered had the guys clued her in on the threat on her life that Joshua received. Joshua and John had said they believed it was an inside job, so to her, it stood to reason that the less who knew about it, the better. Anyway, Desiree's return would flush out the perpetrator all that sooner. She looked at Timmons. Hard. *No*, she reasoned, *Timmons wasn't on duty during the fires. But then again, let Joshua tell it—everyone is a suspect until proven otherwise.* Desiree dismissed the thought.

"I hope you didn't mind, but I've been sleeping in your quarters."

"Not a problem. That's fine, but you know we're going to have to roll out the cot." Desiree laughed at the feigned look of displeasure on Timmons' face.

"I don't mind. You don't snore do you?"

"Not that I know of," Desiree responded.

"Well, go on out there and have a seat. The food will be on the table in a minute."

Desiree walked out of the kitchen and sat down at the long table. "Tulley, when are you returning?"

"The doctor won't release me for another week." Tulley sat at the table. "But he says I'm doing good. That my lungs will have some scar tissue, which is normal, but that they've really cleared up. Besides, the guys say Timmons is one mean cook. I can't let her take my job from me."

"That she is," Heaney began. "But he's been here driving us crazy just about everyday." He smiled broadly and slapped Tulley good-naturedly on the back. "Instead of sitting at home and watching some trash TV, he's been here worrying the wool off our backs."

Desiree laughed; glad to be among her team again. She had missed them, the easy camaraderie they had established and the mental connection they had established. She glanced over at Tulley.

He met her gaze. They nodded at each other, the unspoken gratitude he felt for the woman who had put her own life on the line in an attempt to save his shone in his eyes. He wiped at the mist that had begun to form in the corners of his eyes. He looked away. He was now, more than ever, ashamed of the role he played in attempting to make her first few months at the stationhouse hell. For as long as he lived, he would never forget, and had made up his mind to do everything in his power to make sure women, especially the sisters, were treated equally and fairly at the stationhouses.

"Hey, Timmons. Where's the food?" Carroll called out.

"Yeah! We're starving," Moose added.

After ten minutes, Timmons appeared carrying two covered casserole dishes. She placed them on the table then went back into the kitchen. By the time Timmons finished placing the various bowls and plates on the table, the seated group had a feast for twenty sitting in front of them.

"All right!" Moose pumped his fists in the air. He reached out to remove the lid then quickly drew his hand back when Timmons hit his knuckles with the back of a spoon.

"Brother-man, we say grace around here." She placed her hands on her narrow hips and narrowed her deep set, dark brown eyes. "I do believe I've told you that a thousand times."

Moose rubbed his knuckles. Desiree chuckled at the chided look on Moose's face.

"All stand," Timmons began. "Join hands and bow your heads." Timmons bowed her head and began to pray. "God, thank you for giving us another day. Thank you for Captain Charles and Firefighter Tulley. Lord, protect us today as we travel to the unknown. And most of all, thank you for the food we are about to receive. Let us all say: Amen."

A chorus of amens was heard. Moose looked at Timmons expectantly.

"Go ahead." She chuckled and smiled brightly.

The assembled team feasted on cheese grits, homemade biscuits lathered in butter, bacon and sausage, home fries, eggs and pancakes. They laughed and joked as they ate, with Timmons recalling how the table, with chairs attached, got to be. She winked at Desiree.

At the end of the meal, Tulley insisted on cleaning the dishes. Desiree assisted.

"That girl can burn. If I weren't already married, I'd marry her. Even though my baby can burn."

Desiree nodded as she filled the sink with hot water and added dish detergent. They were silent as they went about the chore. Tulley opened his mouth to speak just as the siren went off. Neither moved. Desiree closed her eyes and inhaled deeply. She opened her eyes and saw Tulley as he stood in front of her.

"It's going to be okay. You've got the best behind you," he said.

Desiree threw the dishtowel into the sink and rushed from the kitchen. She donned her turn out gear, jumped into the cab and held on as Heaney drove the large truck from the stationhouse. She spoke into the hand-held microphone.

"Engine Company #19, 10-4."

"10-4," the dispatcher replied. "Welcome back, Captain."

"Glad to be back."

Desiree looked up at the large three-story, frame house. Flames jutted out of the upstairs windows, embers floated upward toward the blue sky. She ordered Timmons and Moose to the rear of the house, while Carroll hooked up the hose to a nearby hydrant.

"Seems to be contained to the upstairs," Heaney said. He glanced at Desiree. She nodded her head.

"Let's go," she ordered as she began to rush up the front steps. She removed her glove and tested the doorknob. Cool and locked. She stepped to the side as Heaney leveled his ax. The door splintered.

She followed Heaney inside the house. They saw Timmons and Moose come from the rear. Desiree pointed upward. Each checked their oxygen tanks, placed their masks over the heads then ascended the stairs that would lead them to the upper level of the house.

"Carroll. Hoses needed. Stat." Desiree spoke through the mouthpiece.

Timmons tapped Desiree on her shoulder. She pointed to herself then began to climb the stairs. Desiree snatched Timmons back and motioned for her to get behind Moose. She didn't want her to get the wrong idea, and she knew she would have to explain later, but right now, Desiree didn't want to think about allowing another member of her team to take lead. *Not yet, anyway.*

"Hoses here," Heaney spoke. They made it a habit of speaking very little as a means of conserving oxygen.

The team stepped to the side as Carroll carried the hose up the stairs. Desiree stepped in front of him as they climbed the stairs.

The second floor had little smoke. Desiree looked up. She thought she heard a creaking sound. She pulled the heat seeker from her belt and aimed it upward.

"Out!" She screamed and twirled around then reached out and pulled Carroll by the hem of his protective coat. She knew that it was only a matter of minutes before the ceiling would give way.

The team rushed down the stairs. Desiree stood to one side at the front entrance. Her hand tapped each one as they rushed from the house. She followed after the last of her team exited the burning structure. Her heart beat furiously in her chest at the sound of the ceiling as it caved in. She called for back up.

"Ladder #7 needed at 210 E. Seventy-fifth Street."

"10-4, nineteen. ETA, seven minutes."

Moose and Timmons hooked up additional hoses, and together with Carroll and Heaney, trained the forceful water toward the upper story of the house.

Hours later, the fire was out, but not before the large house sustained major damage. Desiree turned in time to see two people run from a car.

"Is this your house?" Desiree asked the man who jumped from the car first. She watched his expression as he nodded and looked on in horror at the charred remains of his house. The woman, who Desiree guessed was his wife, did the same as they stood on the sidewalk. The woman wept silently.

"You're going to need a board up service. And contact your insurance company. I'm Captain Charles of Engine Company #19. Your insurance company may want to know." She walked to the truck, climbed in, and held on as they headed back to the stationhouse.

The rest of the shift crawled by. Desiree tried to stay busy, tried to occupy her mind with any and everything in order to steel her nerves. She explained her actions at the fire to Timmons, who seemed to understand. She played poker for a few hours with Moose and Tulley, sat with Carroll as he studied for the upcoming Lieutenant's exam, held aimless conversations with Heaney and talked on the phone with Joshua. Still, she felt nervous and she knew, without a doubt, that it was only a matter of time before the arsonist would strike. It was the "when" part she found hard to stomach.

As the sun rose, Desiree and her team began to prepare to turn the stationhouse over to the next crew. They checked the hoses, restocked the equipment on the truck, and filled the oxygen tanks. By 7:30, the morning shift began to trickle in and they all approached Desiree and welcomed her back.

She waved goodbye and stepped out into the warm morning, her spirits lifted by the sight of the three little girls from up the street.

She smiled brightly as the three stopped in front of her. Christina stepped closer. "We heard you were hurt." Miranda handed Desiree a card while Hannah played with the cracks in the sidewalk with her sandaled foot.

Desiree took the card from Miranda, opened it then smiled broadly. She knelt down, took the trio into her arms and hugged them tightly. Her eyes misted.

"Girl, thank you so much for the beautiful card. Did the three of you make it?"

"Yup, and we made one for the other guy, too." Miranda beamed.

"Thank you." Desiree stood and wiped the tears from her eyes. She gained her composure. "Where are you three headed this early?"

"Day camp. It started while you were gone," Hannah said.

"We came by here to tell you. That's when the other lady said you were on vacation. But Mr. Moose told us the truth. He said that you were in an accident and at home re … re…," Christina tried to sound out the word.

"Reverberate," Miranda yelled out.

Desiree laughed. "Girls, I think the word is recuperate."

The trio nodded. "We glad to see you. Think you'll be up for another game of hopscotch?" Christina asked.

"I'll be back in two days. You've got yourselves a date. And maybe this time Mr. Moose will play with us."

"Okay. See ya, Miss Captain."

"Have a great day at day camp."

The trio yelled, "We will," over their shoulders as they continued down the block. Desiree watched them; an odd feeling came over her. She wondered what she and Joshua's children would look like. *Children?* She shook her head and continued toward the vehicle. She looked up and smiled.

"Hey beautiful," Joshua said as he walked across the street. "How was your night?"

Desiree met Joshua on the sidewalk. He pulled her into his arms and kissed her long and hard. The intensity and heat of his kiss made her weak.

T the now familiar tingle in her middle signaled that if they didn't stop, soon, she would have him right there on the sidewalk. She gently ended the kiss.

"What are you doing here?"

"Here to escort you home. That is, if you don't mind?"

Desiree smiled. "No, I don't mind."

Joshua signaled behind him. Desiree looked around his large frame to see John as stood near the driver's side of his black SUV. He waved at Desiree then climbed back into the vehicle.

"You and John been at it all night again?" Desiree inquired as she followed Joshua to the rear. He nodded his head as he opened the door then shut it once she was seated.

"I think I know who's the arsonist?" He said once settled next to her. "And hold on to your hat, this is going to be crazy."

Desiree listened in stunned silence as Joshua told her that he and John had a strong sense that the Chief's son was their arsonist. He told her about the logs that he and John poured over them for three days. They finally noticed that Mike's name was on the logs, but according to several of the firefighters at the stationhouse, he was missing in action at several fires his stationhouse had answered. Coincidentally, the same time as the fires Engine Company #19 had responded to. In addition, Heaney had mentioned that he saw Mike at the restaurant fire.

"Unbelievable. Are you guys sure?"

"The logs don't lie. But we're missing one very important key. We need evidence. A can of accelerants, glue, ammonia, soiled shoes. Something that would tie him to those fires," Joshua said as he looked at Desiree through the rear view mirror.

"But why?"

Joshua went on to tell Desiree about the conversation between John and Mike's father. "He wants Mikey to be promoted to captain. And it seems as if Mikey will do whatever his father tells him to. So the way I see it, he'll stop at nothing to get it."

"You think Callahan instructed Mike to start fires?"

"No, I don't think so. But Mikey's twisted enough to come up with some crazed scheme like starting fires."

"Damn," she blew out. "But to kill me over a position? That's maddening."

"We've got him under surveillance. We're watching his every move. But hold on, baby, that's not all of it."

Desiree looked at him, her smooth eyebrows raised high on her forehead. "Can't be any worse."

"Seems as if Mikey has a thing for sisters."

Desiree listened as Joshua went on to tell her how John had seen Mike and Lieutenant Janice Timmons at a bar.

"That's nothing," Desiree said. "Fellow fighters hang out often."

"And have babies?"

"Babies?!"

"Yeah, John did a little snooping and found a picture of a bi-racial child in Janice Timmons' locker. He snooped a little further and found out that Lieutenant Timmons had been on medical leave for about nine months. Just enough time to have a baby, be off for six weeks, then return. None the wiser."

Desiree thought of Lena. She hadn't mentioned that her sister had a baby. "This is too wild."

Desiree grew silent as the news Joshua had told her seeped into her mind. It was all too crazy to be believed, yet she knew that the hearts of humans could be tainted to the point of no return. She had seen it in Chief Callahan. And even saw it in Janice Timmons many years ago.

At her house, Joshua held Desiree's hand as they walked up the steps. She looked up at him. She was grateful that he was by her side to love and protect her. She placed her arm around his waist.

Joshua opened the door and watched as Desiree headed upstairs. He decided to let her be—to allow the information he and John had unearthed to sink in. And when she was ready to talk about it, he'd be here. Just as he had promised.

☙

CHAPTER 19

Nearly three weeks had passed, and not one suspicious fire had broken out. John had placed Mike Junior's every move under surveillance, but nothing out of the ordinary occurred. Junior went to work, went home and went to Janice Timmons' house, where he had spent several nights. Outside of that, John's tail hadn't uncovered a thing. At the stationhouse, the team went on as usual. Lena Timmons went back to B shift and Tulley returned to work. They fought fires, but none even hinted of anything out of the ordinary.

"Two more weeks," Heaney said as Desiree stepped down from the fire truck. She glanced up at him just before she closed the truck's door. Desiree walked around to the back of the large, red engine.

"Two more weeks?"

"Yeah, two more weeks and you'll be on furlough."

Desiree sighed. She hadn't wanted to think of her upcoming furlough or the fact that she wasn't pregnant. Initially when her menses began a week ago she had seemed relieved, but then became sullen when she told Joshua that they wouldn't be parents. She was surprised at the disappointment that had shone in his eyes. He hadn't voiced his thoughts. Instead, he had pulled her into his arms and simply stated, "One day."

"Desiree?" Heaney called her name. "Earth to, Desiree. Lass, what's the matter?"

She dismissed his concern. "Nothing." She walked toward the desk.

"Okay. So, what are you going to do while on furlough?"

"Going to Charlotte," she responded absently as her mind thought about how much she needed that furlough, those seventeen days to regroup. She had long planned on spending two weeks in Charlotte, but she didn't want to leave Joshua. Since her accident, he had practically moved in and had given the excuse of keeping her in his sight as much as possible. To add to it, Joshua's parents were coming to town, and she wanted to meet them, especially his mother who had made it a habit of calling Desiree just because. Desiree liked Joshua's mother, her soft, slight southern accent and her sage wisdom. She knew that their meeting would only be a formality, for she felt as if she'd known Carrie Davis her entire life.

"Well, it's almost quittin' time," Tulley announced as the crew readied the stationhouse for the next shift of firefighters.

Within the hour, the shift had arrived and Desiree, followed by her team, left the stationhouse. There stood Joshua, his wide smile and deep complexion greeted her, just like he had been since her return.

Joshua drove toward Desiree's house. The cell phone attached to his hip rang. "Detective Davis." He nodded his head, glanced over at Desiree then disconnected the call.

He punched in a number. "I've got a tip. Meet me at Desiree's." He disconnected.

"What's going on?" Desiree asked.

"I got a tip. I need to meet someone."

"Not without me."

Joshua pulled the vehicle over to the side and parked. He shifted his large frame so that he could face her. "I'm afraid I have to." He took her hand in his and kissed it. "Baby, don't be difficult. Not now. You have to understand. This is the second call. One I'd hoped to get. And now that it's come, I can't let it go. This is what we've been looking for."

Desiree nodded her head. Though her mind understood, her heart didn't. "At least tell me where you're going."

He released her hand. "Now you know better than that. Besides, I don't want you to come after me. John is going to stay with you."

Desiree removed her hand from his, turned her head away and stared out the passenger window. She heard him huff loudly, then felt the movement of the vehicle as Joshua pulled the vehicle back onto the street and headed toward her house.

Desiree stepped from the car. She waited as Joshua joined her.

"Baby, the minute I'm finished, I'll call you," he promised. "Then I'll be right here." He tilted her chin upward. "Believe me?"

Desiree nodded. Heart beating a million miles a minute, she wrapped her arms around Joshua and held on. She didn't want him to go without her, but she had also come to know that when Joshua Davis said something he meant it. He placed his hands around her and hugged her to his chest. A car stopped in front of Desiree's house. They released each other.

"Hey, you about ready to leave?" John said as he stepped out of his SUV, its windows heavily tinted.

"Yeah. You stay here until I get back."

John nodded then turned slightly to the right and motioned toward the parked SUV. They watched as the passenger side door opened and out stepped Annette. Desiree smiled, glad her matchmaking had finally worked. She had talked about John to Annette for two solid weeks until Annette acquiesced and agreed to meet with John. After their first meeting, Annette had called Desiree and told her what a charming, smart man John was. All Desiree could do was laugh.

"Hey, girl," Desiree said as Annette joined them. "What's up? John broke every traffic rule created by man to get here."

Desiree looked at Joshua, then to John. "Joshua has a tip on who's been starting the fires. He has to meet this informant."

"John," Annette faced him. "Why didn't you say something?"

"Couldn't. When Josh called, I just went into overdrive. Sorry, sweetie."

Desiree raised her eyebrows and looked at Annette. She couldn't wait to hear how she went from Annette to "sweetie."

"Gotta go," Joshua announced. "Walk me to the car." He took Desiree's hand in his and headed back to his sedan. He leaned his body against the vehicle and pulled her to him. "I promise to be back as soon as I can." He looked at the pinched restraint on her face, the apprehension that shone in her eyes. "Kiss me," he ordered softly as he bent his head. His lips touched hers. She closed her eyes and felt the searing heat consume her entire body as his tongue found and mated with hers.

"Hey guys, get a room, will ya," Annette teased.

Desiree smiled. She turned to see Annette and John as they stood close, their sides touching, hands entwined.

"Okay, baby. I'll see you soon. Besides, there's something I want to talk to you about." He winked, his handsome face made even more so with his alluring smile.

She waved then joined John and Annette on the sidewalk. They entered the house.

"Why don't you go on up and get some sleep. I'll wake you in a couple of hours," Annette said as they entered the house.

Desiree walked up the stairs, entered her bedroom then sat on the edge of the bed. She looked around the room. Joshua's cologne sat on top of her chest of drawers. The shorts and T-shirt he liked to lounge in lay neatly folded at the foot of the bed. She stood and walked over to the window. She closed her eyes and did the only thing she could do. She prayed.

"Finally," the image said as it walked around to face Joshua. "Wake up. I didn't hit you that damn hard." The image slapped Joshua across his face. Joshua's head popped back with the sudden sting. He opened his eyes and attempted to focus on the white shirt that stood in front of him. "Glad you could make it. It's been a long time, Detective Davis."

Joshua shook his head. His eyes trailed up the shirt, past the nametag to the face above the collar. "What the…?"

"Surprised? Not as surprised as Captain Charles is going to be at hearing of your untimely death. See, I knew that you'd come. That's the dumb cowboy in you. And knowing you, Detective Davis, I'll bet you a box of old fashioned donuts that you didn't tell Charles where you were going. Did you?"

Joshua watched as Janice Timmons circled him. He tried to move then realized that he was tied to a chair. The last thing he remembered was entering the burnt shell of the warehouse where Desiree and Tulley had been injured. As soon as he had stepped in, he felt a heavy object connect with his head then all went black. He looked up at Timmons. The wild look in her eyes put him on high alert. He knew that he had to tread lightly with her, else she'd kill him; but, he also knew he needed her to talk, to at least tell him why she had hit him and tied him up.

"Okay, Lt. Timmons. What gives?" he asked, his voice modulated.

She sneered at him. "I'll tell you what gives. It's having to suffer the indignity of watching someone who you know you're better than continually get the breaks. I should have been the first black female captain, not the almighty Charles." Janice began to pace, her soft-soled shoes kicked at rubbish from the fire as she moved. "Crazy me. I thought that being with Mike would help. I just had no clue that his father was a real, in living color, racist. I thought it was all an act. Then, I got wind of your boy, Paglinini. And I just knew that if Mike's dad got the assistant commissioner's spot, then I'd be elevated to captain." Janice stopped suddenly. She grabbed Joshua by the collar and leaned over, her nose inches from his. "But nooo, Mike's crazy-assed daddy ruined it all."

"So, what does all this have to do with me?"

Janice began to laugh. The sound was mercurial. Joshua shivered from its odd cadence. "Well, at first I was going to off your girlfriend. I hear you two are quite an item." She paused and smiled at him. "But then after you rescued her, I got an even better idea. If you're out of the picture, she'll be so broken up that she won't even want to be Battalion Chief, much less a firefighter. And this would clear the way for both me and Mike to elevate quickly. Besides, you were getting too close. When you and Paglinini showed up at the stationhouse, I knew I had to act fast."

"So, you think that Desiree would give up that easily?"

Janice tilted her head to the side. "Let's put it this way. If she doesn't, she'll be joining you." She snapped her fingers then walked over to a pile of rubbish. "You know this warehouse use to be a temporary morgue during World War II. It housed many a dead soldier. It even had the nerve to have a 'colored' section for the black soldiers." She pulled a plastic bottle from her back pocket. "You know, this stuff is great for starting fires. You want to know where I learned it from? Captain Charles. She gave a presentation once to firefighters on accelerants. You mix a little glue with the right amount of ammonia and oil and presto, strike a match, and in an instant you've got an uncontrollable blaze. One that takes water forever to extinguish."

Joshua watched her as she gathered more rubbish and placed it neatly in the pile. He had to think, had to clear his mind. All this time he thought that Mike was responsible for the fires and for the note, but he had it all wrong. *Or did I?*

"Where does Mike fit into all of this?"

Lena smiled slightly then pulled a picture from her left breast pocket. Her eyes took on a dream like state as she stared at the picture. "My baby." She looked at Joshua. He noticed the anger had returned to her eyes. "Mike's a drunk. He wouldn't know what to do. When he told his father that we had a child, his grandson, Callahan almost had a coronary. Imagine, Callahan's son, his offspring, sired a child with a nigger woman."

Joshua could not believe that he was witnessing Timmons in all of her maddening glory. He flexed his biceps. She had tied the rope tight. He moved his hands, secured behind him, and felt his cell phone attached to the belt of his pants. He knew the phone was on, but couldn't remember where the send button was. He fumbled with the numbers then pressed several buttons.

She returned to the pile. "Mike started drinking a lot more after the birth of our son. He couldn't handle the pressure. Even said he didn't want to be a firefighter, that his father had wanted him to and forced him to join the department. Me?" She pointed to herself. "I've always wanted to be a firefighter. I used to start fires then put them out."

"Janice, killing me won't solve anything. It won't get you that promotion. It won't make Callahan think you're any better than before."

"Think so?" she laughed. "I happen to disagree. I think it will get me exactly what I want. The promotion that's due me—that Desiree took from me. Mike, the baby and I together as a family and Callahan will have no choice but to accept me: his daughter-in-law, who's the mother of his only grandson, a captain. Then after a year or so, even Battalion Chief."

"I think you're making a big mistake, Janice. Let me go and allow me to help you."

"Are you saying I'm crazy, Detective Davis?"

"No, I'm not. You just need someone to talk to. Someone to help."

"That sounds like crazy to me." She placed her hands on her narrow hips. "Okay, this looks good." She poured the mixture over the pile. "Detective Davis, it's been live. Gotta go." She pulled a book of matches from her pants pocket, removed a match, struck it against the back of the book then tossed it into the pile of rubble.

The sound of the ringing phone startled Desiree. She rushed over to the phone and knocked it off the nightstand. She picked it up and placed it to her ear.

"Hello?" she spoke into the receiver. "Hello?" She repeated then became silent. She listened to the phone then began to yell. A second later, John and Annette appeared in her doorway.

"Joshua's in trouble."

CHAPTER 20

Desiree contacted the 911 Center and had Joshua's cell phone tracked. Once they knew the location, John ran from the house with Desiree and Annette close on his heels. John didn't have time to protest as he jumped behind the wheel of his SUV then floored the accelerator. The sound and smell of rubber permeated the warm, late morning air. John pushed the vehicle to ninety miles an hour as he expertly bobbed and wove in and out of traffic.

"That's the warehouse, John," Desiree said. "My God. Hurry."

In what seemed an eternity to Desiree, they finally arrived at the warehouse. Desiree didn't wait for the car to come to a stop. She bolted from the vehicle and ran toward the burnt shell. As she got closer, she smelled the scent of the accelerants used at several of the fires she and her men had fought. Then she saw the smoke.

As she reached the side entrance, the door swung open and narrowly missed knocking her to the ground. She eyed Mike as he carried Joshua across his back. She watched as he placed Joshua on the ground then disappeared back into the burning warehouse. Desiree grabbed Joshua by his wrists and drug him further away.

"Mike went back in," Desiree said to John when he appeared by her side. He spoke into a hand-held walkie-talkie.

"Joshua? Honey, wake up," Desiree pleaded, the tears in her eyes blurred her vision. In the distance she heard the sirens. "Here that, baby? They're on their way. Hang in there. Please, God! Hang in there."

As the fire truck arrived, followed by an ambulance, Desiree looked up to see Mike exit the warehouse carrying Janice Timmons in his arms. He cradled her to his chest as he walked past them toward the street.

❦

Desiree ran along side the gurney. A feeling of déjà vu rushed through her body. She looked down at Joshua, his face calm and peaceful. On the ride in the ambulance to the hospital, she prayed, not sure of the extent of his injuries.

If not for Mike, Joshua would have burned alive.

"Ma'am, you can't go in there." A nurse appeared and gently escorted Desiree to a nearby waiting room. As the hours passed, firefighters joined them, along with Desiree's parents, the men of Engine Company #19 and a few investigators from Joshua's unit.

A doctor finally stepped into the room. "Family of Joshua Davis." Everyone who wasn't sitting jumped to their feet. "Wow. What a big family," the doctor replied. "He's going to be alright. He has a mild concussion and can go home if there is someone that will be with him at least for the night." The doctor chuckled. "And from the looks of it, there are a lot of you."

"Can I see him?" Desiree asked as she stepped forward.

"You must be Desiree." She nodded. "When he came to, you were the first person he asked about." The doctor smiled. "Sure. He's down the hall in unit three."

"Thank you," she replied then bolted from the waiting room. She rushed down the hall. The numbers over the curtained cubicles blurred. She heard him before she saw him.

She snatched back the curtain. Joshua was propped up with his cell phone to his ear.

"No, Mom, I'm fine. Desiree's here. Talk to her." He handed her the phone.

Desiree spoke with Carrie Davis and assured her that she'd take good care of her son. She ended the call with a promise to contact her tomorrow.

Desiree sat the phone down. She looked at Joshua, the man who had so readily risked his own safety for her, the man who had promised and proved that he loved her. She walked over to the bed as Joshua stretched out his arms. Desiree laid in them, reveled in the warmth of them. Nothing, and she meant nothing, would ever separate them.

"I'm ready to go home, baby." Joshua held Desiree as she stroked the side of his face.

"Then let's take you home."

The waves rolled over Desiree's bare feet as she walked along the shoreline. She glanced over her shoulder. She felt him before she saw him. Desiree smiled as he came up behind her, stopped her then wrapped his arms around her waist. He kissed her on the side of her face.

"It seems as if the parents are getting along well."

"They sure are," Desiree responded. "You're mom is great and your dad is a riot. I loved hearing the stories of you as a kid. You were a bad little something, weren't you."

"Not as bad as you, my little linebacker."

A week after Joshua's release, Desiree took her furlough. Now that the case had been solved, she insisted that he accompany her since he was off recovering. He had agreed, but with one caveat.

"I've got to go and see Abel."

"Would you like for me to go with you?"

"No, it's something I have to do. I'll be back tomorrow, and then we'll head to South Carolina."

She kissed his lips and waved as he stepped from her home and got into his car.

For an hour and a half, he drove southwest along Interstate 55, glancing at the directions he had gotten from MapQuest. He exited the highway and followed the directions until he came upon a large imposing building surrounded by several rows of fence topped with razor wire and electronic sensors. His eyes rested on the sign. Pontiac Corrections Center. The place Abel had called home for ten years.

Joshua followed the signs and parked in the visitors' lot. He walked slowly toward the entrance and looked up at the towers manned by armed guards.

"I'm here to visit Abel Davis," he said to a guard posted behind a desk. The man's dark thick neck and large arms gave the appearance that they were one. "My name is Joshua Davis." Joshua pulled out his drivers license and birth certificate.

The guard took the documents then looked through a log and located Abel's name. He looked up at Joshua. "Y'all look alike. You his brother?"

"Yes."

"Okay, your name is on the list. Stand over there with them."

Joshua followed the guard's orders and walked to the opposite side of the somber room. He looked at the people near him, watched their faces and wondered if they visited often. He knew he hadn't.

After forty-five minutes, a door opened and out stepped a small woman, dressed in a navy suit, her blonde hair pulled back from her face, clutching a clipboard to her chest. The room fell silent as the woman began to recite the rules and regulations for visiting inmates. The woman ended by informing the visitors that they would be searched adding that now was the time to leave if they were carrying any type of contraband.

Joshua endured another hour, which included a thorough search of the loafers, socks, jeans and matching shirt he wore. He smiled grimly at the two young guards, who he guessed were no older than twenty-one, as they went through his wallet and turned over his loafers.

"Hey, you a detective?" one of guards asked.

He nodded his head. "For the Chicago Fire Department."

The other guard simply looked at him and continued sorting through Joshua's personal belongings.

Joshua sighed and was relieved that the search had ended. He found it unsettling to have someone search you, frisk you down, then go through your pockets, their hands too close for comfort.

"Okay, Detective Davis. Right over here."

Joshua looked at the guard who had searched his wallet He wanted to know why he wasn't following the other visitors. He raised his eyebrows.

"We give a little leeway with protected citizens. Come with me."

Joshua followed, the soles of his shoes squeaked on the highly polished floor. He passed several men dressed in orange jump suits with their numbers stenciled on the left breast pocket and "Illinois Department of Corrections" emblazoned on the back.

They stopped at a large door. Joshua peered through the thick glass then jumped when the guard next to him barked out an order. "Open on thirteen." At the sound of the lock being disengaged, they stepped in. Once that door shut, the other in front of them opened. He looked around. His eyes took in the various men walking about interspersed with guards.

They stopped at another door, this one leading into what looked like a lounge surrounded by thick glass. The room had four tan chairs and a wooden table in the middle. The windows were sealed with bars. And a closed circuit camera sat next to a television mounted above their heads in the corner of the lounge.

"Wait here. Your brother will be down in a minute. You're the first visitor he's gotten in six months."

Joshua nodded his head and sat in one of the chairs. He knew Abel's last visitors had been their parents. He flinched as the door shut with a loud thud.

He watched as the inmates strolled by and looked in at him. Sizing him up. He refused to look away, even though a part of him hadn't wanted to challenge any of them in this maximum-security facility.

He watched as a man, surrounded by two guards, approached the lounge, his arms and legs shackled in chains. Joshua's eyes misted as he watched his brother shuffle-walk toward the lounge. He stood as the guard who escorted him appeared and unlocked the door.

They remained silent as Abel's escorts unlocked the chains then stepped back, closing the door behind them.

"You guys have one hour," one of the guards said as he folded his arms about him and assumed a wide-legged stance.

"Joshua," Abel said as he stepped forward. He wrapped his arms around Joshua and held him tight.

"Davis!" the guard barked. "You know the rules. No contact."

Abel stepped back then sat in the chair across from Joshua. One of the guards came to stand behind Joshua.

Joshua looked into his brother's face, his eyes so like his own, and saw the resignation in them.

"So, how's it going?" Joshua sat and absorbed his brother's presence, the bald head and beard.

Abel huffed at the question and glanced over Joshua's shoulder. Joshua could see his eyes tear, and he reached out and grabbed his brother's hands, which rested, palms down, on top of the table. All the pain and realization of the situation slammed into Joshua hard. For the first time, Joshua had no anger toward his one and only brother. The emotion had been instantly replaced with remorse—remorse for allowing his own pain to keep him from Abel.

"I'm sorry, Josh. I really am."

Joshua nodded. "No need to—"

"No, I should have been there for you, man. Helped you. But no, my stupidity got in the way. That's why I'm in this place."

Joshua thought of all their years together and the ones apart. He and Abel had been inseparable growing up. Abel had taught him to play baseball, football and baseball. Had been their to cheer him on at every game. Had always been there, except that one time.

The peace that had eluded Joshua finally rested within him. "I forgive you, Abel. I do."

Abel hung his head. His shoulders heaved sporadically as his tears dropped to the table below him. "Thank you," he whispered then lifted his head, allowing the unchecked tears to cleanse them.

Joshua wiped the tears from his own eyes with the sleeve of his shirt and nodded.

The guards had been kind as one hour led into two then into three as Joshua and Abel talked about everything, including Desiree.

At the end of their visit, Abel stood first. Joshua rose then grabbed his hand. Their eyes met.

"I'll be back," Joshua said as he gripped Abel's hand tightly. "I promise."

"You better. I want to see the pictures from the wedding."

Joshua nodded and watched as the guards stepped forward and placed Abel back in chains. Abel shuffled out of the lounge. He turned once, smiled brightly then disappeared from Joshua's sight.

EPILOGUE

After leaving Pontiac, Joshua drove back to Chicago and to Desiree. He told her of his visit with his brother, the peace he found and the regret he held for being angry with his brother for being in prison when Serena died.

Desiree had simply nodded as she pulled Joshua into her arms and held him.

Once they arrived on the island, they secluded themselves in each other's arms, experiencing a seemingly endless passion neither had ever experienced.

During their final week, their parents, Annette and John joined them. For the first time since Janice Timmons had been arrested for arson and the attempted murder of Desiree and Joshua, they spoke of the incident. According to John, Janice Timmons was angry that she had been passed over countless times for promotions—the one she did get had been done so as a bribe from Callahan, to buy her silence over the child, who was close to five years old. As for the note, Mike Junior admitted to writing the note and placing it in Joshua's mailbox. Mike also admitted he didn't know who had started the fires until he over-head some firefighters talk about Janice's crazed berating of her sister, Lena, at a fire that Desiree should have been at, but wasn't due to her injuries.

Still, the person who had placed the calls remained a mystery. Since Janice Timmons arrest, she hadn't uttered a word. John ended the conversation with a question.

"Case solved. Are you ready to join me?"

Joshua looked at Desiree. She nodded her head. Joshua looked at John. "Well, I guess you've got yourself a Chief of Investigations. When do we start?"

"In two weeks. Be ready, because, brother, we're gonna turn the department upside down."

Joshua laughed then turned serious. "What about Desiree?"

"What about her?"

Desiree stood and walked over to the railing of the sun deck. Annette joined her.

"Sister, why don't you go for it?" Desiree said to Annette.

"Can't. We're dating." She pointed to John, then to herself. "Besides, I think you'd make a great Battalion Chief."

Desiree dared not look at Joshua. Battalion Chief was a plum position with many responsibilities. She thought of the stationhouses she'd have under her, the scores of men and women who'd be under her charge. And though she knew she could do the job, she wanted more time to think on it. *But*, she thought, *at least Callahan is gone*

Callahan had retired immediately after Janice Timmons was arrested and the news of his blatant racist attitude hit the newspapers. During his reign, several of his stunts resulted in resignations and missed opportunities for advancement.

"Let me think on it, okay, John?" Desiree said.

"Sure."

Joshua took Desiree by the hand and led her away from their best friends' ears.

"Baby," Joshua turned Desiree to face him. "We haven't had that talk."

"What talk?" She looked up at him.

"You know the one I told you just before I went to the warehouse."

"Okay. Talk."

Joshua looked down into Desiree's eyes. He thought of how blessed he was to find true love twice in his life. "I talked to your dad last night."

"I thought you two would never go to bed."

"Well, what we talked about was important."

"What did you two talk about?"

Joshua fished around the pocket of his shorts. "I told him that I'd take care of you for the rest of my life. That he wouldn't mind having me as a son-in-law. That is, if you'll have me as a husband?"

Desiree looked at the diamond solitaire and knew just what he was asking her. She knew that no matter what, that he'd always be her knight. "Yes, Joshua. Yes," she responded, knowing their blaze could not be extinguished in one day. This blaze would sustain them for a lifetime.

ABOUT THE AUTHOR

Blaze is **Barbara Keaton's** fifth romance for Genesis Press, Inc. An avid reader, Barbara lives on the South Side of Chicago with her ornery cat, General Patton, and works for the Chicago Transit Authority. She holds a Bachelor of Arts degree in Communication from Columbia College Chicago and a Master of Science in Journalism from Roosevelt University. She has always had a love and passion for the written word and credits her late grandfather, Thomas Hill, and the black religious order of the Oblate Sisters of Providence, for instilling those virtues in her.

Excerpt from

HAND IN GLOVE

BY

ANDREA JACKSON

Release Date: December 2005

CHAPTER 1

Tyson McAllister stepped onto one of the patios at the rear of the Kingston estate. *A sistah could get used to this life.* She paused and gazed at the mansion with its windows sparkling in the sun. Even at this early hour, servants bustled through the house preparing breakfast and tidying up. Turning to take in the spectacular view, she watched the rising sun as it filtered through the trees that ringed the grounds, laying a shimmer of magic to the swimming pool waters and the Italian marble tiles of the extensive patios. She could hear the chirrup of birds in the woods.

A wry smile curved her mouth as she methodically stretched her muscles in preparation for her morning jog. Sometimes she couldn't believe how far she had come. She still couldn't believe her luck in landing this assignment to help cover a big house party in a wealthy suburb of Atlanta, Georgia. But the morning was too intoxicating to waste thinking those thoughts. Light-footed and confident, she jogged along the hedges that ringed the patio; sure, nothing could stop her now. She felt invincible, until she slammed into a hard body coming around the corner of the hedges and fell on her butt with the breath knocked out of her.

There was a startled silence as Ty gathered her shattered thoughts. Jarred more than hurt, she began to giggle hysterically. It figured. Every time she thought she had it made, life knocked her on her ass. Ty McAllister couldn't forget that she had to watch out for herself every step of the way.

As the other runner helped her up with apologetic concern, she breathlessly assured him she was unhurt. Taking in his appearance, the breath swooshed out of her again.

The man before her epitomized the old cliché tall, dark and handsome. In tight-fitting leggings, a pullover jersey with a hood and high-priced running shoes, he could be a model in some touched-up photo in a physical fitness magazine. His exercise clothes emphasized his trim waist and narrow hips, yet at the same time seemed to show off the broadness of his chest and shoulders. His legs stretched fantastically long, the powerful muscles in his thighs accentuated by the sheen of the leggings. *Is he real?* The casual touch of his hands assured her that he was vibrantly real.

He thrust out his hand with a grin. "Hi. I'm Victor."

She gulped and took the hand. "Ty," she managed to respond to his slight Spanish accent.

He scrutinized her from head to toe, warm approval revealed in his flickering smile. "Are you going for a run?"

"Huh? Oh, yeah." She frowned. *Good grief, I sound like an idiot. I had better start acting like a television producer.* "Were you out already? How's the trail?"

"I just got back. It's beautiful down by the gardens. I love this time of morning." He glanced toward the east and lifted his chin to take a deep breath. Ty's senses went into a tailspin once more. *Wow, that sensual mouth, that strong jaw line.* He seemed unaware of his effect on her emotions.

"Uh-huh," she sighed, reining in her reaction once more. "Yeah, great morning. You must have been out early. Did you have a good workout?"

"Yes, but you're the only person I've seen so far."

"Really? I guess most folks are sleeping in."

"I guess so. Maybe we can talk over breakfast when you get back?"

Her heart did another little flutter. "Maybe," she said, with a slight shrug. "I'd better get going now."

She eased past him, turned with a wave then picked up her pace. He was still watching her when she turned the corner.

Heartthrob! She felt all warm and tingly with attraction. He wasn't precisely handsome, she decided; yet something about that square jaw, penetrating black eyes and well-conditioned body made a woman take a second look. And of course, he possessed that devastating slow smile that enticed like honey oozing from an overturned hive. She shook her head over her own whimsy. She wasn't about to indulge in a weekend flirtation. Ty McAllister never did foolish things like that. Her career had been the center of her life for some time. To avoid distractions from the challenge and competition of her job, she'd dumped her last serious relationship. She had no time for a steady boyfriend or social life. No time for coddling some man's fragile ego. She knew how to focus on what needed to be done.

She wasn't here to mingle with the guests, she reminded herself. She was here to work. This was the first big on-location assignment since her promotion to producer. A twinge of nerves sent a shiver down her spine. She had to prove her ability to her boss, Patty Sheldon, as well as the network executives.

Still, she couldn't help wondering exactly who this Victor was. He had to be a guest here at the party, which gave him immediate status. This house party was a small part of one of Atlanta's annual traditions. The rivalry between Clark Atlanta University and Morehouse College, two premier Black schools, was almost one hundred years old. The annual football face off in September was an opportunity to raise scholarship money for both schools. The days preceding the game were filled with lively rivalry and energetic festivity among the alumni and the community. No doubt, Victor was one of the successful alumni.

She didn't see her heart-throb for the rest of the morning. After her morning jog, she went straight to her room to change and get to work. By that afternoon, she had all but forgotten him as she directed a taping sequence for the show. The director was busy with Patty taping interviews, while she and the camera operator recorded some background sequences. She watched a dozen or more laughing, fashionable women burst out of the double doors of the mansion. They ignored the large staring lens of a television camera aimed at them.

"Steady, Pete, steady," Ty murmured to the cameraman. She watched the scene over his shoulder as he videotaped. This would definitely show the upscale nature of the party. Most of these women, wives of prominent celebrities and executives from around the country, seemed to spend most of their time on their appearance or their entertainment. She hadn't seen so much fake hair and designer clothes since the last Grammy Awards on television. She wondered what would turn up if the glittering surface were scratched.

She felt a little smile tug her lips as she continued to shadow the camera operator. Trust Patty to find any dirt to uncover. The woman was a bloodhound when it came to gossip. She wasn't naïve, but Patty's ability to sniff out secrets still disconcerted her at times.

"Backing up," warned Pete in a low voice. Keeping her hand on his shoulder, Ty started to ease backward so that he could swing the lens on the women as they walked across the green lawn toward the tennis courts.

"Ouch!" So of course, she was the one to bump into someone, jostling the cameraman and almost losing her footing.

Pete lowered the video cam and glared at her in exasperation. She turned and found herself facing two more annoyed individuals.

One of them was Vanessa Sweetlove, a close friend of the host, Duke Kingston. The other was a man with a beard and thick glasses. Ty had noticed them with their heads bent together when she and Pete first set up a few minutes ago.

"Watch where you're going with that thing!" shrilled Vanessa.

"Cameras?" Her companion scowled, his lips pouting from saggy jowls. "What the hell are you trying to do to me, Vanessa? Don't you appreciate my position? I can't be seen here! Those reporter parasites can ruin everything. Everything!"

In his poorly fitting polyester suit, he turned and scurried into the house, leaving Ty gazing after him.

Now that reaction seemed a little extreme, she mused. Most of the people at this fling were glad for a little promotion. This guy didn't quite fit in with the other men at the house party, many of whom occupied positions of power in corporate offices all over the South. Mr. Cheap Suit didn't have that executive air.

Vanessa Sweetlove showed no sign of fleeing. Ty observed a beautiful, hazel-eyed woman of color with peachy skin and sandy hair. Chiffon in bright ocean colors floated around her shapely curves. She frowned at Ty. "Honey, if you can't stay out of the way of the guests, I'll have Duke ask you to leave."

"I apologize," Ty said. She nodded to Pete, who began rolling up cords and collecting his lights.

"Miss Sweetlove, isn't it?" Ty went on in her best professional voice. "I'm Patty Sheldon's producer. I understand that you're a well-known psychic. Perhaps you could give me a few minutes of your time later, so that I can ask some preliminary questions for Patty. I'm sure she'd love to have you on the show. Have you seen *Eye on Atlanta*?" As she named the popular local talk show, she pasted on a smile to hide her real thoughts. *Or maybe you can read your crystal ball on the 1-800 Psychic Rip-off Line.*

Ty's preliminary research had revealed that Vanessa Sweetlove was "involved" with Duke Kingston. Vanessa had suddenly dropped her weekly radio call-in talk show, "Sweetlove Predictions" just a few weeks ago. The tabloids speculated that she was preparing to venture into a new area. Ty had a shrewd idea that Duke Kingston would finance the new area.

At the mention of publicity, Vanessa's frown cleared, replaced by smiling approval. "I'd love to talk to Patty. I think your audience will find my powers unique and fascinating."

"Good," Ty said, her mind racing to find an excuse to put Vanessa off until later. "I'll just go and check Patty's calendar. I'll see you at dinner, won't—" she slid a step to the rear in preparation for flight. "Ouch!" Once more, she slammed into something warm and solid. This seemed to be her day for bumbling into people.

Hands caught her from behind, and she twisted around to free herself. "Excuse me. Oh, it's you!" she exclaimed and felt her mouth stretch into a wide, admiring smile.

"Easy there. Oh, hi!"

Just like this morning, the sound of that voice sent a shiver of bone-melting sensual awareness down her spine, and she found herself gulping to get her emotions under control as she turned to face good-looking Victor. This time she noticed that when his generous chiseled lips stretched in a smile, a little indentation appeared on one side of his mouth.

They both recovered at the same time; he released her and she stepped away.

"Hi," he said, still smiling that slightly lopsided grin. "Did you enjoy your run this morning?"

"Mr. Santiago," cooed Vanessa Sweetlove's fluting voice behind her. Ty had almost forgotten about the beautiful psychic. "Mr. Santiago, I've been looking all over for you!"

The name sank into Ty's brain. She froze, staring at him in consternation. *He was Victor Santiago?* She'd heard all about the mysterious, ruthless, and fabulously successful investment consultant who'd popped up on Duke Kingston's doorstep last night. The guests had been buzzing about him all day, and Ty had hoped to get some footage of him. The last thing she'd expected was that he'd turn out to be *this* heart-stopping brother.

She might have imagined that his smile tightened a little as he turned toward Vanessa. "Were you? I don't believe we've met, have we, Miss…?"

"Vanessa." The psychic stepped up and hooked her arm into his. "I'm helping Duke entertain the guests. You must tell me if there's anything you need to make your stay more pleasant." She fluttered her lashes at him with seductive invitation.

Victor hesitated, casting another look at Ty. She hastily busied herself with a notebook she had managed to hang onto through all the jostling.

"Well," said Victor. "I did want to ask you about the gentleman you were talking to a minute ago. I believe we're acquainted."

"Dr. Franklin? Shall we go and find him?" Vanessa began to tug Victor's arm with firm determination.

He hung back. "I'll see you at dinner, Ty?" he asked.

She avoided his compelling gaze. "Oh, I expect I'll be working," she mumbled. "I'll see you around."

Vanessa, chattering, led him away. Ty peeped after them from beneath her lashes. *Trouble*, she decided. *No thanks.* Tyson McAllister knew how to focus on what was important.

Victor forced himself to lend an attentive ear to Vanessa's flirtatious prattle. Something fresh and soothing about Ty attracted him. Perhaps he'd have time to pursue an acquaintance with the young producer later this weekend. Despite his oddly compelling attraction to Ty McAllister, he did need to focus on his primary goal.

He and Vanessa found Franklin standing at the edge of the side lawn watching while some guests performed cheers for their favorite college team.

"How do you do?" Victor said after Vanessa introduced him.

Franklin's gaze shifted, avoiding Victor's face, as he hesitantly took the hand Victor extended. He grunted a brief acknowledgement.

"I thought I might have met you when I attended Morehouse a few years ago," Victor went on. "I majored in history under Dr. Berengi. Do you know him?"

Franklin stiffened. "I've always been at Clark-Howard," he muttered.

"Yes? I thought you might know Dr. Berengi since your field is history, too. He's one of the leading authorities on the African Diaspora."

"Berengi," Franklin said as if the name curdled his tongue. "Berengi is a do-gooding show-off who's managed to get a couple of books published. I have a lot of problems with his theories."

"In what areas?" asked Victor with an air of interest. "I thought his book on the Nakisisi was considered a standard."

"Berengi knows nothing—" began Franklin in a strident voice.

"You men aren't going to start discussing history!" exclaimed Vanessa with a little laugh. "This is a party, gentlemen. Wouldn't you rather talk about who'll win the game this weekend?"

Victor flashed her a smile. "Sorry to bore you. Why don't the professor and I go inside so you can get back to your other guests?"

She took a quick step closer to Victor as if to hang on to him. "Well, I—"

"I was just about to go to my room anyway," said Franklin in a quieter tone. Tight-lipped, he added, "Excuse me, Santiago. It was nice meeting you."

"Perhaps we can talk about the Nakisisi later then," said Victor.

Franklin's only response was a non-committal grunt as he turned and walked away.

Victor offered Vanessa an apologetic smile.

"Maybe you and I could talk about the Nakisisi," she said over the rowdy crowd.

"Are you familiar with the tribe?"

"Perhaps. A little," she said. Then she smiled. "But we'll talk later. When it's quieter."

He let her change the topic. How much did Vanessa know? She enjoyed a close relationship with Kingston, apparently. Perhaps she might prove useful to him. He had a couple more days to try to get the information he had come for.

Ty spent the remainder of the afternoon setting up camera angles around the house and grounds, storyboarding ideas, talking to Patty, and taking pages of notes.

As she studied the notes on the guests, she saw that there were several interesting leads to follow up. As she had come to expect, many of these seemingly upright citizens hid personal baggage, some more dramatic than others. She only had to pick which would work best for the show.

This wasn't a simple party; this was high stakes business, the way the wealthy and powerful did it. She had a feeling that there were some interesting, secret dealings going on beneath the festivities, and this party promised to provide plenty of footage for Patty's show. Duke Kingston had invited a number of leading black Georgia businessmen; people who contributed heavily to the scholarship funds of the Atlanta universities.

Kingston was one of the city's most notorious businesspersons. Some dozen years ago as a handsome young man with charm and a fascinating Caribbean accent, he had snared a wealthy older widow in matrimony. The new Mrs. Kingston, known to have chronic health problems, had died just a few months ago. After a brief period of mourning, the bereaved husband was now living large, partying, wheeling and dealing as hard as he could.

As evening approached, Ty retreated to the mansion's magnificent library to work on her notes. She'd found the library was the least used room in the house.

As she walked in, a man sitting on one of the couches behind a low coffee table lifted his head with a frown.

"What are you doing here?" he demanded.

Ty recognized Vanessa's flustered companion from this morning, still wearing the same rumpled blue suit. The gruffness of his tone set her defenses alight.

"Am I disturbing you?" she asked coldly. Her gaze flickered down to the papers spread on the table before him. He began to rake them inside a scuffed leather briefcase, without regard for neatness.

"Yes, you're disturbing me," he snarled. "What are you doing, following me around with that camera?"

"I'm not following you."

"Do I look like a fool? I know your kind. You stay away from me. You come near me with that camera again and I'll smash it! Do you hear me? I'll have you thrown out of this house!"

"Excuse me?" Her voice turned even chillier. "Mr. Kingston made an agreement with Ms. Sheldon to record this weekend. I think you're overreacting. Believe me, you're not the type our show takes an interest in, Mr.—,"

He didn't supply his name, but descended into a strident rant about reporters and privacy, his voice rising with every word. She remembered, though, that Vanessa had called him Dr. Franklin.

"What's going on in here?" demanded a new voice from the doorway, which Ty had left opened behind her.

She and the irate Franklin turned to face their host, Duke Kingston. He was a mahogany-skinned man of medium height, in fairly good shape without looking as if he worked too hard at it. His Armani suit was clearly custom-tailored, with creases sharp enough to cut. His thin mustache was so perfectly trimmed it might have been drawn on. Ty had already decided he had the practiced smoothness of a pretty boy hopelessly in love with himself.

Franklin sputtered at him, "Why have you brought these television people here, Kingston? I won't have it! They'll mess up everything if you don't get rid of them. I demand it! They go or I go!"

Ty gaped at the blustering man, all her internal alarms clanging. *What the hell was this guy hiding? Who was he to deliver ultimatums to a man as influential as Duke Kingston was?*

"Calm down, Franklin," Kingston said, lifting his palms in a soothing gesture. "There's no need to upset yourself." He turned to Ty, his expression going stern. "Ms. McCall, isn't it?"

"McAllister," Ty corrected, her throat tight with anger.

"I've allowed Ms. Sheldon to bring her crew into my home as a favor. I advise you to stay away from my guests. I wouldn't like to have to make a complaint to your employer." Kingston still had a faint Caribbean accent, which would have been intriguing at any other time.

Ty was in no mood to appreciate it just now as she felt her blood boil. "Don't concern yourself," she spat out in a low, furious tone. "I'm sure I can manage to keep to my *place* without disturbing any of your guests."

With a jerky turn, Ty stalked from the room. *How dare that man speak to me as if I were one of his servants?* She started to climb the stairs, but paused on hearing the front doorbell.

Standing at the banister over the entrance foyer below, Ty saw a uniformed maid open the door and admit more guests, dressed in glittering, evening finery. A smiling Kingston emerged from the library to greet them.

Ty turned and stumbled along the second floor hallway. She didn't think she had the stomach to sit through dinner with these people tonight. She would work in her room.

BLAZE

2005 Publication Schedule

January

A Heart's Awakening
Veronica Parker
$9.95
1-58571-143-8

Falling
Natalie Dunbar
$9.95
1-58571-121-7

February

Echoes of Yesterday
Beverly Clark
$9.95
1-58571-131-4

A Love of Her Own
Cheris F. Hodges
$9.95
1-58571-136-5

Higher Ground
Leah Latimer
$19.95
1-58571-157-8

March

Misconceptions
Pamela Leigh Starr
$9.95
1-58571-117-9

I'll Paint a Sun
A.J. Garrotto
$9.95
1-58571-165-9

Peace Be Still
Colette Haywood
$12.95
1-58571-129-2

April

Intentional Mistakes
Michele Sudler
$9.95
1-58571-152-7

Conquering Dr. Wexler's Heart
Kimberley White
$9.95
1-58571-126-8

Song in the Park
Martin Brant
$15.95
1-58571-125-X

May

The Color Line
Lizzette Grayson Carter
$9.95
1-58571-163-2

Unconditional
A.C. Arthur
$9.95
1-58571-142-X

Last Train to Memphis
Elsa Cook
$12.95
1-58571-146-2

June

Angel's Paradise
Janice Angelique
$9.95
1-58571-107-1

Suddenly You
Crystal Hubbard
$9.95
1-58571-158-6

Matters of Life and
    Death
Lesego Malepe, Ph.D.
$15.95
1-58571-124-1

2005 Publication Schedule (continued)

July

Class Reunion
Irma Jenkins/John
  Brown
$12.95
1-58571-123-3

Wild Ravens
Altonya Washington
$9.95
1-58571-164-0

August

Path of Thorns
Annetta P. Lee
$9.95
1-58571-145-4

Timeless Devotion
Bella McFarland
$9.95
1-58571-148-9

Life Is Never As It Seems
J.J. Michael
$12.95
1-58571-153-5

September

Beyond the Rapture
Beverly Clark
$9.95
1-58571-130-6

Blood Lust
J. M. Jeffries
$9.95
1-58571-138-1

Rough on Rats and
  Tough on Cats
Chris Parker
$12.95
1-58571-154-3

October

A Will to Love
Angie Daniels
$9.95
1-58571-141-1

Taken by You
Dorothy Elizabeth Love
$9.95
1-58571-162-4

Soul Eyes
Wayne L. Wilson
$12.95
1-58571-147-0

November

A Drummer's Beat to
  Mend
Kei Swanson
$9.95
1-58571-171-3

Sweet Reprecussions
Kimberley White
$9.95
1-58571-159-4

Red Polka Dot in a
  World of Plaid
Varian Johnson
$12.95
1-58571-140-3

December

Hand in Glove
Andrea Jackson
$9.95
1-58571-166-7

Blaze
Barbara Keaton
$9.95
1-58571-172-1

Across
Carol Payne
$12.95
1-58571-149-7

Other Genesis Press, Inc. Titles

Erotic Anthology	Assorted	$8.95
Eve's Prescription	Edwina Martin Arnold	$8.95
Everlastin' Love	Gay G. Gunn	$8.95
Fate	Pamela Leigh Starr	$8.95
Forbidden Quest	Dar Tomlinson	$10.95
Fragment in the Sand	Annetta P. Lee	$8.95
From the Ashes	Kathleen Suzanne	$8.95
	Jeanne Sumerix	
Gentle Yearning	Rochelle Alers	$10.95
Glory of Love	Sinclair LeBeau	$10.95
Hart & Soul	Angie Daniels	$8.95
Heartbeat	Stephanie Bedwell-Grime	$8.95
I'll Be Your Shelter	Giselle Carmichael	$8.95
Illusions	Pamela Leigh Starr	$8.95
Indiscretions	Donna Hill	$8.95
Interlude	Donna Hill	$8.95
Intimate Intentions	Angie Daniels	$8.95
Just an Affair	Eugenia O'Neal	$8.95
Kiss or Keep	Debra Phillips	$8.95
Love Always	Mildred E. Riley	$10.95
Love Unveiled	Gloria Greene	$10.95
Love's Deception	Charlene Berry	$10.95
Mae's Promise	Melody Walcott	$8.95
Meant to Be	Jeanne Sumerix	$8.95
Midnight Clear	Leslie Esdaile	$10.95
(Anthology)	Gwynne Forster	
	Carmen Green	
	Monica Jackson	
Midnight Magic	Gwynne Forster	$8.95
Midnight Peril	Vicki Andrews	$10.95
My Buffalo Soldier	Barbara B. K. Reeves	$8.95
Naked Soul	Gwynne Forster	$8.95
No Regrets	Mildred E. Riley	$8.95
Nowhere to Run	Gay G. Gunn	$10.95

Object of His Desire	A. C. Arthur	$8.95
One Day at a Time	Bella McFarland	$8.95
Passion	T.T. Henderson	$10.95
Past Promises	Jahmel West	$8.95
Path of Fire	T.T. Henderson	$8.95
Picture Perfect	Reon Carter	$8.95
Pride & Joi	Gay G. Gunn	$8.95
Quiet Storm	Donna Hill	$8.95
Reckless Surrender	Rochelle Alers	$8.95
Rendezvous with Fate	Jeanne Sumerix	$8.95
Revelations	Cheris F. Hodges	$8.95
Rivers of the Soul	Leslie Esdaile	$8.95
Rooms of the Heart	Donna Hill	$8.95
Shades of Brown	Denise Becker	$8.95
Shades of Desire	Monica White	$8.95
Sin	Crystal Rhodes	$8.95
So Amazing	Sinclair LeBeau	$8.95
Somebody's Someone	Sinclair LeBeau	$8.95
Someone to Love	Alicia Wiggins	$8.95
Soul to Soul	Donna Hill	$8.95
Still Waters Run Deep	Leslie Esdaile	$8.95
Subtle Secrets	Wanda Y. Thomas	$8.95
Sweet Tomorrows	Kimberly White	$8.95
The Color of Trouble	Dyanne Davis	$8.95
The Price of Love	Sinclair LeBeau	$8.95
The Reluctant Captive	Joyce Jackson	$8.95
The Missing Link	Charlyne Dickerson	$8.95
Three Wishes	Seressia Glass	$8.95
Tomorrow's Promise	Leslie Esdaile	$8.95
Truly Inseperable	Wanda Y. Thomas	$8.95
Twist of Fate	Beverly Clark	$8.95
Unbreak My Heart	Dar Tomlinson	$8.95
Unconditional Love	Alicia Wiggins	$8.95
When Dreams A Float	Dorothy Elizabeth Love	$8.95

Whispers in the Night	Dorothy Elizabeth Love	$8.95
Whispers in the Sand	LaFlorya Gauthier	$10.95
Yesterday is Gone	Beverly Clark	$8.95
Yesterday's Dreams, Tomorrow's Promises	Reon Laudat	$8.95
Your Precious Love	Sinclair LeBeau	$8.95

Order Form

Mail to: Genesis Press, Inc.
P.O. Box 101
Columbus, MS 39703

Name _____

Address _____

City/State _____ Zip _____

Telephone _____

Ship to (if different from above)

Name _____

Address _____

City/State _____ Zip _____

Telephone _____

Credit Card Information

Credit Card # _____ ☐ Visa ☐ Mastercard

Expiration Date (mm/yy) _____ ☐ AmEx ☐ Discover

Qty.	Author	Title	Price	Total

Use this order
form, or call
1-888-INDIGO-1

Total for books _____

Shipping and handling:
  $5 first two books,
  $1 each additional book _____

Total S & H _____

Total amount enclosed _____

Mississippi residents add 7% sales tax